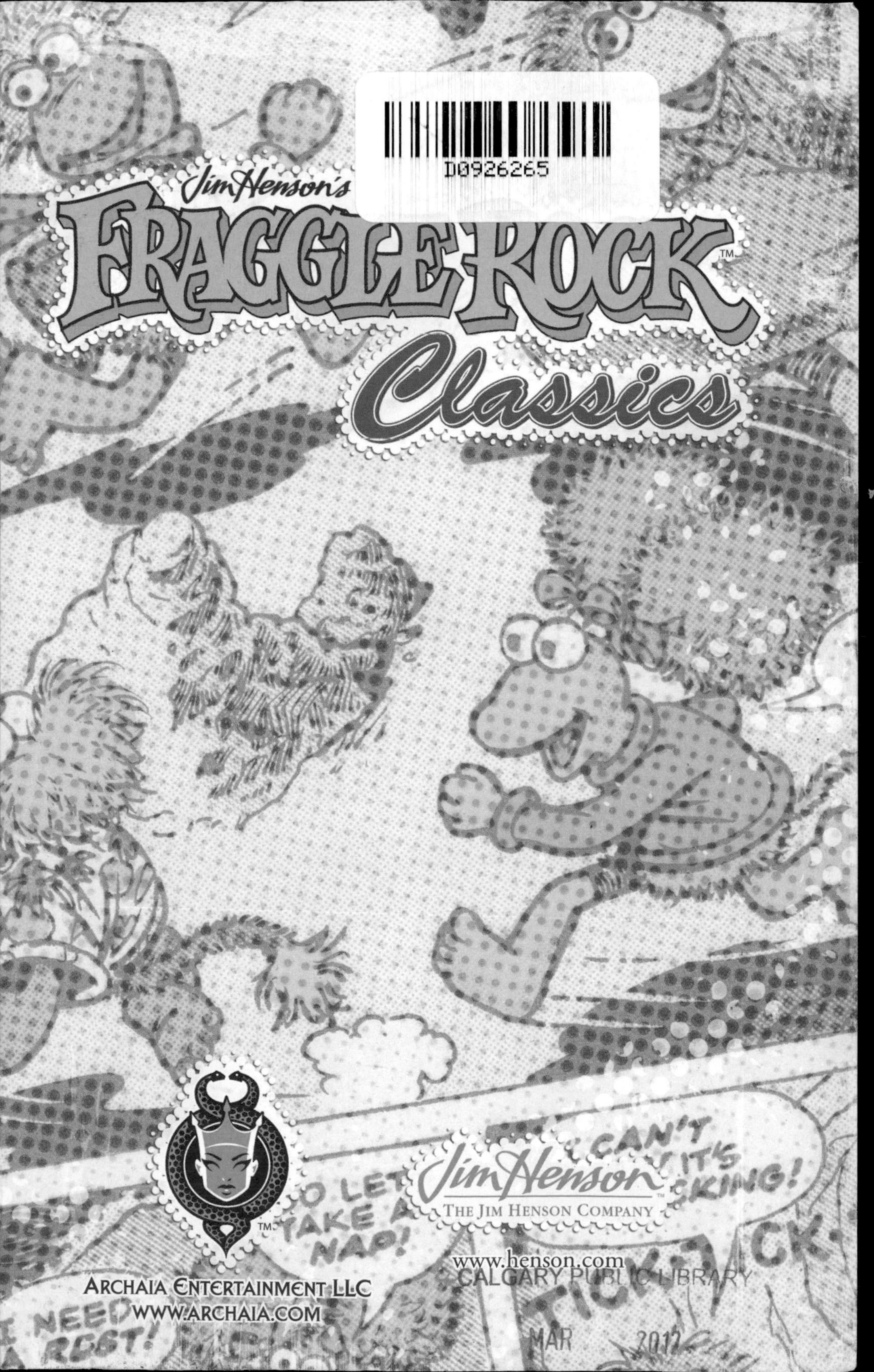

Jim Henson's
FRAGGLE ROCK™
Classics

Jim Henson™
THE JIM HENSON COMPANY
www.henson.com

ARCHAIA ENTERTAINMENT LLC
WWW.ARCHAIA.COM

Sid Jacobson, *Editor, Original Series*
Tom DeFalco, *Executive Editor, Original Series*
Jim Shooter, *Editor-in-Chief, Original Series*
Stephen Christy and Rebecca Taylor, *Editors, Collected Edition*
Scott Newman, *Designer*
Grace Dremer, *Letterer*

Archaia Entertainment LLC

PJ Bickett, *CEO*
Mark Smylie, *CCO*
Mike Kennedy, *Publisher*
Stephen Christy, *Editor-in-Chief*

Published by **Archaia**

Archaia Entertainment LLC
1680 Vine Street, Suite 1010
Los Angeles, California, 90028, USA
www.archaia.com

FRAGGLE ROCK CLASSIC VOLUME ONE. November 2011. FIRST PRINTING

Originally published as FRAGGLE ROCK VOL. 1 #1-4 by Marvel Comics in 1985.

10 9 8 7 6 5 4 3 2 1

ISBN: 1-936393-22-0

ISBN 13: 978-1-936393-22-0

ARCHAIA.
NEW STORIES. NEW WORLDS.™

Jim Henson
THE JIM HENSON COMPANY

APPROVED
BY THE
COMICS
CODE
AUTHORITY

Jim Henson's™
FRAGGLE ROCK™
Classics

Written by **STAN KAY**

Illustrated by **MARIE SEVERIN**

Restoration and Colors by
BRIAN NEWMAN
JOANNA ESTEP
Cover by
JAKE MYLER

Special Thanks to
BRIAN HENSON, LISA HENSON, JIM FORMANEK, NICOLE GOLDMAN,
MARYANNE PITTMAN, MELISSA SEGAL, HILLARY HOWELL,
JILL PETERSON, TIM BEEDLE AND THE ENTIRE HENSON TEAM!

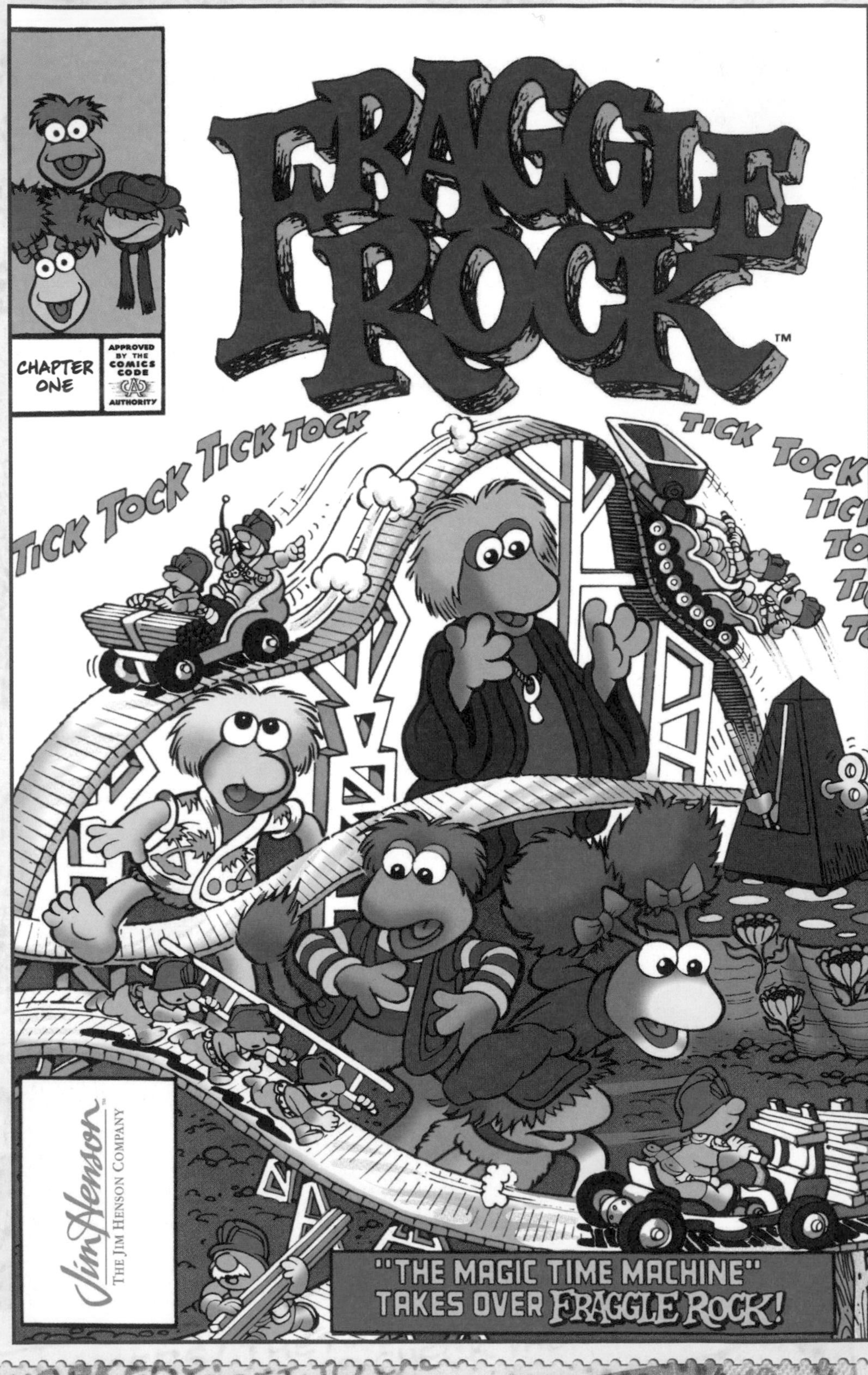
FRAGGLE ROCK™
CHAPTER ONE
APPROVED BY THE COMICS CODE AUTHORITY
TICK TOCK TICK TOCK
TICK TOCK
Jim Henson
THE JIM HENSON COMPANY
"THE MAGIC TIME MACHINE" TAKES OVER FRAGGLE ROCK!

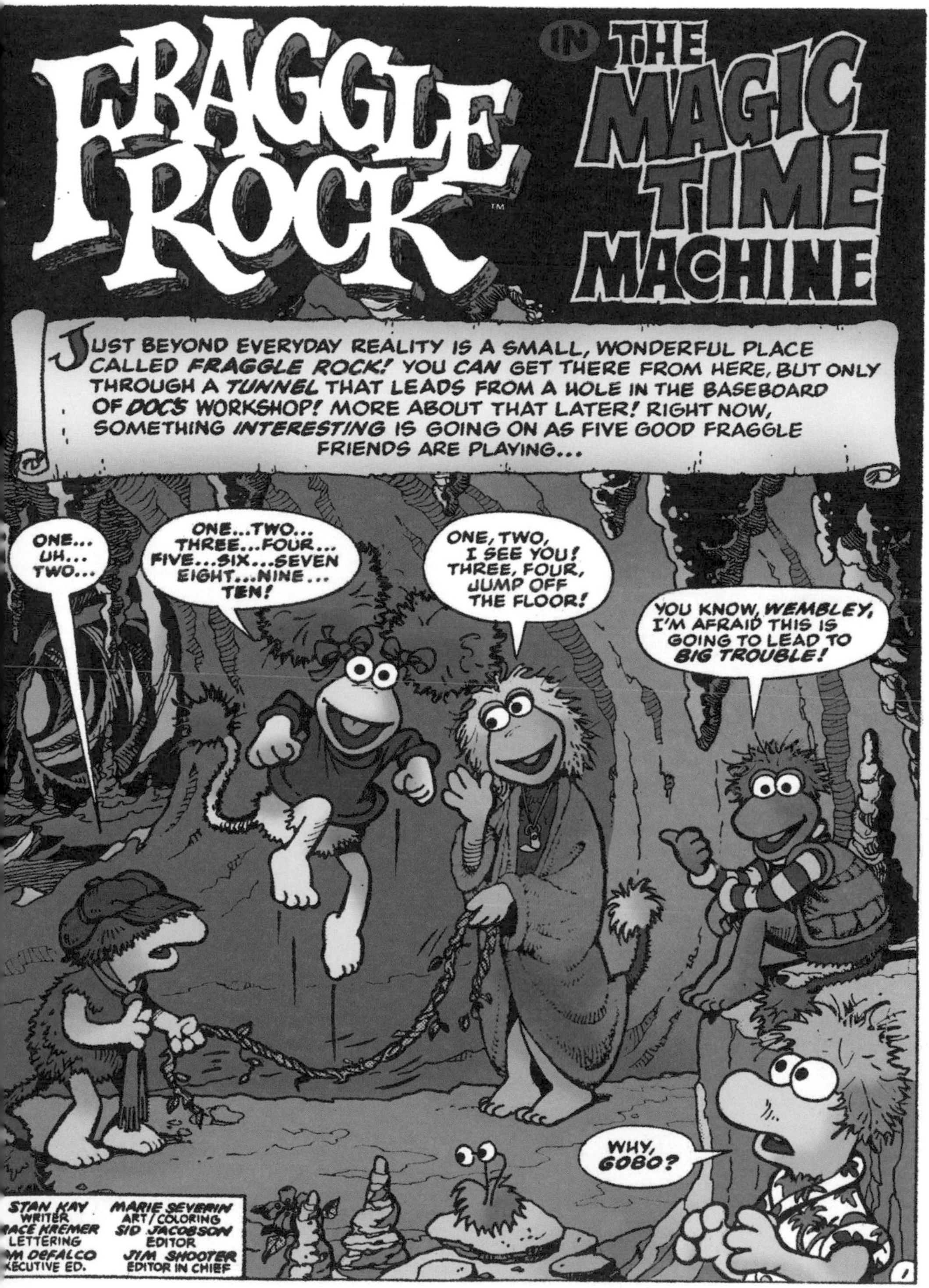
FRAGGLE ROCK™
IN
THE MAGIC TIME MACHINE
JUST BEYOND EVERYDAY REALITY IS A SMALL, WONDERFUL PLACE CALLED FRAGGLE ROCK! YOU CAN GET THERE FROM HERE, BUT ONLY THROUGH A TUNNEL THAT LEADS FROM A HOLE IN THE BASEBOARD OF DOC'S WORKSHOP! MORE ABOUT THAT LATER! RIGHT NOW, SOMETHING INTERESTING IS GOING ON AS FIVE GOOD FRAGGLE FRIENDS ARE PLAYING...
ONE... UH... TWO...
ONE...TWO... THREE...FOUR... FIVE...SIX...SEVEN EIGHT...NINE... TEN!
ONE, TWO, I SEE YOU! THREE, FOUR, JUMP OFF THE FLOOR!
YOU KNOW, WEMBLEY, I'M AFRAID THIS IS GOING TO LEAD TO BIG TROUBLE!
WHY, GOBO?
STAN KAY WRITER
MARIE SEVERIN ART/COLORING
ACE KREMER LETTERING
SID JACOBSON EDITOR
M DEFALCO KECUTIVE ED.
JIM SHOOTER EDITOR IN CHIEF
1

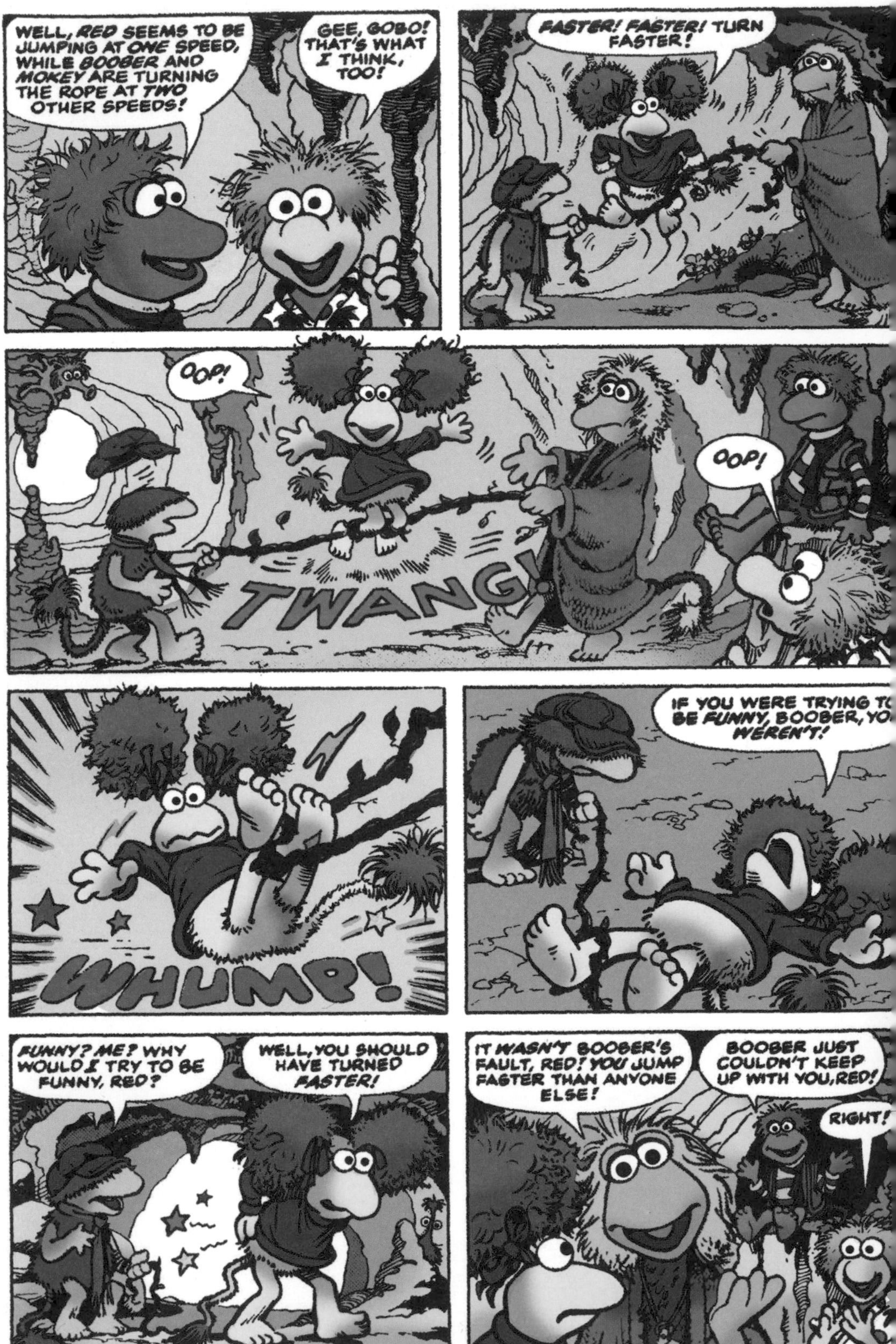
WELL, RED SEEMS TO BE JUMPING AT ONE SPEED, WHILE BOOBER AND MOKEY ARE TURNING THE ROPE AT TWO OTHER SPEEDS!
GEE, GOBO! THAT'S WHAT I THINK, TOO!
FASTER! FASTER! TURN FASTER!
OOP!
OOP!
TWANG!
WHUMP!
IF YOU WERE TRYING TO BE FUNNY, BOOBER, YO WEREN'T!
FUNNY? ME? WHY WOULD I TRY TO BE FUNNY, RED?
WELL, YOU SHOULD HAVE TURNED FASTER!
IT WASN'T BOOBER'S FAULT, RED! YOU JUMP FASTER THAN ANYONE ELSE!
BOOBER JUST COULDN'T KEEP UP WITH YOU, RED!
RIGHT!

WELL, HE SHOULD HAVE *TRIED!* JUMPING *FAST* IS THE WAY TO GO!

ONE TWO THREE FOUR FIVE SIX SEVEN EIGHT NINE TEN ELEVEN TWELVE THIRTEEN FOURTEEN FIFTEEN SIXTEEN SEVENTEEN EIGHTEEN NINETEEN TWENTY

WOW! RED IS JUMPING IN QUADRUPLE TIME!

SPEAKING OF TIME...

IT MUST BE TIME FOR A *POSTCARD* FROM MY *UNCLE TRAVELING MATT,* WHO'S OUT EXPLORING THE WORLD BEYOND!

ARE YOU GOING TO TRAVEL INTO *OUTER SPACE,* GOBO?

THAT'S WHERE I *HAVE* TO GO FOR UNCLE MATT'S POSTCARD, WEMBLEY!

SEE YOU ALL *LATER!*

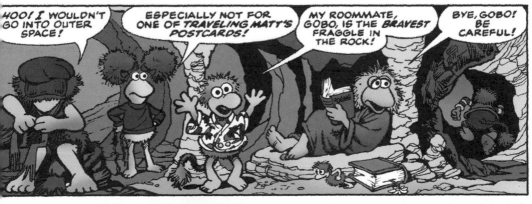

HOO! I WOULDN'T GO INTO OUTER SPACE!

ESPECIALLY NOT FOR ONE OF *TRAVELING MATT'S* POSTCARDS!

MY ROOMMATE, GOBO, IS THE *BRAVEST* FRAGGLE IN THE ROCK!

BYE, GOBO! BE CAREFUL!

BOING

IT'S TOO BAD EVERYONE WAS JUMPING ROPE AT *DIFFERENT SPEEDS...*

...BUT BOOBER WILL NEVER *LEARN* TO KEEP UP WITH RED!

HEY! WHAT *STRANGE* MUSIC! IT'S COMING FROM THE *TUNNEL* TO OUTER SPACE!

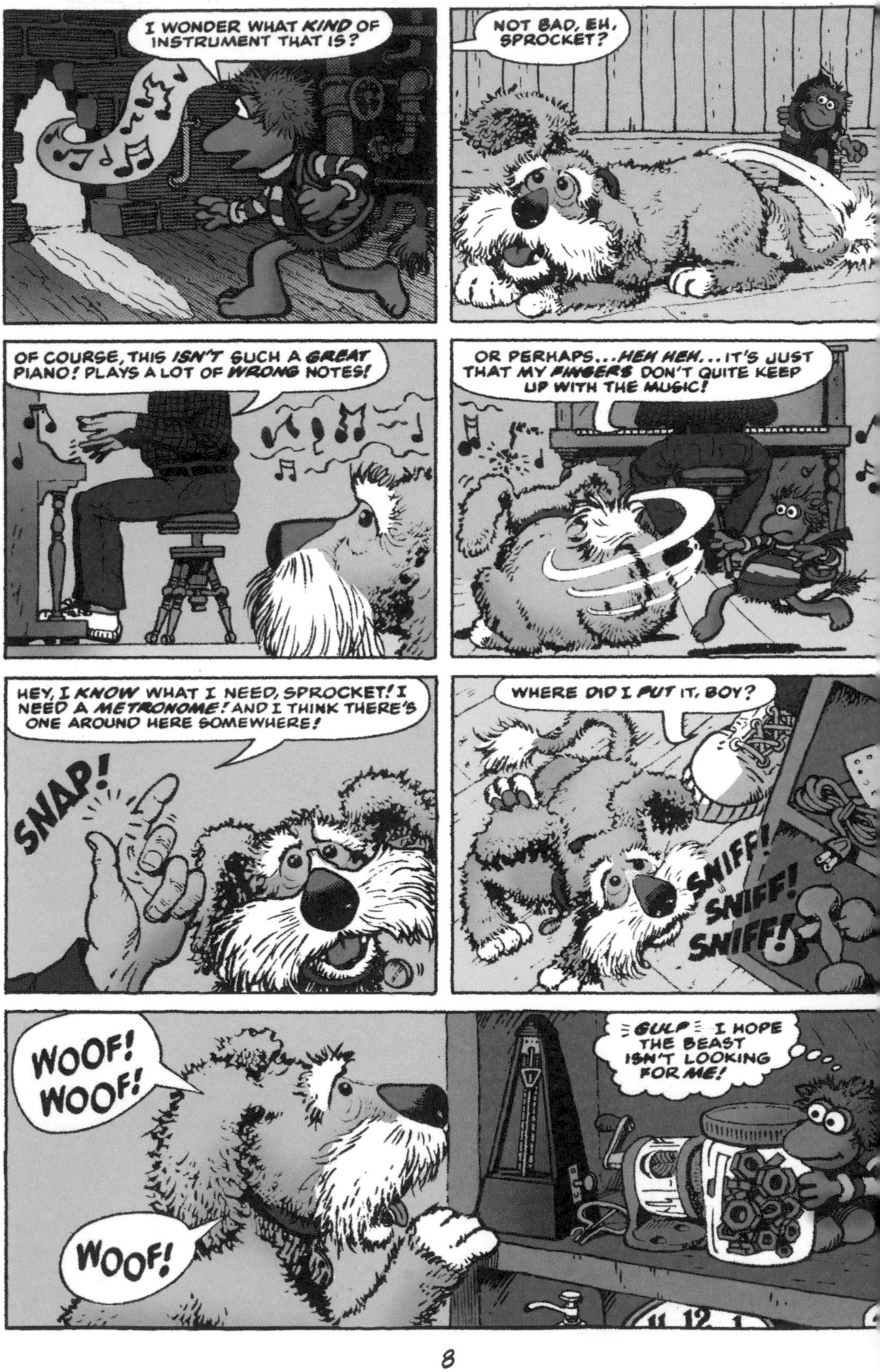
I WONDER WHAT KIND OF INSTRUMENT THAT IS?
NOT BAD, EH, SPROCKET?
OF COURSE, THIS ISN'T SUCH A GREAT PIANO! PLAYS A LOT OF WRONG NOTES!
OR PERHAPS... HEH HEH... IT'S JUST THAT MY FINGERS DON'T QUITE KEEP UP WITH THE MUSIC!
HEY, I KNOW WHAT I NEED, SPROCKET! I NEED A METRONOME! AND I THINK THERE'S ONE AROUND HERE SOMEWHERE!
SNAP!
WHERE DID I PUT IT, BOY?
SNIFF! SNIFF! SNIFF!
WOOF! WOOF!
WOOF!
GULP I HOPE THE BEAST ISN'T LOOKING FOR ME!

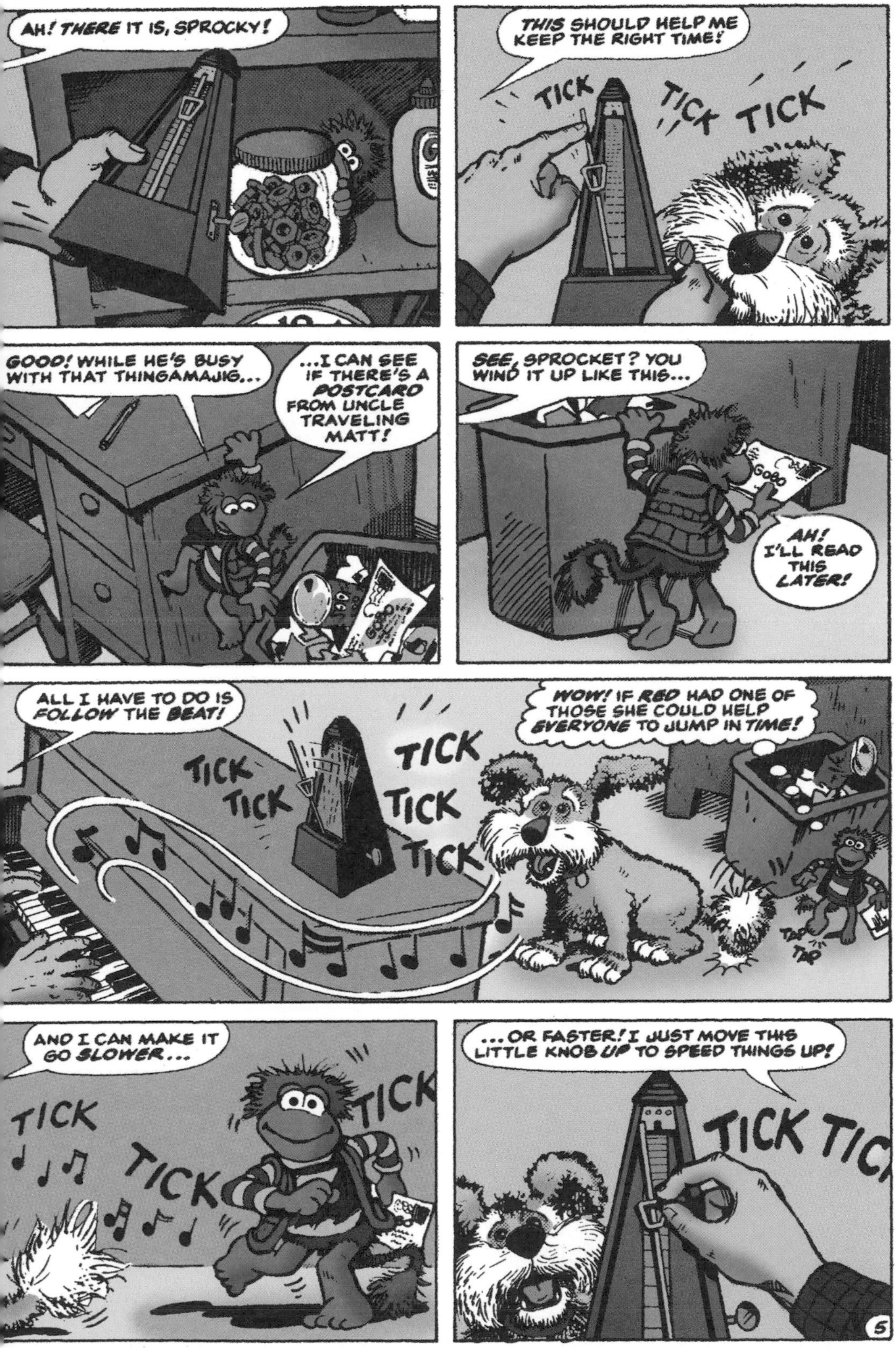
AH! THERE IT IS, SPROCKY!
THIS SHOULD HELP ME KEEP THE RIGHT TIME!
TICK
TICK
TICK
GOOD! WHILE HE'S BUSY WITH THAT THINGAMAJIG...
...I CAN SEE IF THERE'S A POSTCARD FROM UNCLE TRAVELING MATT!
SEE, SPROCKET? YOU WIND IT UP LIKE THIS...
GOBO
AH! I'LL READ THIS LATER!
ALL I HAVE TO DO IS FOLLOW THE BEAT!
TICK
TICK
TICK
TICK
TICK
WOW! IF RED HAD ONE OF THOSE SHE COULD HELP EVERYONE TO JUMP IN TIME!
AND I CAN MAKE IT GO SLOWER...
TICK
TICK
TICK
...OR FASTER! I JUST MOVE THIS LITTLE KNOB UP TO SPEED THINGS UP!
TICK
5

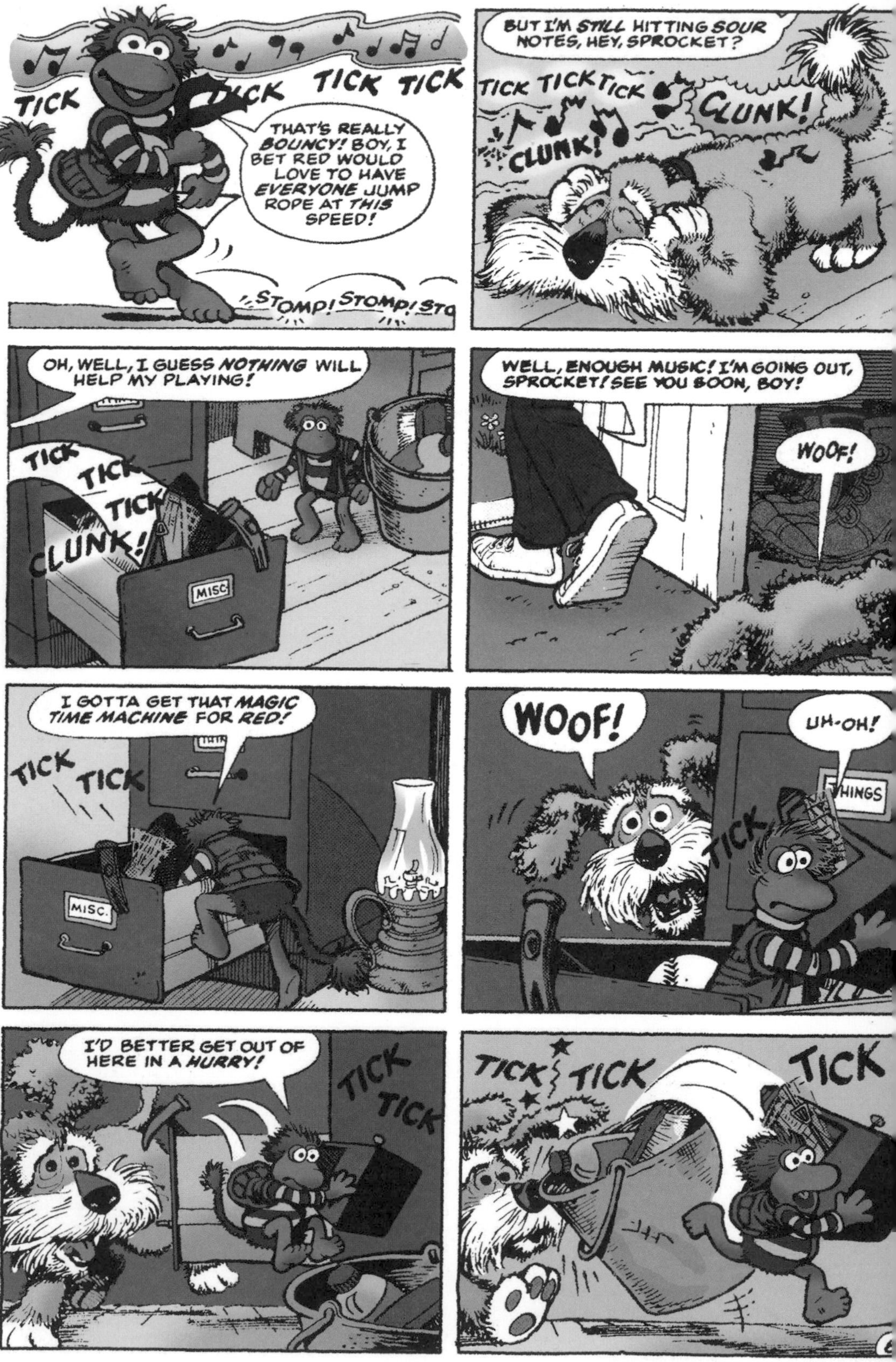

TICK
ICK
TICK TICK
THAT'S REALLY BOUNCY! BOY, I BET RED WOULD LOVE TO HAVE EVERYONE JUMP ROPE AT THIS SPEED!
STOMP! STOMP! STO
BUT I'M STILL HITTING SOUR NOTES, HEY, SPROCKET?
TICK TICK TICK
CLUNK!
CLUNK!
OH, WELL, I GUESS NOTHING WILL HELP MY PLAYING!
TICK
TICK
TICK
CLUNK!
MISC.
WELL, ENOUGH MUSIC! I'M GOING OUT, SPROCKET! SEE YOU SOON, BOY!
WOOF!
I GOTTA GET THAT MAGIC TIME MACHINE FOR RED!
TICK
TICK
MISC.
WOOF!
UH-OH!
HINGS
TICK
I'D BETTER GET OUT OF HERE IN A HURRY!
TICK
TICK
TICK
TICK
TICK

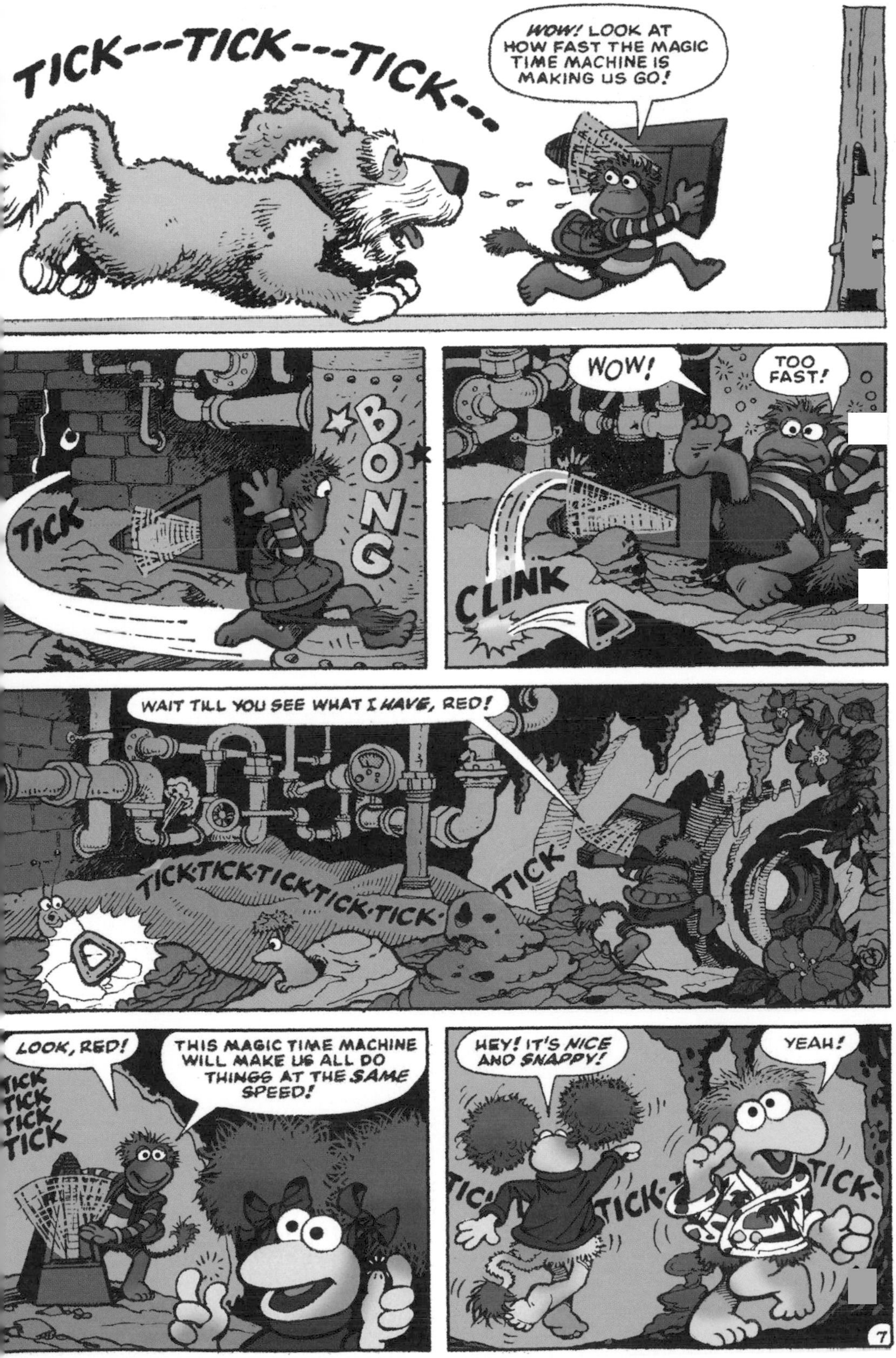
TICK---TICK---TICK---
WOW! LOOK AT HOW FAST THE MAGIC TIME MACHINE IS MAKING US GO!
TICK
BONG
WOW!
TOO FAST!
CLINK
WAIT TILL YOU SEE WHAT I HAVE, RED!
TICK·TICK·TICK·TICK·TICK·
TICK
LOOK, RED!
TICK TICK TICK TICK
THIS MAGIC TIME MACHINE WILL MAKE US ALL DO THINGS AT THE SAME SPEED!
HEY! IT'S NICE AND SNAPPY!
YEAH!
TICK-
TICK-
7

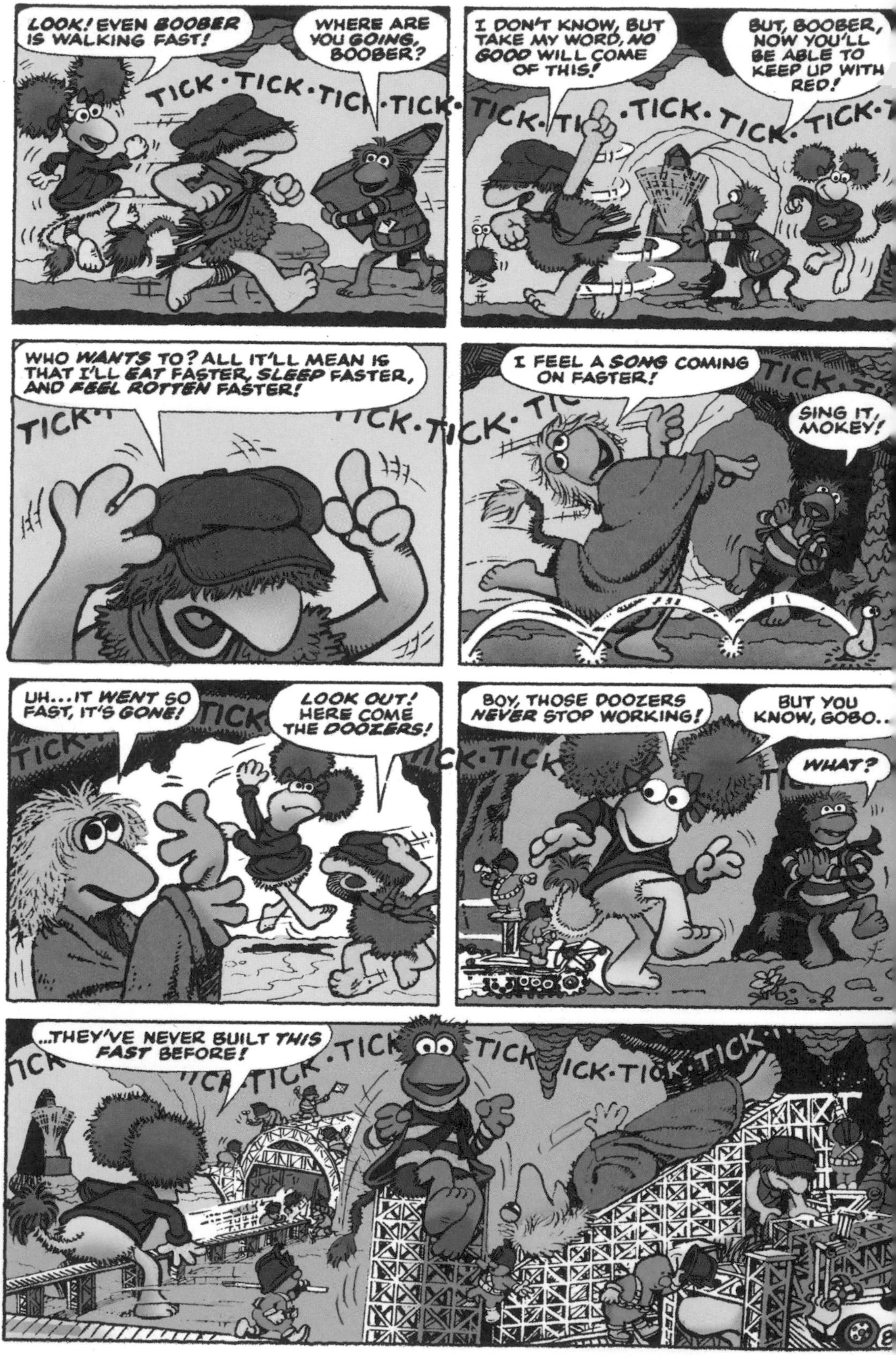
LOOK! EVEN BOOBER IS WALKING FAST!
WHERE ARE YOU GOING, BOOBER?
TICK·TICK·TICK·TICK·TICK·TICK·TICK·TICK·TICK
I DON'T KNOW, BUT TAKE MY WORD, NO GOOD WILL COME OF THIS!
BUT, BOOBER, NOW YOU'LL BE ABLE TO KEEP UP WITH RED!
WHO WANTS TO? ALL IT'LL MEAN IS THAT I'LL EAT FASTER, SLEEP FASTER, AND FEEL ROTTEN FASTER!
I FEEL A SONG COMING ON FASTER!
SING IT, MOKEY!
UH... IT WENT SO FAST, IT'S GONE!
LOOK OUT! HERE COME THE DOOZERS!
BOY, THOSE DOOZERS NEVER STOP WORKING!
BUT YOU KNOW, GOBO...
WHAT?
...THEY'VE NEVER BUILT THIS FAST BEFORE!

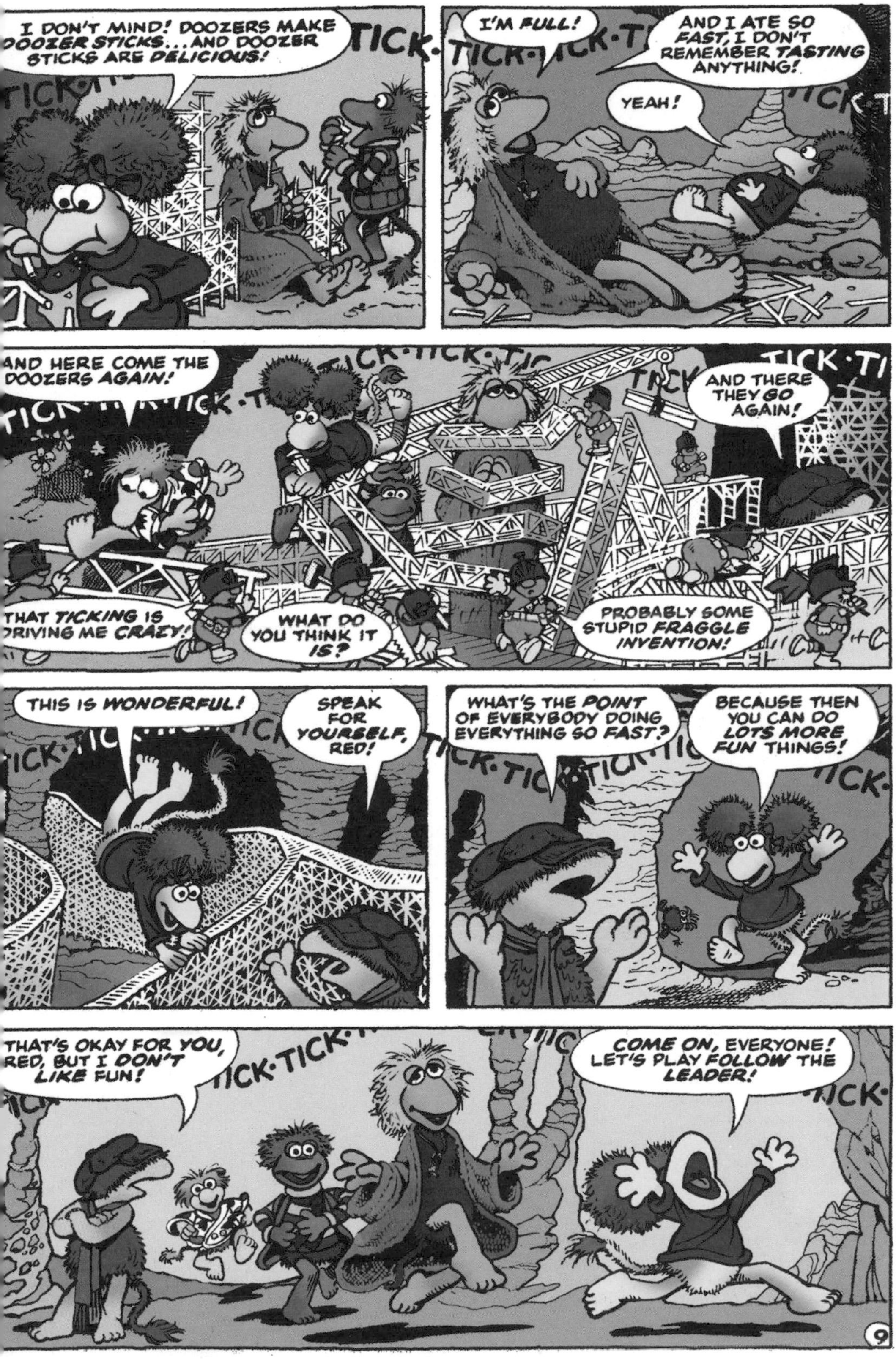
I DON'T MIND! DOOZERS MAKE DOOZER STICKS... AND DOOZER STICKS ARE DELICIOUS!
TICK·TICK·TICK·TI
I'M FULL!
AND I ATE SO FAST, I DON'T REMEMBER TASTING ANYTHING!
YEAH!
AND HERE COME THE DOOZERS AGAIN!
AND THERE THEY GO AGAIN!
THAT TICKING IS DRIVING ME CRAZY!
WHAT DO YOU THINK IT IS?
PROBABLY SOME STUPID FRAGGLE INVENTION!
THIS IS WONDERFUL!
SPEAK FOR YOURSELF, RED!
WHAT'S THE POINT OF EVERYBODY DOING EVERYTHING SO FAST?
BECAUSE THEN YOU CAN DO LOTS MORE FUN THINGS!
THAT'S OKAY FOR YOU, RED, BUT I DON'T LIKE FUN!
TICK·TICK·
COME ON, EVERYONE! LET'S PLAY FOLLOW THE LEADER!
9

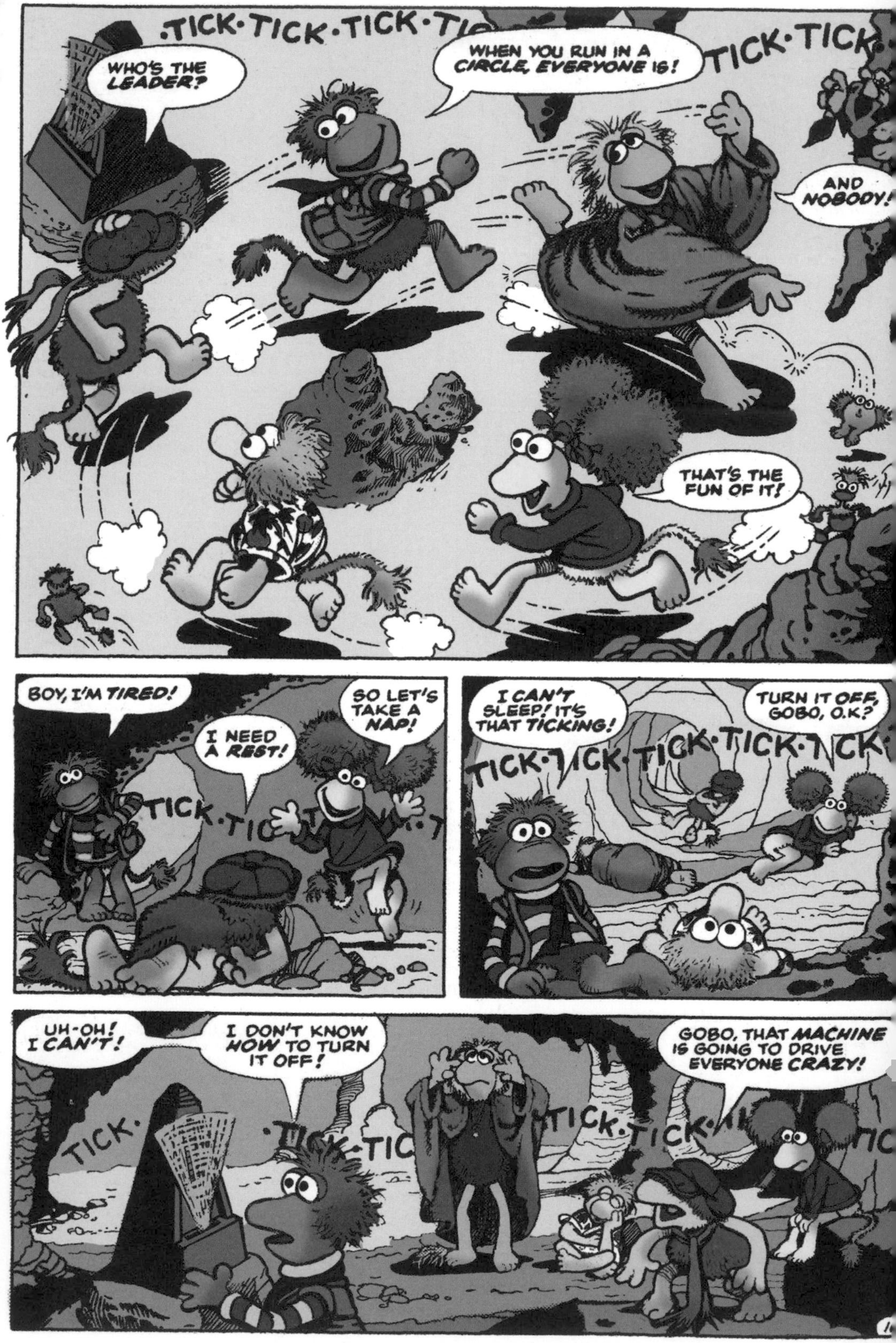
TICK·TICK·TICK·
WHO'S THE LEADER?
WHEN YOU RUN IN A CIRCLE, EVERYONE IS!
TICK·TICK
AND NOBODY!
THAT'S THE FUN OF IT!
BOY, I'M TIRED!
I NEED A REST!
SO LET'S TAKE A NAP!
I CAN'T SLEEP! IT'S THAT TICKING!
TURN IT OFF, GOBO, O.K.?
TICK·TICK·TICK·TICK·
UH-OH! I CAN'T!
I DON'T KNOW HOW TO TURN IT OFF!
GOBO, THAT MACHINE IS GOING TO DRIVE EVERYONE CRAZY!
TICK·
TICK·TICK

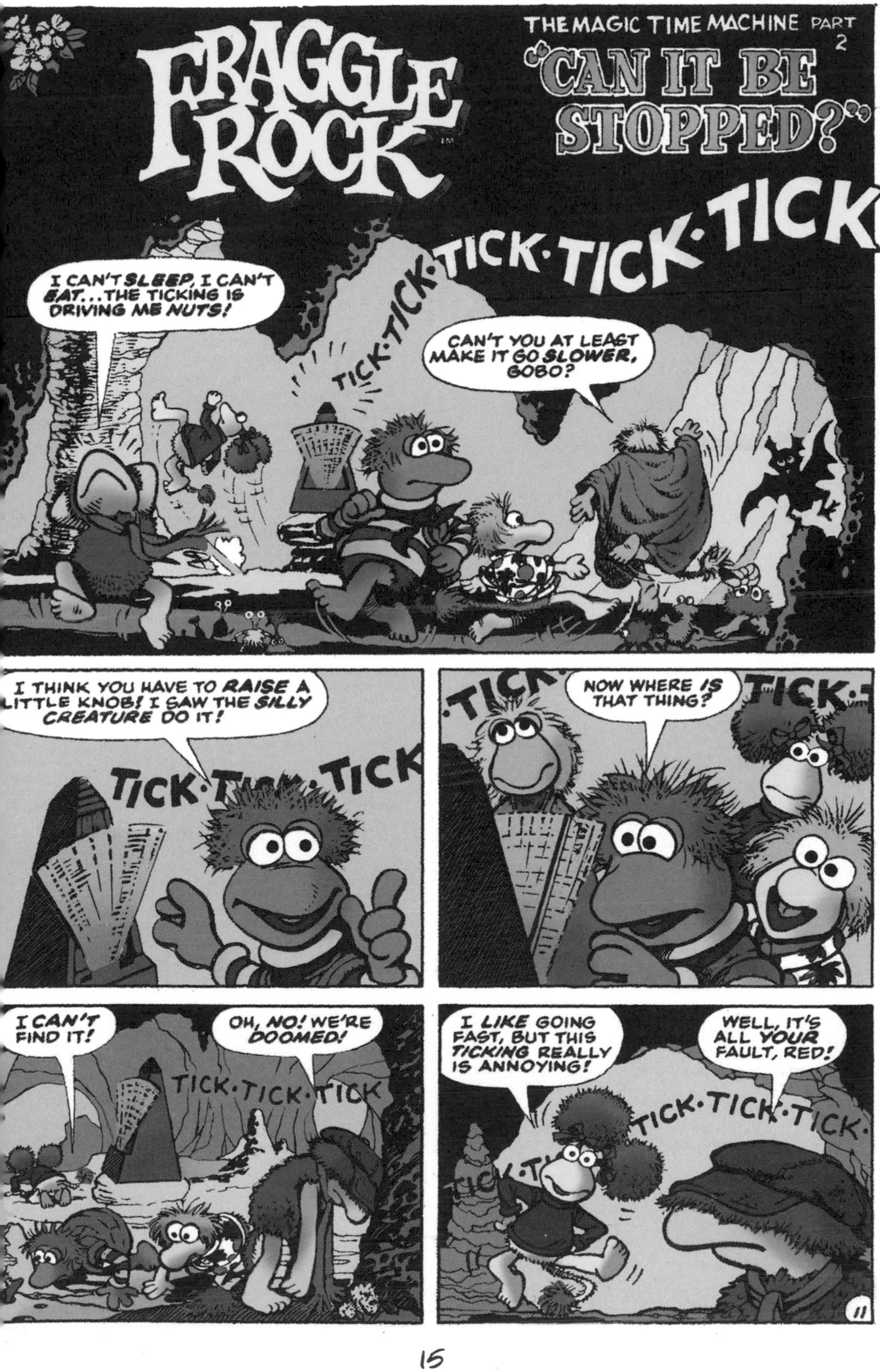
FRAGGLE ROCK TM
THE MAGIC TIME MACHINE PART 2
"CAN IT BE STOPPED?"
TICK·TICK·TICK·TICK·TICK·TICK
I CAN'T SLEEP, I CAN'T EAT...THE TICKING IS DRIVING ME NUTS!
CAN'T YOU AT LEAST MAKE IT GO SLOWER, GOBO?
I THINK YOU HAVE TO RAISE A LITTLE KNOB! I SAW THE SILLY CREATURE DO IT!
TICK·T ·TICK
NOW WHERE IS THAT THING?
TICK·
I CAN'T FIND IT!
OH, NO! WE'RE DOOMED!
TICK·TICK·TICK
I LIKE GOING FAST, BUT THIS TICKING REALLY IS ANNOYING!
WELL, IT'S ALL YOUR FAULT, RED!
TICK·TICK·TICK·TICK·
11

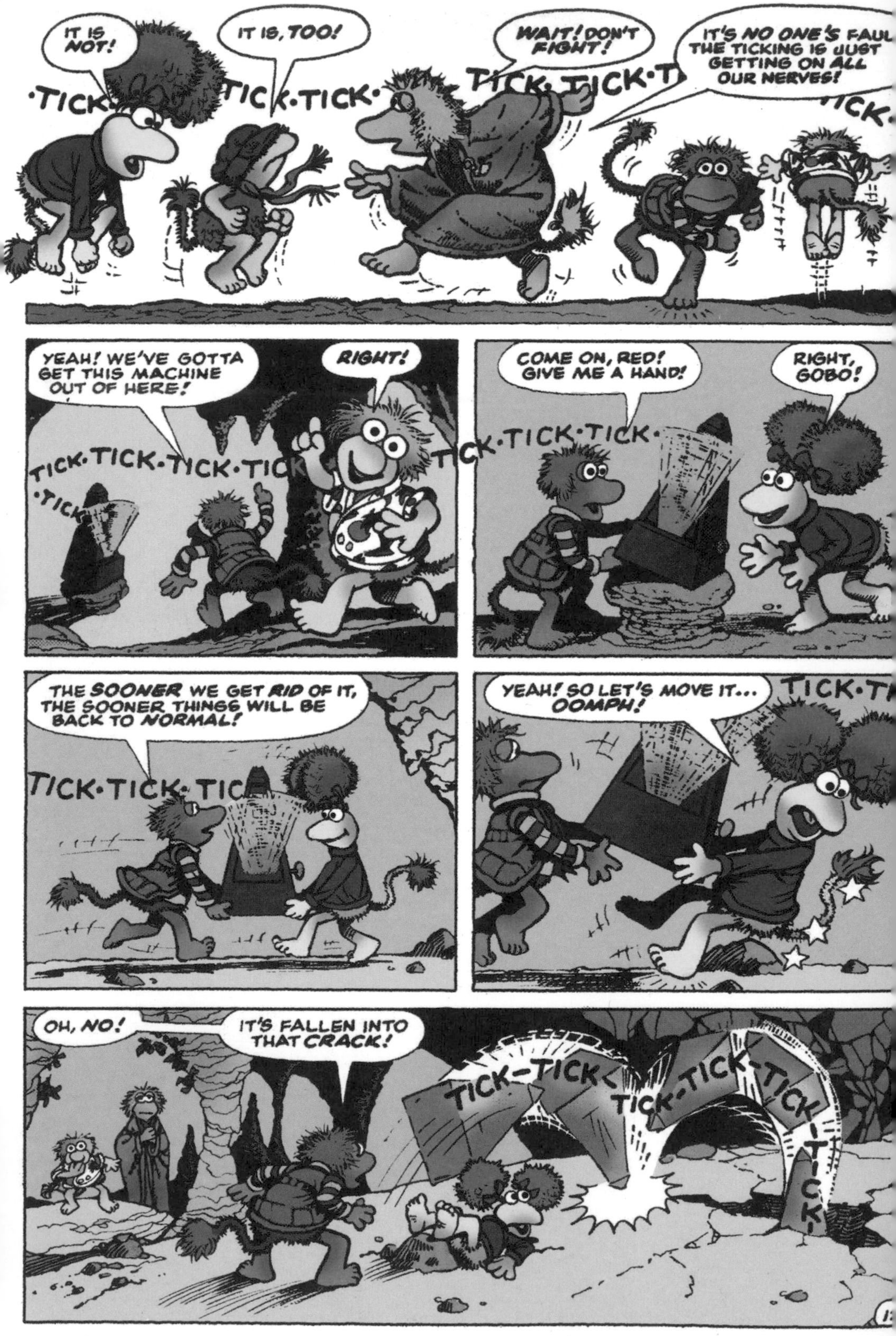
IT IS NOT!
·TICK·
IT IS, TOO!
TICK·TICK·
WAIT! DON'T FIGHT!
TICK·TICK·T
IT'S NO ONE'S FAUL THE TICKING IS JUST GETTING ON ALL OUR NERVES!
ICK·
YEAH! WE'VE GOTTA GET THIS MACHINE OUT OF HERE!
RIGHT!
TICK·TICK·TICK·TIC
·TICK
COME ON, RED! GIVE ME A HAND!
RIGHT, GOBO!
TICK·TICK·TICK·
THE SOONER WE GET RID OF IT, THE SOONER THINGS WILL BE BACK TO NORMAL!
TICK·TICK·TIC
YEAH! SO LET'S MOVE IT... OOMPH!
TICK·T
OH, NO!
IT'S FALLEN INTO THAT CRACK!
TICK-TICK-TICK-TICK-TICK-TICK

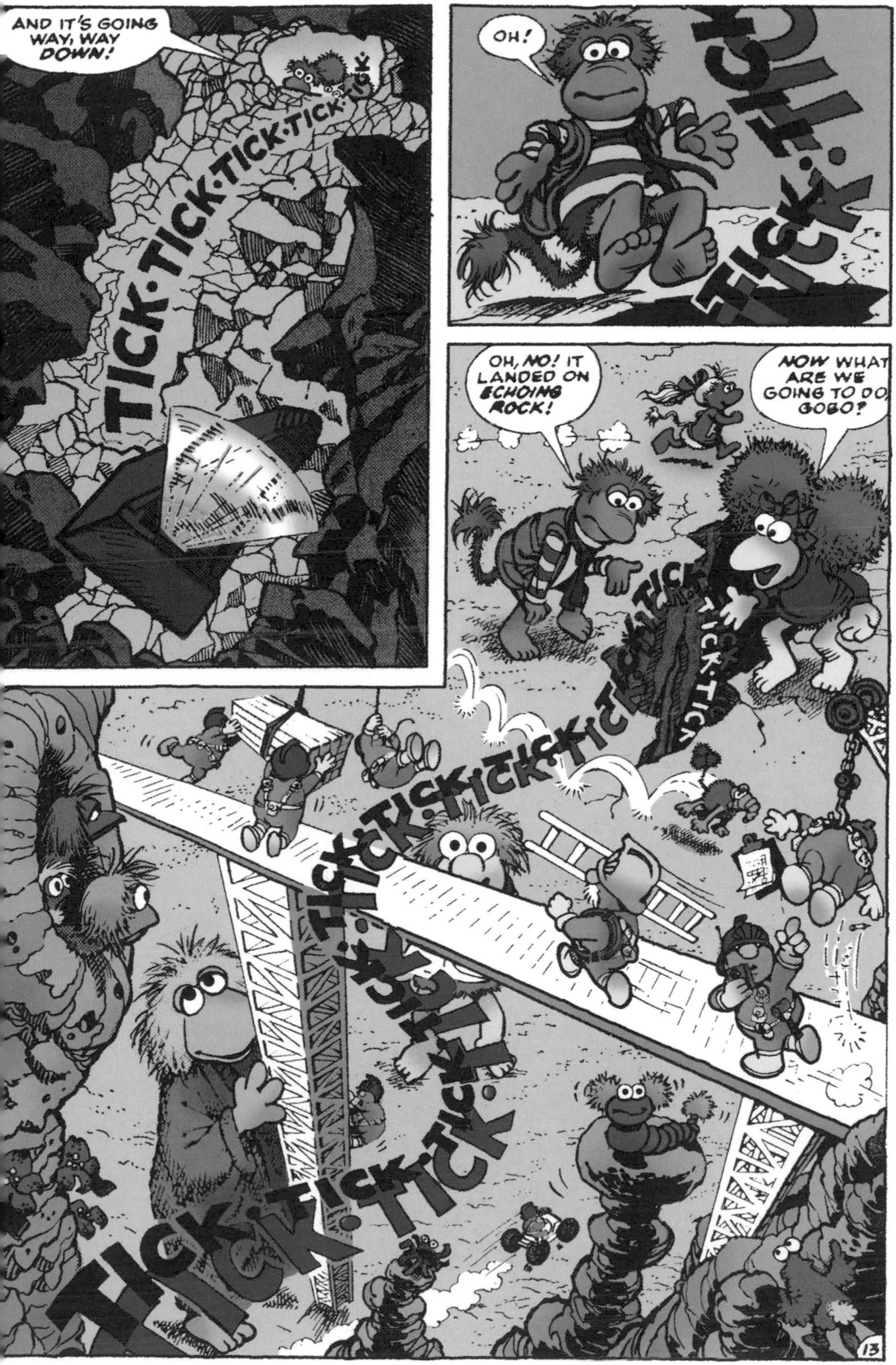
AND IT'S GOING WAY, WAY DOWN!
TICK·TICK·TICK·TICK·TICK
OH!
TICK·TICK
OH, NO! IT LANDED ON ECHOING ROCK!
NOW WHAT ARE WE GOING TO DO, GOBO?
TICK·TICK·TICK
TICK·TICK·TICK·TICK
TICK·TICK·TICK·TICK
13

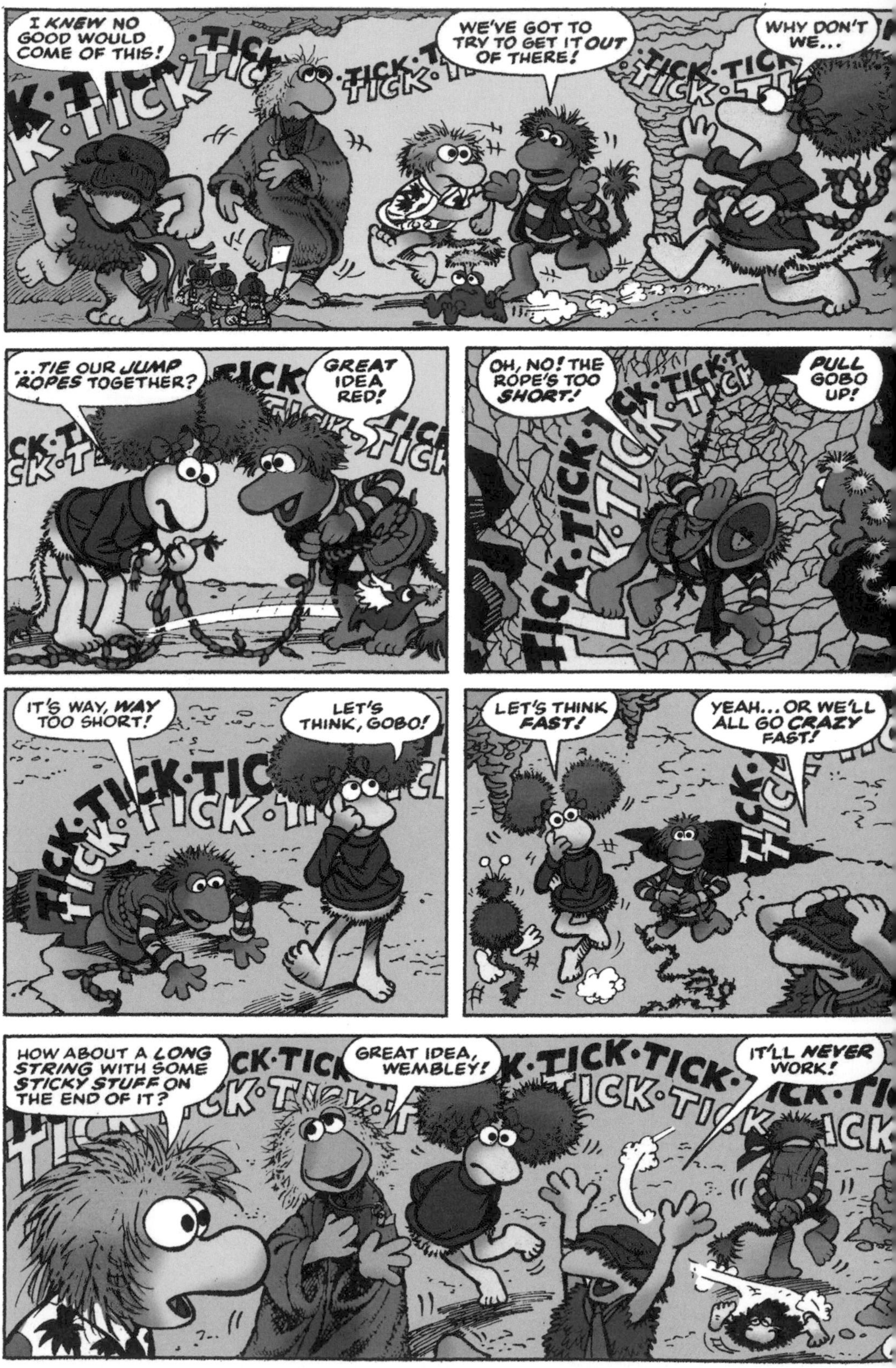
I KNEW NO GOOD WOULD COME OF THIS!
WE'VE GOT TO TRY TO GET IT OUT OF THERE!
WHY DON'T WE...
TICK·TICK·TICK
...TIE OUR JUMP ROPES TOGETHER?
GREAT IDEA RED!
OH, NO! THE ROPE'S TOO SHORT!
PULL GOBO UP!
IT'S WAY, WAY TOO SHORT!
LET'S THINK, GOBO!
LET'S THINK FAST!
YEAH...OR WE'LL ALL GO CRAZY FAST!
HOW ABOUT A LONG STRING WITH SOME STICKY STUFF ON THE END OF IT?
GREAT IDEA, WEMBLEY!
IT'LL NEVER WORK!

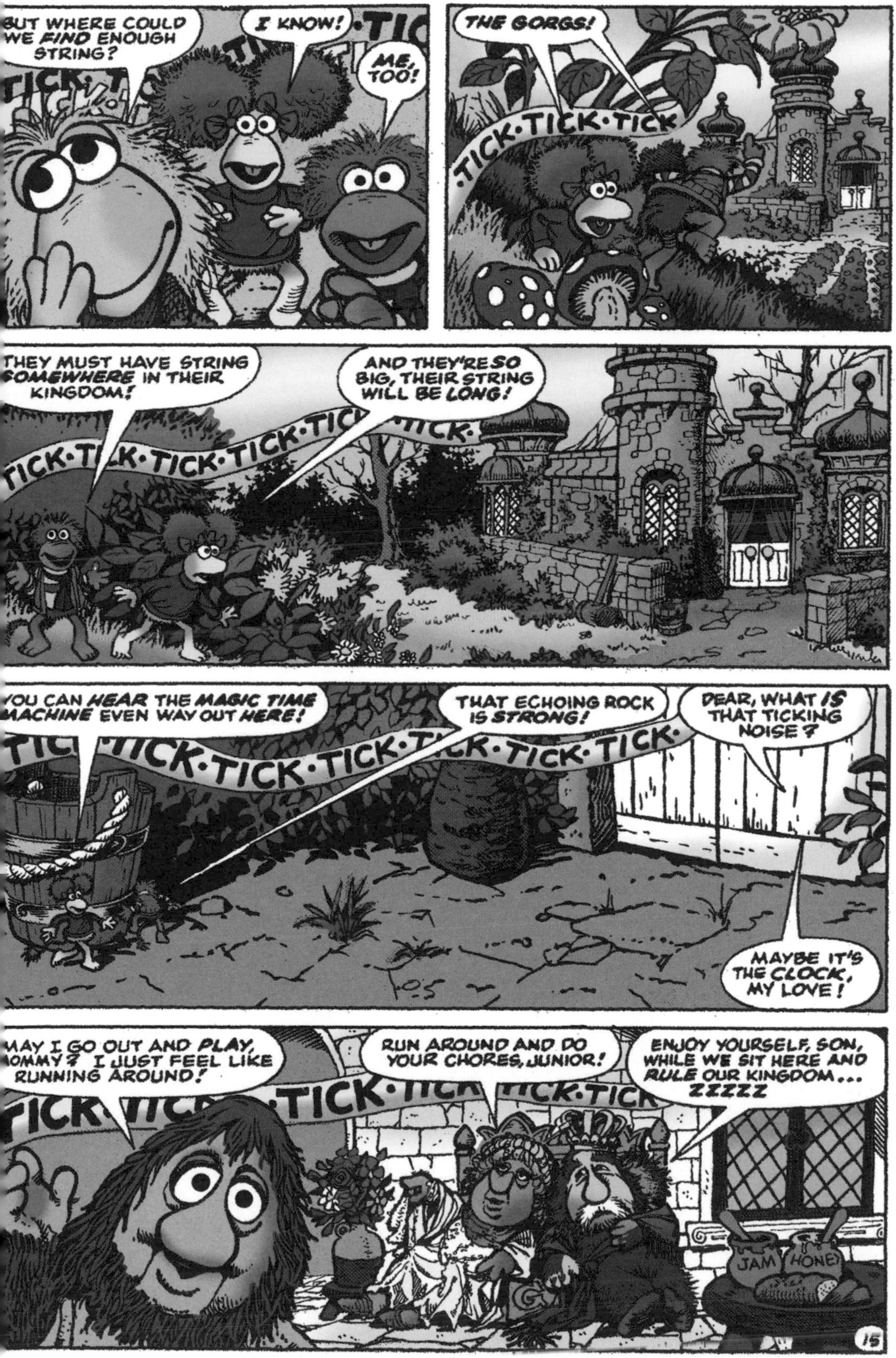
BUT WHERE COULD WE FIND ENOUGH STRING?
I KNOW!
ME, TOO!
TICK
THE GORGS!
TICK·TICK·TICK
THEY MUST HAVE STRING SOMEWHERE IN THEIR KINGDOM!
AND THEY'RE SO BIG, THEIR STRING WILL BE LONG!
TICK·TICK·TICK·TICK·TICK·TICK·
YOU CAN HEAR THE MAGIC TIME MACHINE EVEN WAY OUT HERE!
THAT ECHOING ROCK IS STRONG!
DEAR, WHAT IS THAT TICKING NOISE?
TICK·TICK·TICK·TICK·TICK·TICK·TICK·
MAYBE IT'S THE CLOCK, MY LOVE!
MAY I GO OUT AND PLAY, MOMMY? I JUST FEEL LIKE RUNNING AROUND!
RUN AROUND AND DO YOUR CHORES, JUNIOR!
ENJOY YOURSELF, SON, WHILE WE SIT HERE AND RULE OUR KINGDOM... ZZZZZ
TICK·TICK·TICK·TICK·TICK
JAM
HONEY
15

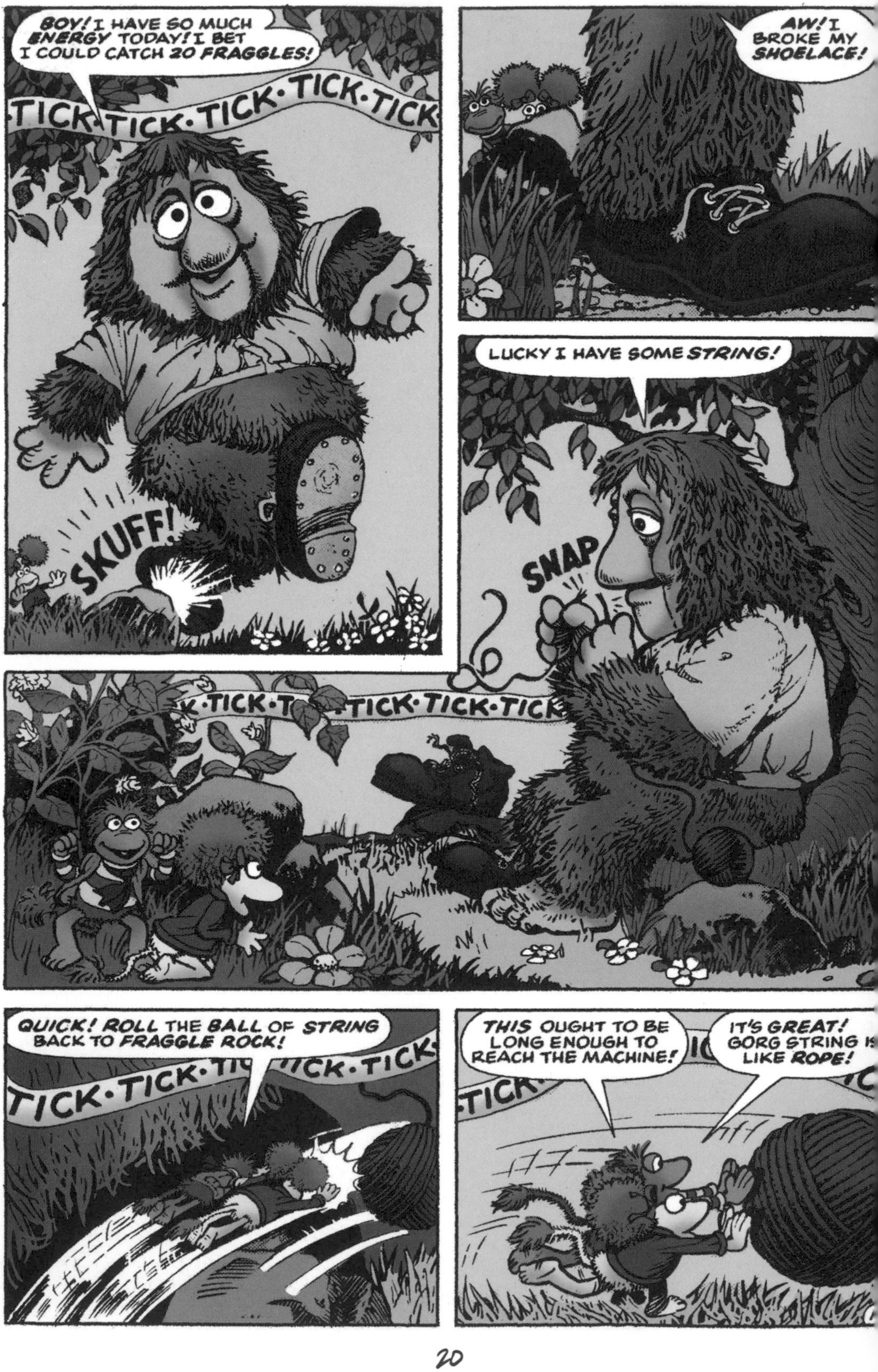
BOY! I HAVE SO MUCH ENERGY TODAY! I BET I COULD CATCH 20 FRAGGLES!
TICK·TICK·TICK·TICK·TICK
SKUFF!
AW! I BROKE MY SHOELACE!
LUCKY I HAVE SOME STRING!
SNAP
K·TICK·T TICK·TICK·TICK
QUICK! ROLL THE BALL OF STRING BACK TO FRAGGLE ROCK!
TICK·TICK·TI ICK·TICK·
THIS OUGHT TO BE LONG ENOUGH TO REACH THE MACHINE!
IT'S GREAT! GORG STRING IS LIKE ROPE!

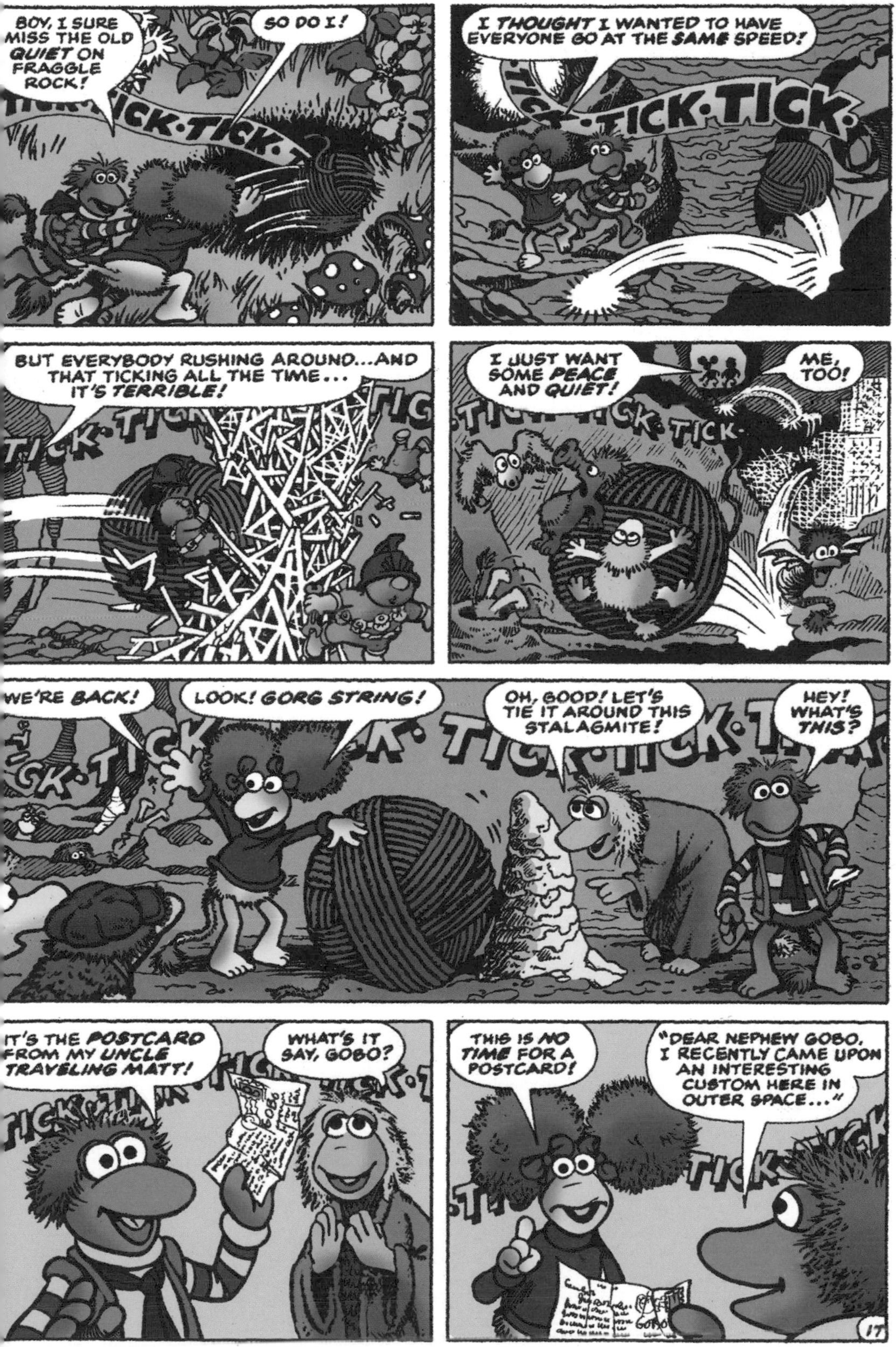
BOY, I SURE MISS THE OLD QUIET ON FRAGGLE ROCK!
SO DO I!
TICK·TICK·TICK·
I THOUGHT I WANTED TO HAVE EVERYONE GO AT THE SAME SPEED!
TICK·TICK·TICK·
BUT EVERYBODY RUSHING AROUND...AND THAT TICKING ALL THE TIME... IT'S TERRIBLE!
I JUST WANT SOME PEACE AND QUIET!
ME, TOO!
TICK·TICK·TICK·
WE'RE BACK!
LOOK! GORG STRING!
OH, GOOD! LET'S TIE IT AROUND THIS STALAGMITE!
HEY! WHAT'S THIS?
TICK·TICK·TICK·
IT'S THE POSTCARD FROM MY UNCLE TRAVELING MATT!
WHAT'S IT SAY, GOBO?
THIS IS NO TIME FOR A POSTCARD!
"DEAR NEPHEW GOBO, I RECENTLY CAME UPON AN INTERESTING CUSTOM HERE IN OUTER SPACE..."
17

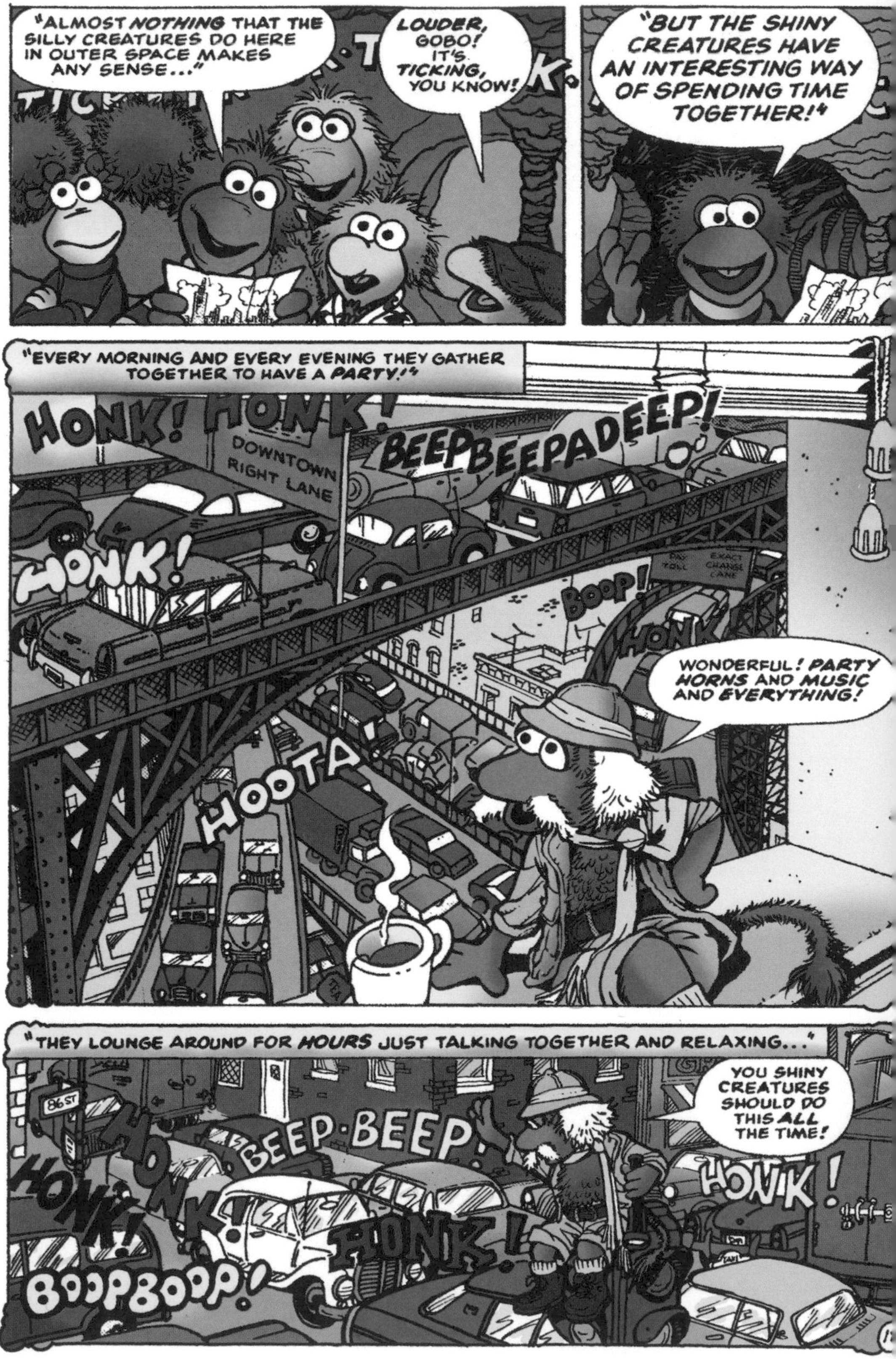
"ALMOST NOTHING THAT THE SILLY CREATURES DO HERE IN OUTER SPACE MAKES ANY SENSE..."
LOUDER, GOBO! IT'S TICKING, YOU KNOW!
"BUT THE SHINY CREATURES HAVE AN INTERESTING WAY OF SPENDING TIME TOGETHER!"
"EVERY MORNING AND EVERY EVENING THEY GATHER TOGETHER TO HAVE A PARTY!"
HONK! HONK!
DOWNTOWN RIGHT LANE
BEEP BEEPADEEP!
HONK!
PAY TOLL
EXACT CHANGE LANE
BOOP!
HONK
WONDERFUL! PARTY HORNS AND MUSIC AND EVERYTHING!
HOOTA
"THEY LOUNGE AROUND FOR HOURS JUST TALKING TOGETHER AND RELAXING..."
86 ST
YOU SHINY CREATURES SHOULD DO THIS ALL THE TIME!
HONK
BEEP-BEEP!
HONK!
HONK!
BOOPBOOP!
HONK!

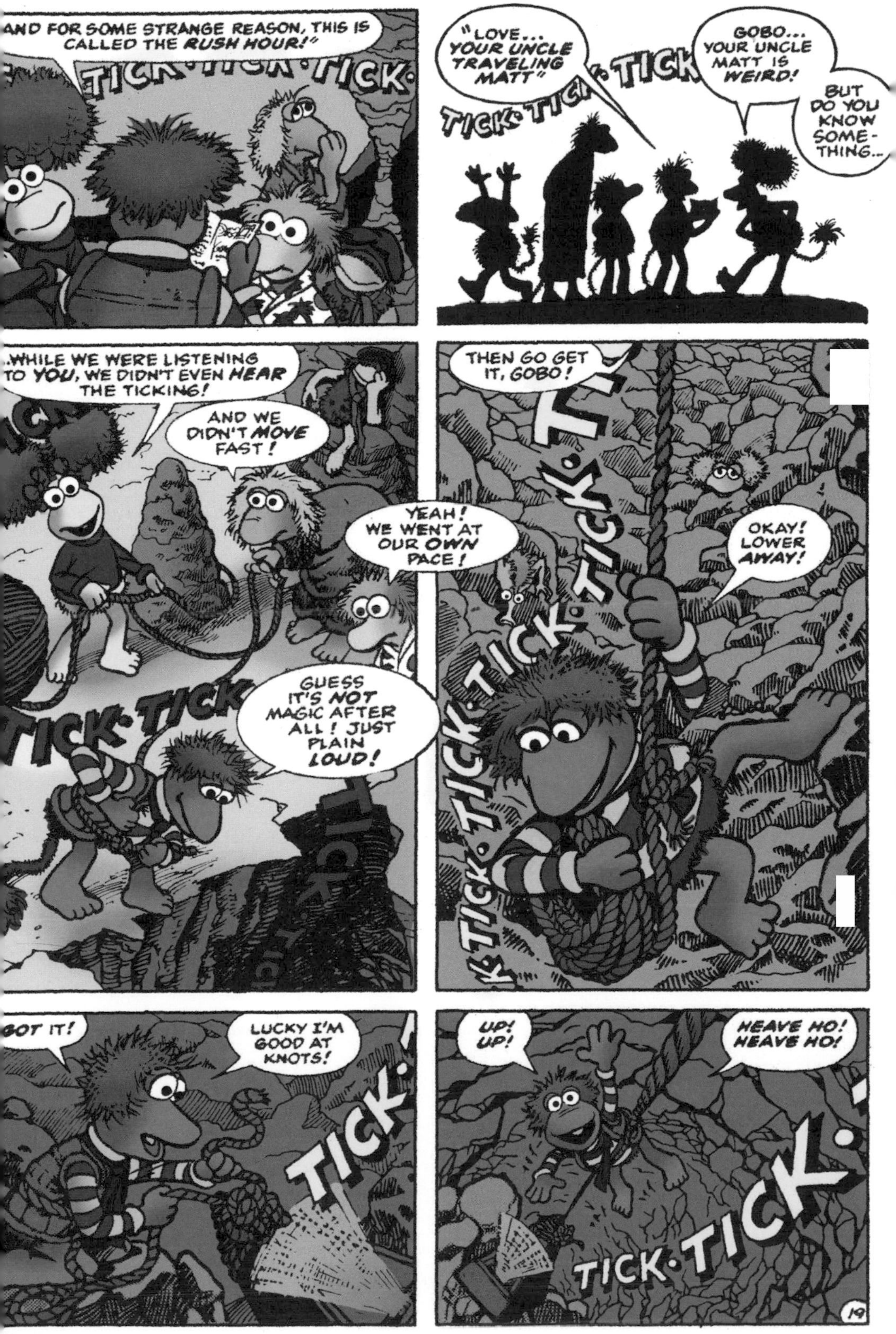
AND FOR SOME STRANGE REASON, THIS IS CALLED THE RUSH HOUR!"
TICK·TICK·TICK·
"LOVE... YOUR UNCLE TRAVELING MATT"
TICK·TICK·TICK
GOBO... YOUR UNCLE MATT IS WEIRD!
BUT DO YOU KNOW SOME-THING...
...WHILE WE WERE LISTENING TO YOU, WE DIDN'T EVEN HEAR THE TICKING!
AND WE DIDN'T MOVE FAST!
YEAH! WE WENT AT OUR OWN PACE!
TICK·TICK
GUESS IT'S NOT MAGIC AFTER ALL! JUST PLAIN LOUD!
TICK
THEN GO GET IT, GOBO!
OKAY! LOWER AWAY!
TICK·TICK·TICK·TICK·TICK·
GOT IT!
LUCKY I'M GOOD AT KNOTS!
TICK·
UP! UP!
HEAVE HO! HEAVE HO!
TICK·TICK·TICK·
19

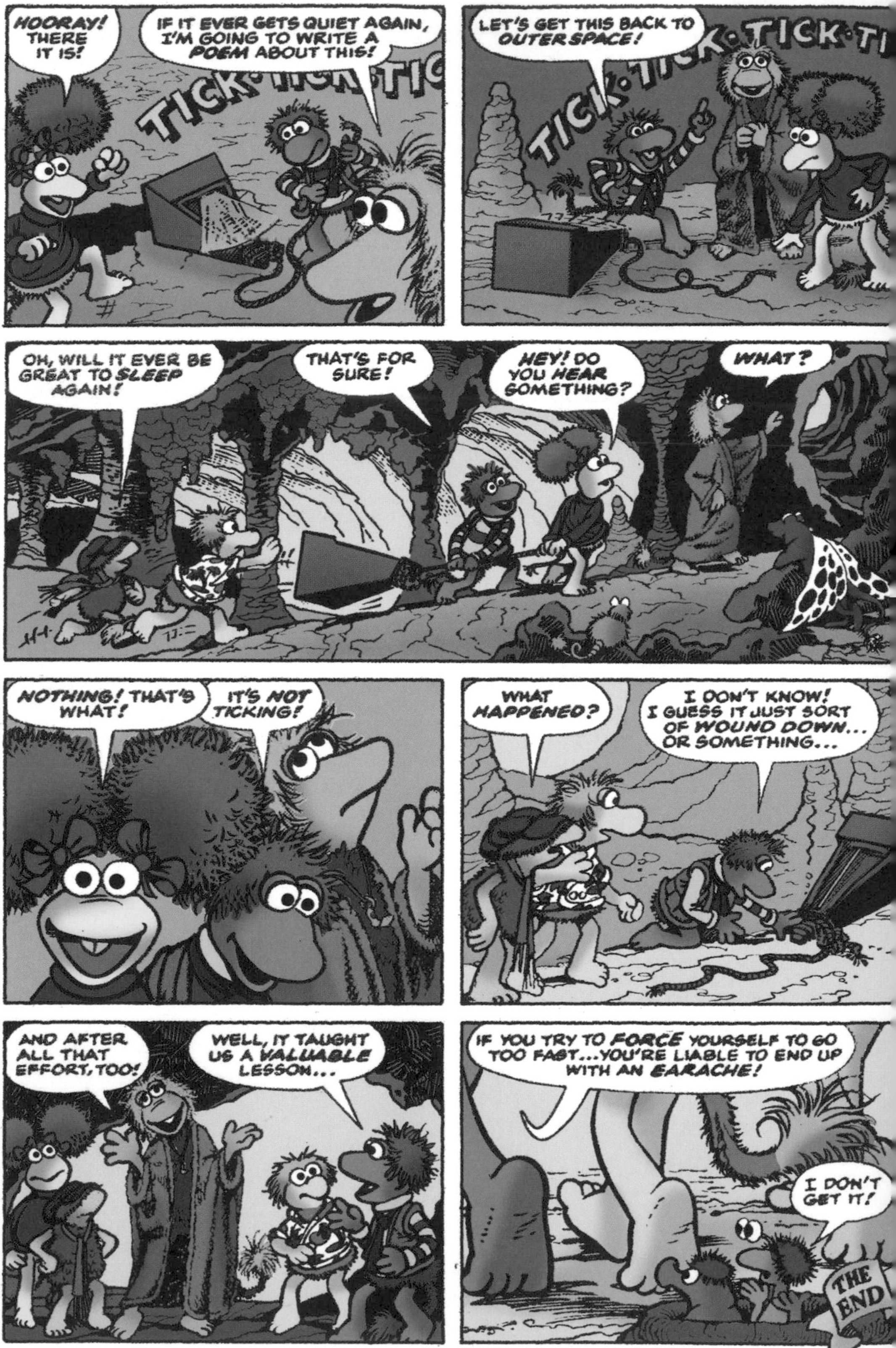
HOORAY! THERE IT IS!
IF IT EVER GETS QUIET AGAIN, I'M GOING TO WRITE A POEM ABOUT THIS!
TICK·TICK·TIC
LET'S GET THIS BACK TO OUTER SPACE!
TICK·TICK·TICK·TI
OH, WILL IT EVER BE GREAT TO SLEEP AGAIN!
THAT'S FOR SURE!
HEY! DO YOU HEAR SOMETHING?
WHAT?
NOTHING! THAT'S WHAT!
IT'S NOT TICKING!
WHAT HAPPENED?
I DON'T KNOW! I GUESS IT JUST SORT OF WOUND DOWN... OR SOMETHING...
AND AFTER ALL THAT EFFORT, TOO!
WELL, IT TAUGHT US A VALUABLE LESSON...
IF YOU TRY TO FORCE YOURSELF TO GO TOO FAST...YOU'RE LIABLE TO END UP WITH AN EARACHE!
I DON'T GET IT!
THE END

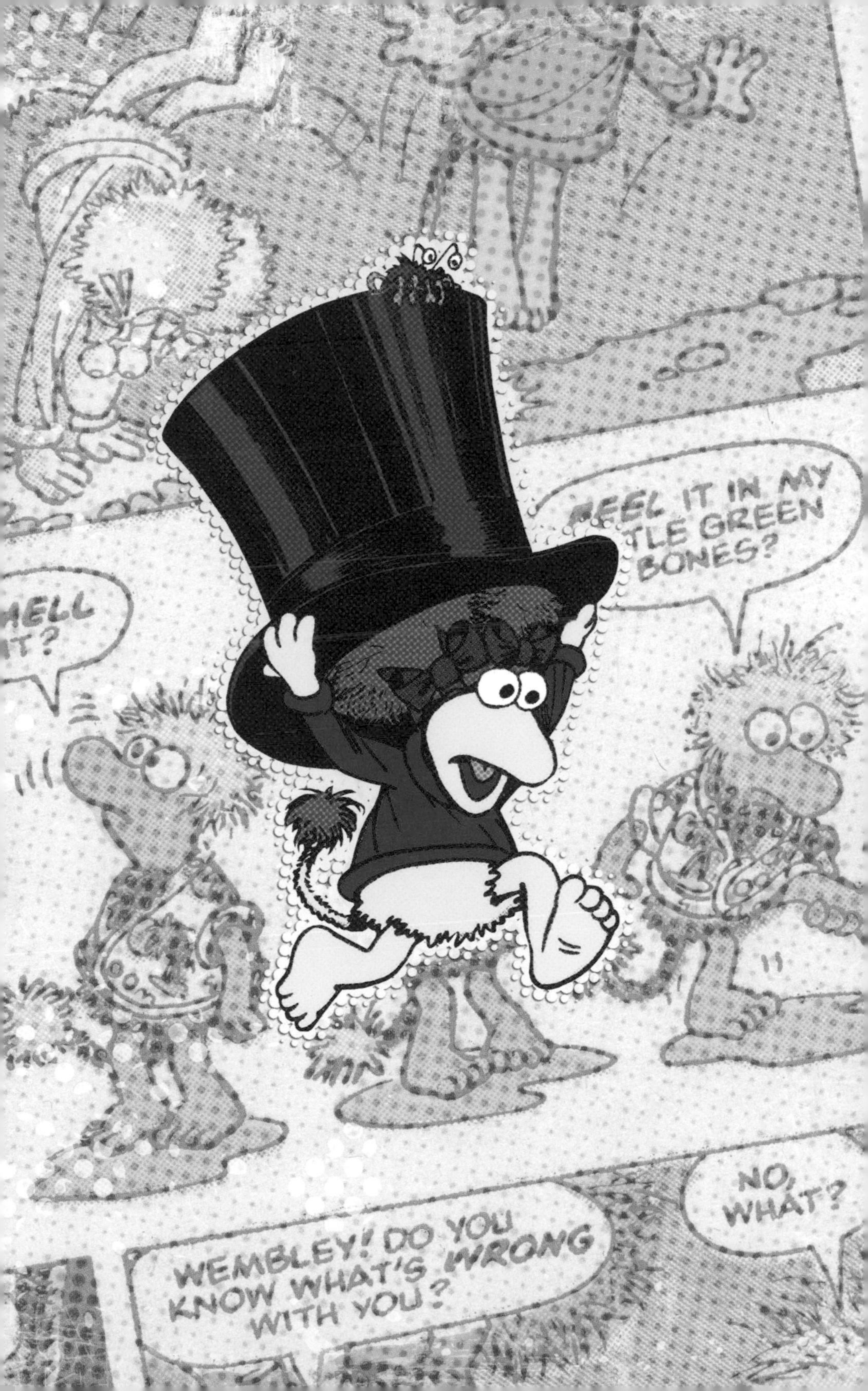

MELL
IT?
EEL IT IN MY
TLE GREEN
BONES?
WEMBLEY! DO YOU KNOW WHAT'S *WRONG* WITH YOU?
NO, WHAT?

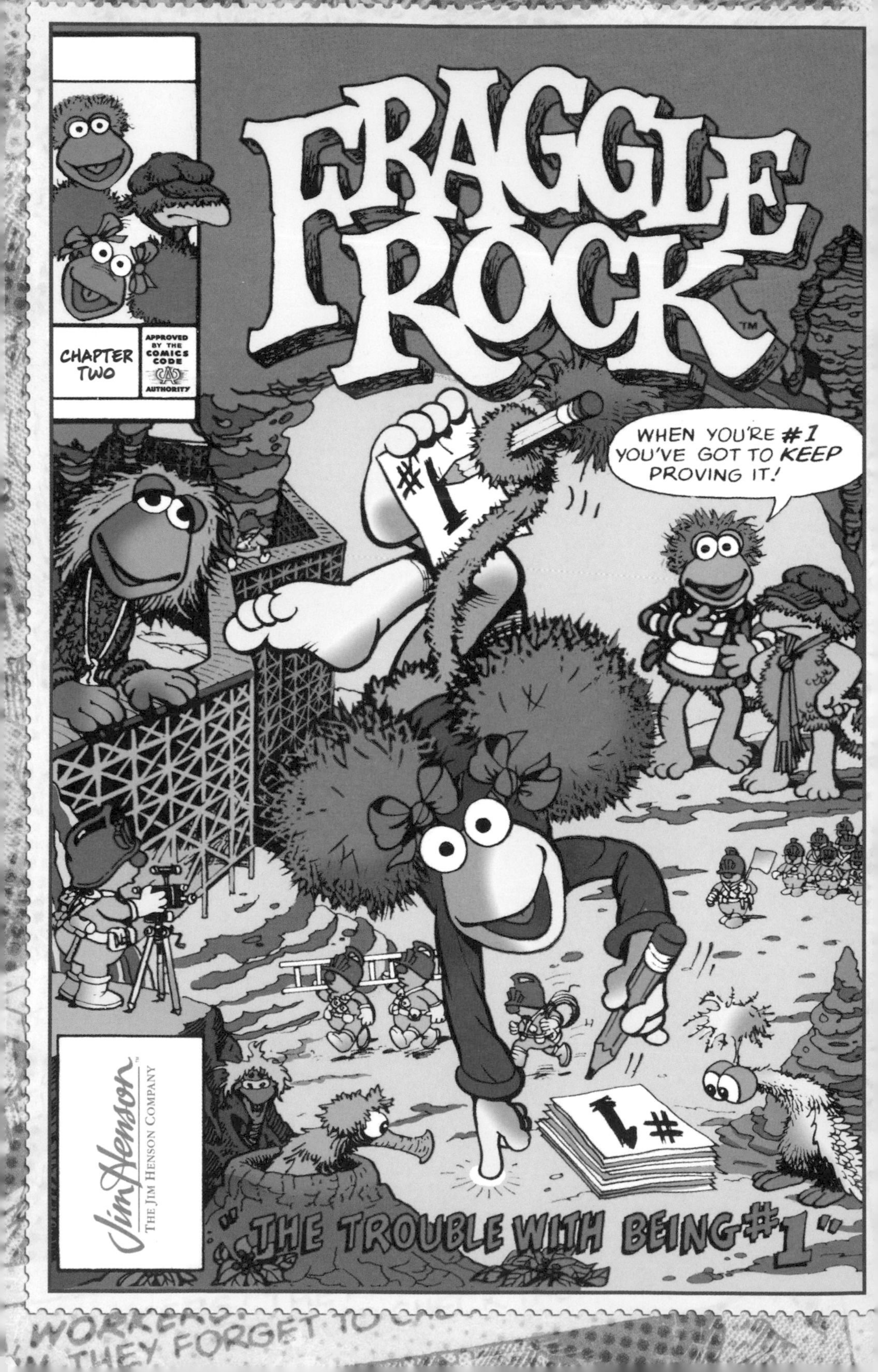
FRAGGLE ROCK™
CHAPTER TWO
APPROVED BY THE COMICS CODE AUTHORITY
WHEN YOU'RE #1 YOU'VE GOT TO KEEP PROVING IT!
#1
Jim Henson™
THE JIM HENSON COMPANY
"THE TROUBLE WITH BEING #1"

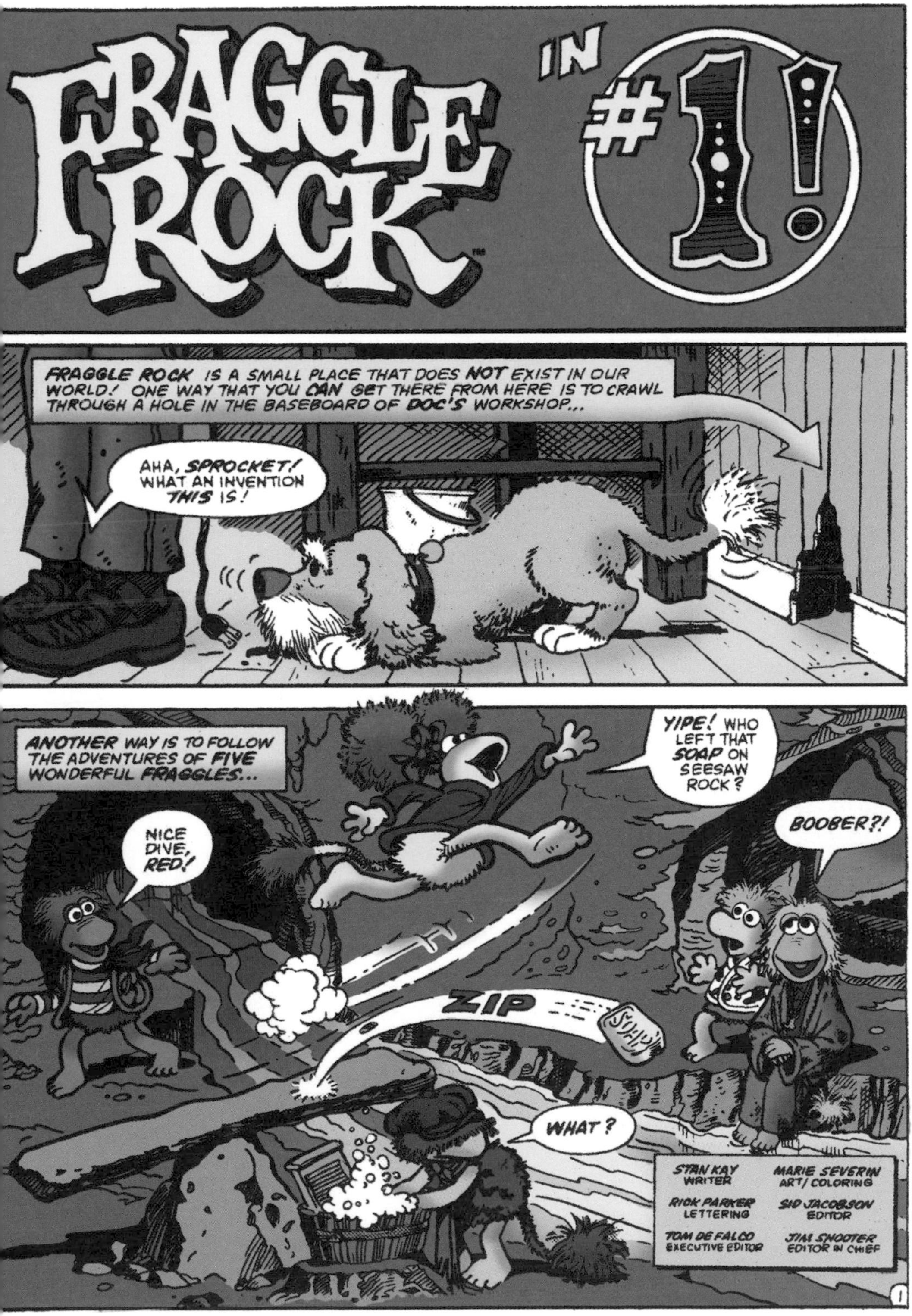
FRAGGLE ROCK IN #1!
FRAGGLE ROCK IS A SMALL PLACE THAT DOES NOT EXIST IN OUR WORLD! ONE WAY THAT YOU CAN GET THERE FROM HERE IS TO CRAWL THROUGH A HOLE IN THE BASEBOARD OF DOC'S WORKSHOP...
AHA, SPROCKET! WHAT AN INVENTION THIS IS!
ANOTHER WAY IS TO FOLLOW THE ADVENTURES OF FIVE WONDERFUL FRAGGLES...
YIPE! WHO LEFT THAT SOAP ON SEESAW ROCK?
NICE DIVE, RED!
BOOBER?!
ZIP
SOAP
WHAT?
STAN KAY WRITER
MARIE SEVERIN ART/COLORING
RICK PARKER LETTERING
SID JACOBSON EDITOR
TOM DE FALCO EXECUTIVE EDITOR
JIM SHOOTER EDITOR IN CHIEF
1

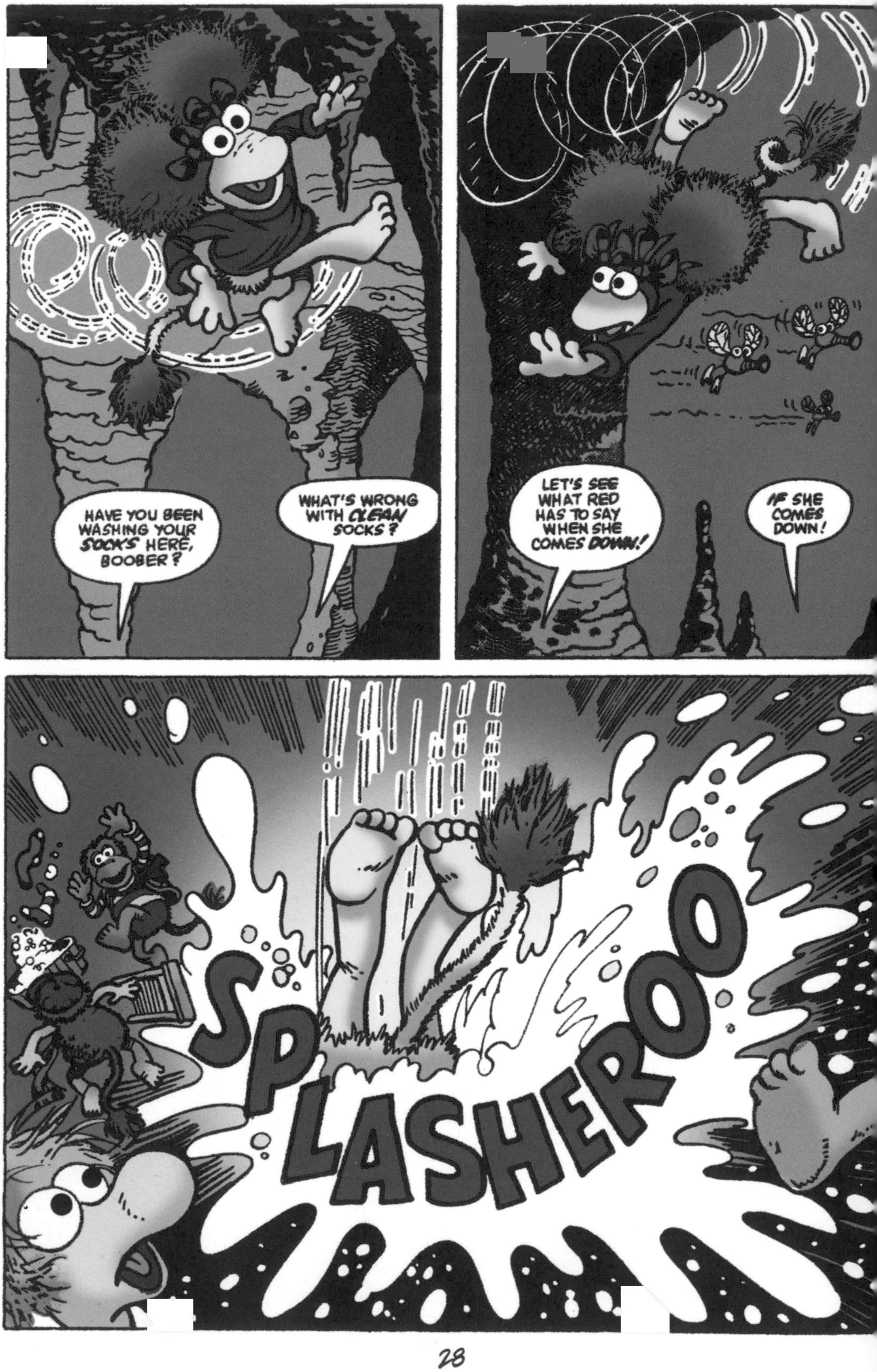

HAVE YOU BEEN WASHING YOUR SOCKS HERE, BOOBER?
WHAT'S WRONG WITH CLEAN SOCKS?
LET'S SEE WHAT RED HAS TO SAY WHEN SHE COMES DOWN!
IF SHE COMES DOWN!
SPLASHEROO

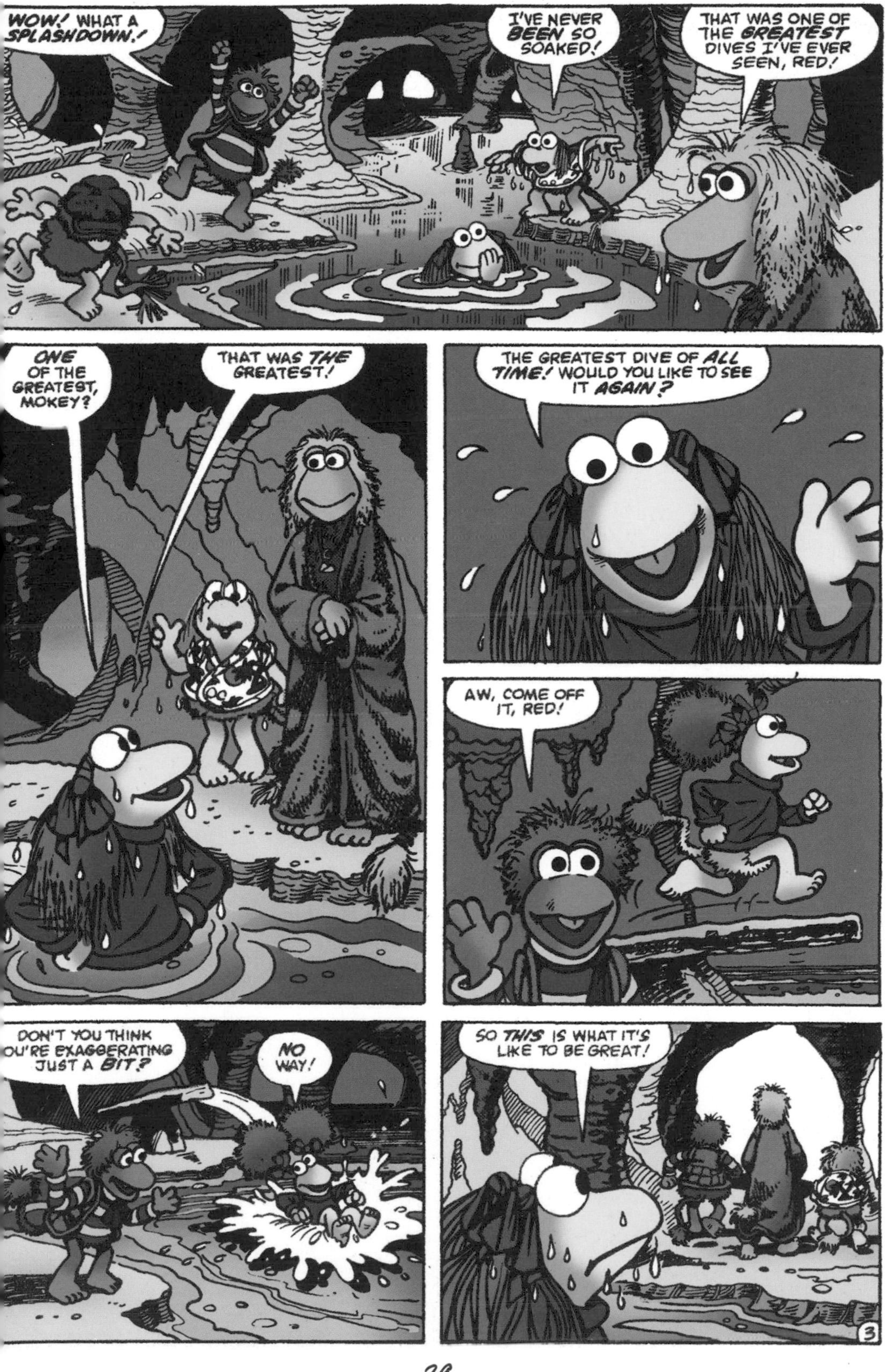

WOW! WHAT A SPLASHDOWN!
I'VE NEVER BEEN SO SOAKED!
THAT WAS ONE OF THE GREATEST DIVES I'VE EVER SEEN, RED!
ONE OF THE GREATEST, MOKEY?
THAT WAS THE GREATEST!
THE GREATEST DIVE OF ALL TIME! WOULD YOU LIKE TO SEE IT AGAIN?
AW, COME OFF IT, RED!
DON'T YOU THINK YOU'RE EXAGGERATING JUST A BIT?
NO WAY!
SO THIS IS WHAT IT'S LIKE TO BE GREAT!
3

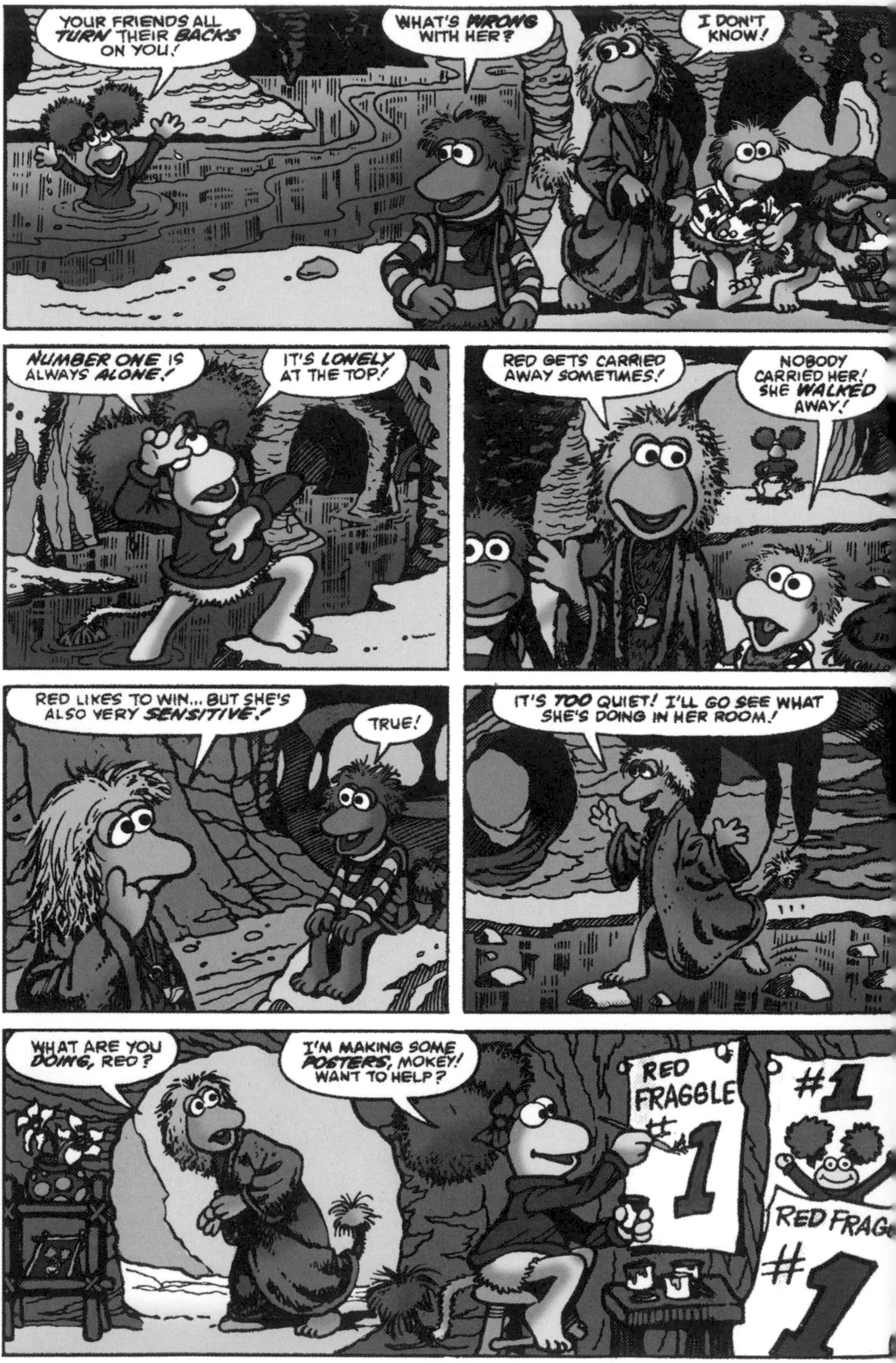

YOUR FRIENDS ALL TURN THEIR BACKS ON YOU!
WHAT'S WRONG WITH HER?
I DON'T KNOW!
NUMBER ONE IS ALWAYS ALONE!
IT'S LONELY AT THE TOP!
RED GETS CARRIED AWAY SOMETIMES!
NOBODY CARRIED HER! SHE WALKED AWAY!
RED LIKES TO WIN... BUT SHE'S ALSO VERY SENSITIVE!
TRUE!
IT'S TOO QUIET! I'LL GO SEE WHAT SHE'S DOING IN HER ROOM!
WHAT ARE YOU DOING, RED?
I'M MAKING SOME POSTERS, MOKEY! WANT TO HELP?
RED FRAGGLE #1
#1
RED FRAG
#1

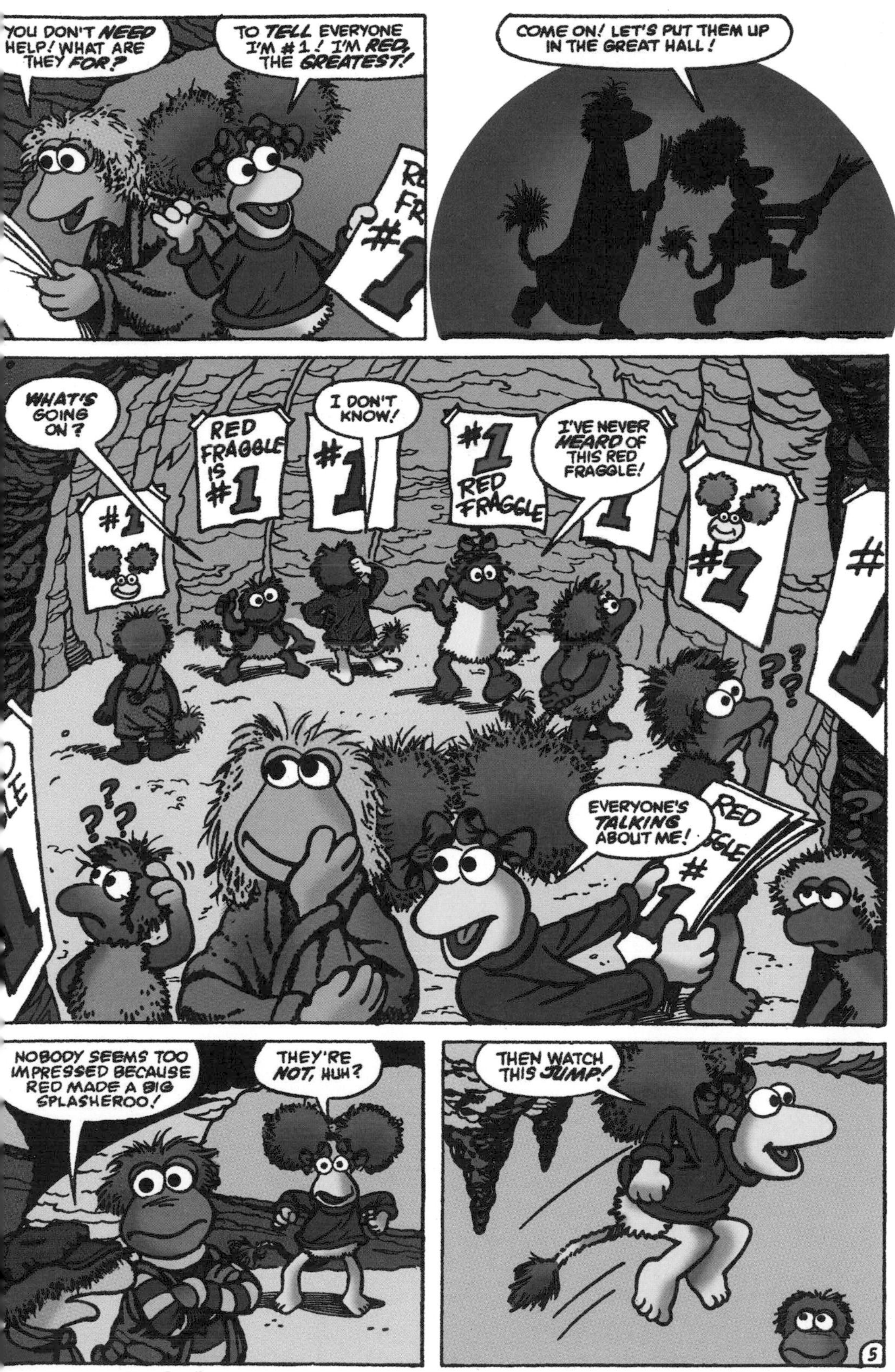
YOU DON'T NEED HELP! WHAT ARE THEY FOR?
TO TELL EVERYONE I'M #1! I'M RED, THE GREATEST!
COME ON! LET'S PUT THEM UP IN THE GREAT HALL!
WHAT'S GOING ON?
RED FRAGGLE IS #1
I DON'T KNOW!
#1 RED FRAGGLE
I'VE NEVER HEARD OF THIS RED FRAGGLE!
EVERYONE'S TALKING ABOUT ME!
NOBODY SEEMS TOO IMPRESSED BECAUSE RED MADE A BIG SPLASHEROO!
THEY'RE NOT, HUH?
THEN WATCH THIS JUMP!
5

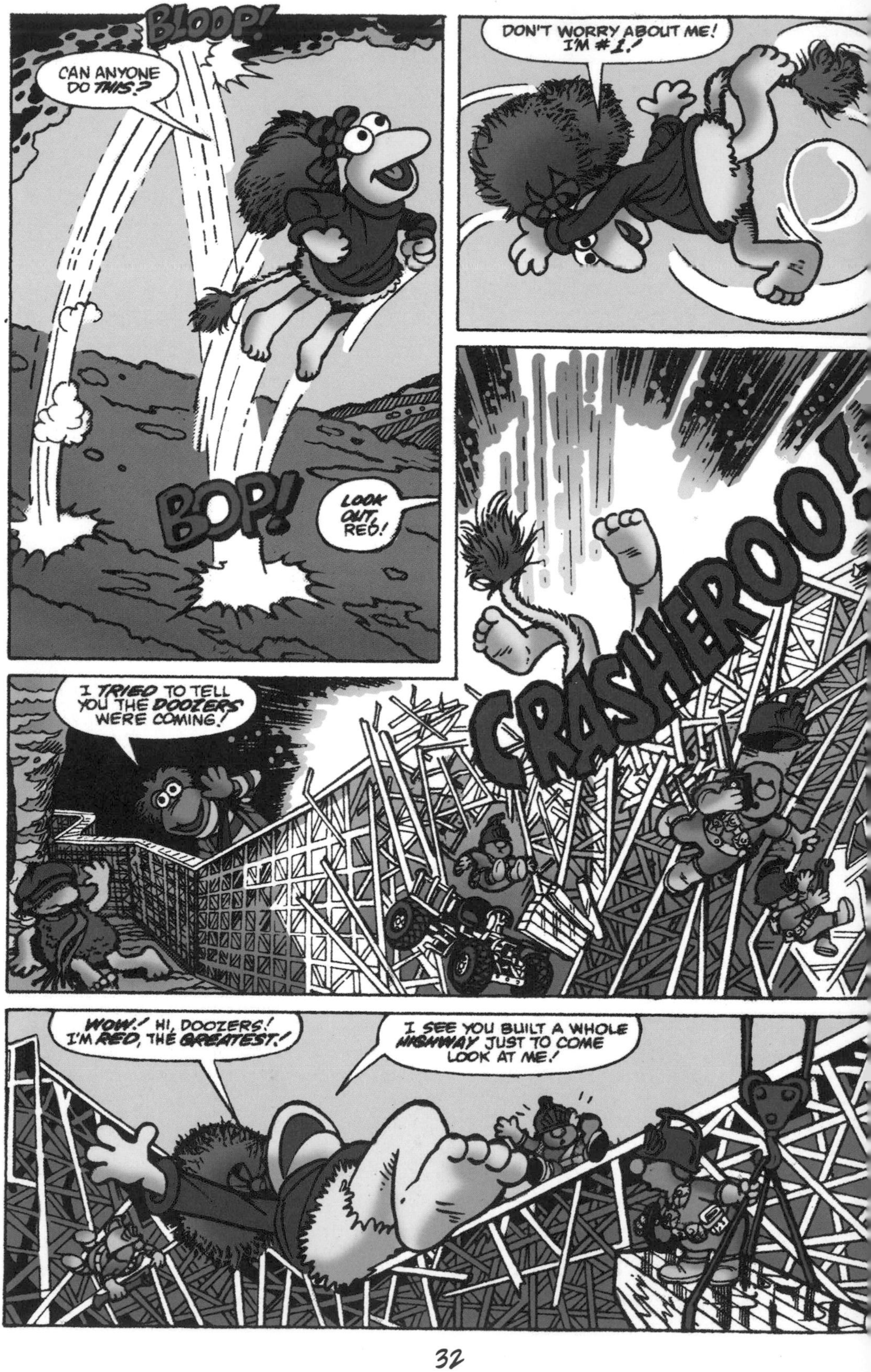
BLOOP!
CAN ANYONE DO THIS?
BOP!
LOOK OUT, RED!
DON'T WORRY ABOUT ME! I'M #1!
CRASHEROO!!
I TRIED TO TELL YOU THE DOOZERS WERE COMING!
WOW! HI, DOOZERS! I'M RED, THE GREATEST!
I SEE YOU BUILT A WHOLE HIGHWAY JUST TO COME LOOK AT ME!

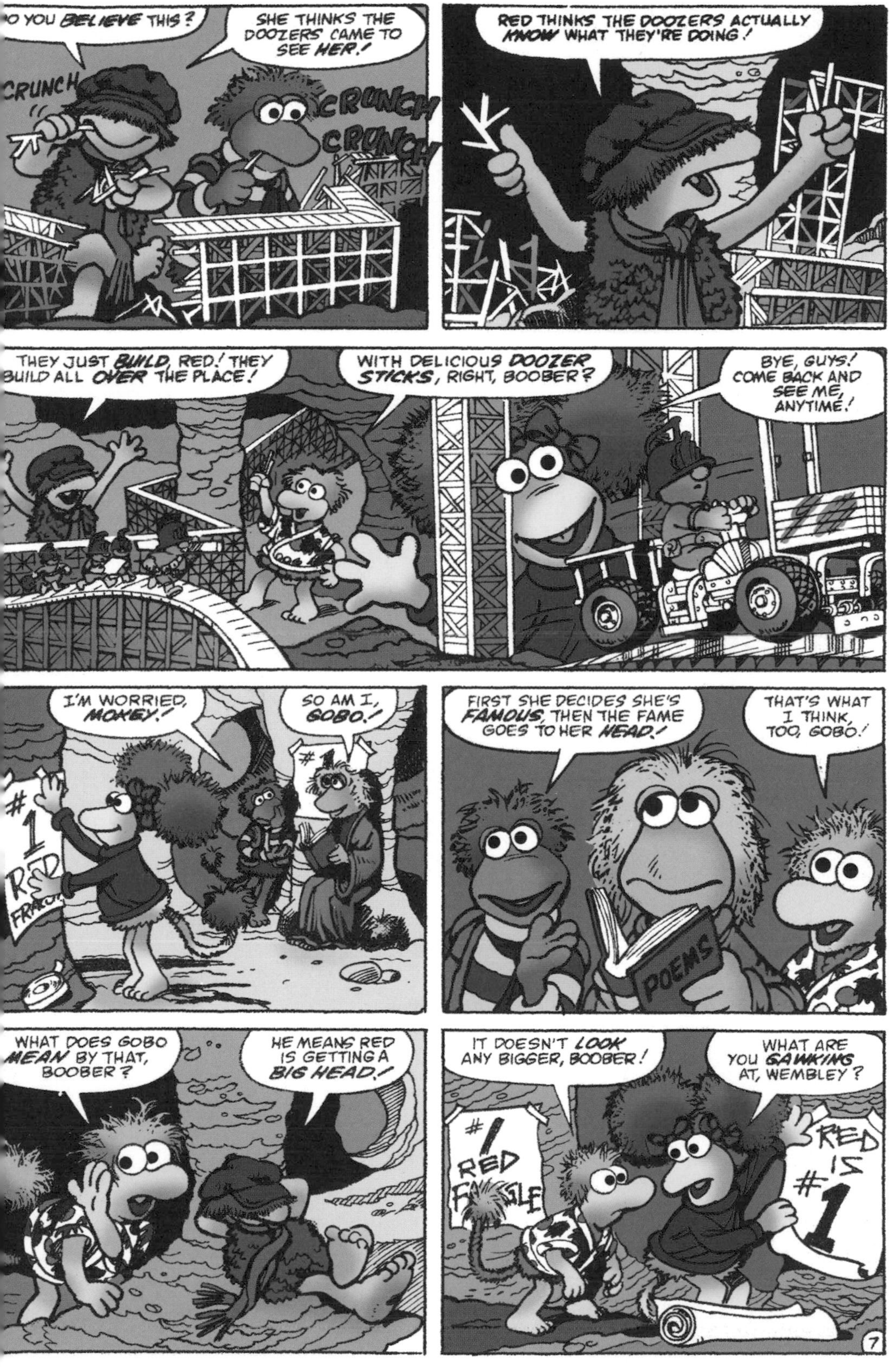

...O YOU BELIEVE THIS?
SHE THINKS THE DOOZERS CAME TO SEE HER!
CRUNCH
CRUNCH
CRUNCH
RED THINKS THE DOOZERS ACTUALLY KNOW WHAT THEY'RE DOING!
THEY JUST BUILD, RED! THEY BUILD ALL OVER THE PLACE!
WITH DELICIOUS DOOZER STICKS, RIGHT, BOOBER?
BYE, GUYS! COME BACK AND SEE ME, ANYTIME!
I'M WORRIED, MOKEY!
SO AM I, GOBO!
FIRST SHE DECIDES SHE'S FAMOUS, THEN THE FAME GOES TO HER HEAD!
THAT'S WHAT I THINK, TOO, GOBO!
POEMS
WHAT DOES GOBO MEAN BY THAT, BOOBER?
HE MEANS RED IS GETTING A BIG HEAD!
IT DOESN'T LOOK ANY BIGGER, BOOBER!
WHAT ARE YOU GAWKING AT, WEMBLEY?
RED IS #1
7

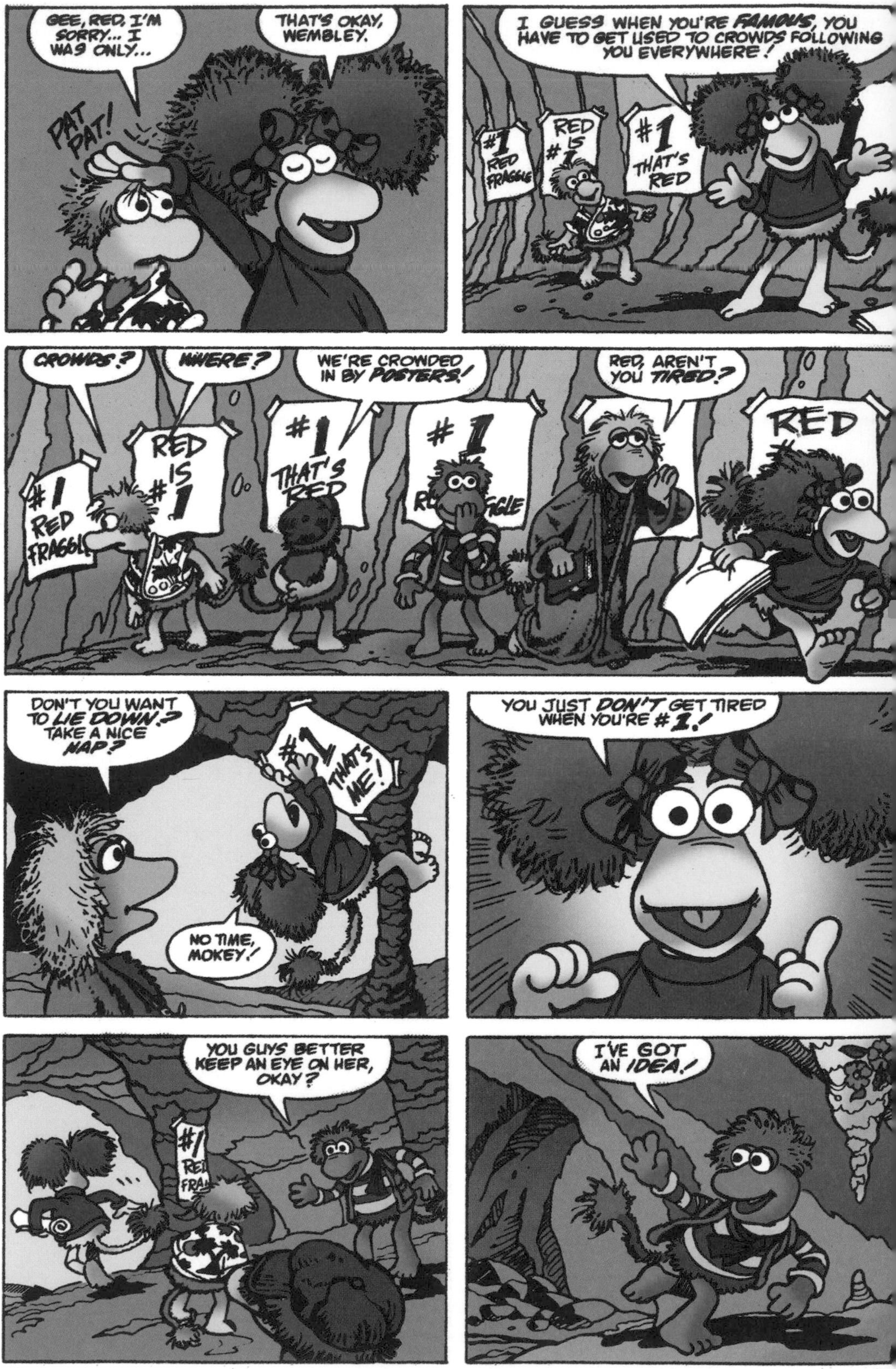
GEE, RED, I'M SORRY... I WAS ONLY...
THAT'S OKAY, WEMBLEY.
PAT PAT!
I GUESS WHEN YOU'RE FAMOUS, YOU HAVE TO GET USED TO CROWDS FOLLOWING YOU EVERYWHERE!
#1 RED FRAGGLE
RED IS #1
#1 THAT'S RED
CROWDS?
WHERE?
WE'RE CROWDED IN BY POSTERS!
RED, AREN'T YOU TIRED?
RED
DON'T YOU WANT TO LIE DOWN? TAKE A NICE NAP?
#1 THAT'S ME!
NO TIME, MOKEY!
YOU JUST DON'T GET TIRED WHEN YOU'RE #1!
YOU GUYS BETTER KEEP AN EYE ON HER, OKAY?
I'VE GOT AN IDEA!

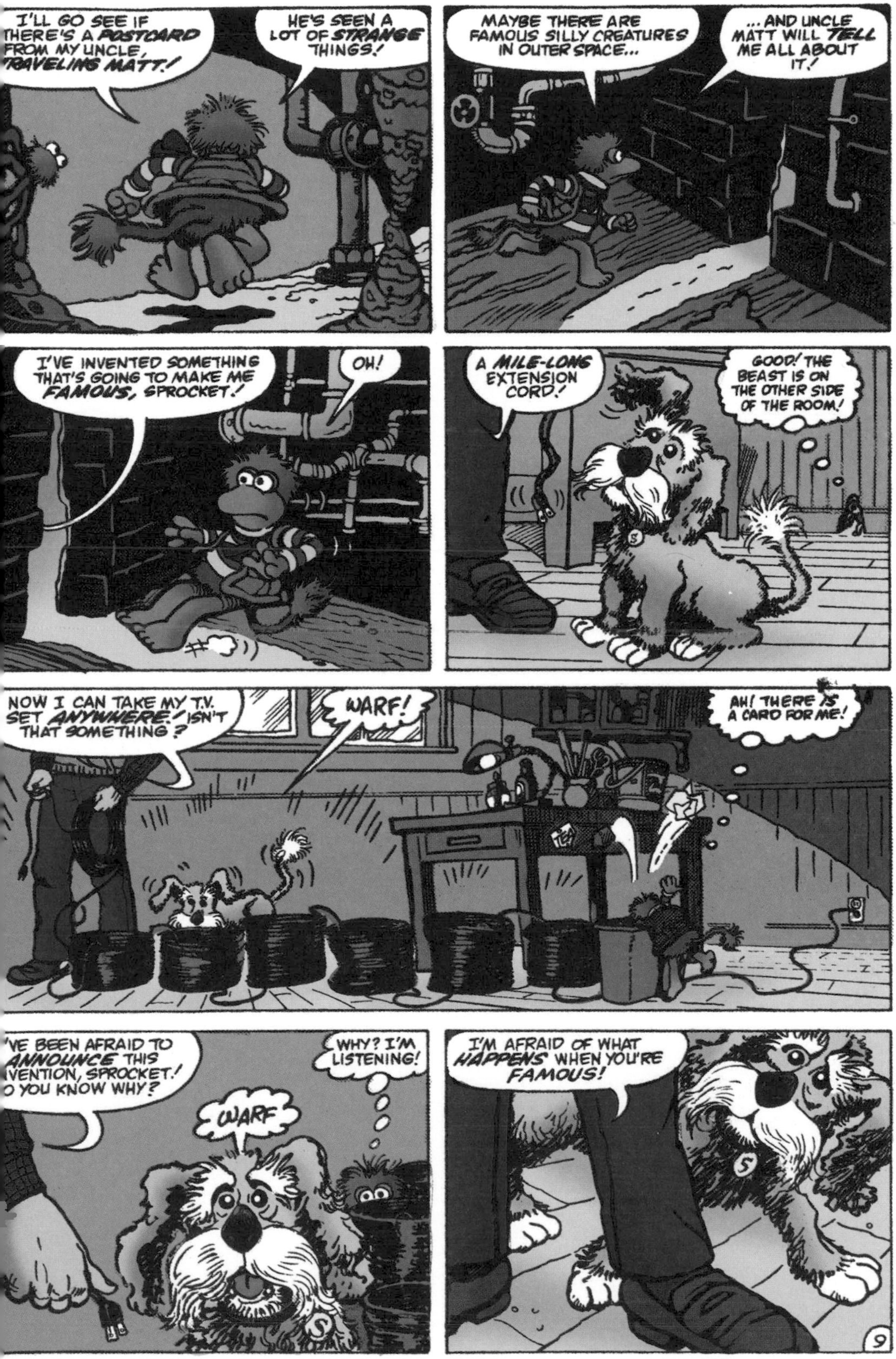
I'LL GO SEE IF THERE'S A POSTCARD FROM MY UNCLE, TRAVELING MATT!
HE'S SEEN A LOT OF STRANGE THINGS!
MAYBE THERE ARE FAMOUS SILLY CREATURES IN OUTER SPACE...
...AND UNCLE MATT WILL TELL ME ALL ABOUT IT!
I'VE INVENTED SOMETHING THAT'S GOING TO MAKE ME FAMOUS, SPROCKET!
OH!
A MILE-LONG EXTENSION CORD!
GOOD! THE BEAST IS ON THE OTHER SIDE OF THE ROOM!
NOW I CAN TAKE MY T.V. SET ANYWHERE! ISN'T THAT SOMETHING?
WARF!
AH! THERE IS A CARD FOR ME!
TEA
'VE BEEN AFRAID TO ANNOUNCE THIS VENTION, SPROCKET! O YOU KNOW WHY?
WHY? I'M LISTENING!
WARF
I'M AFRAID OF WHAT HAPPENS WHEN YOU'RE FAMOUS!
9

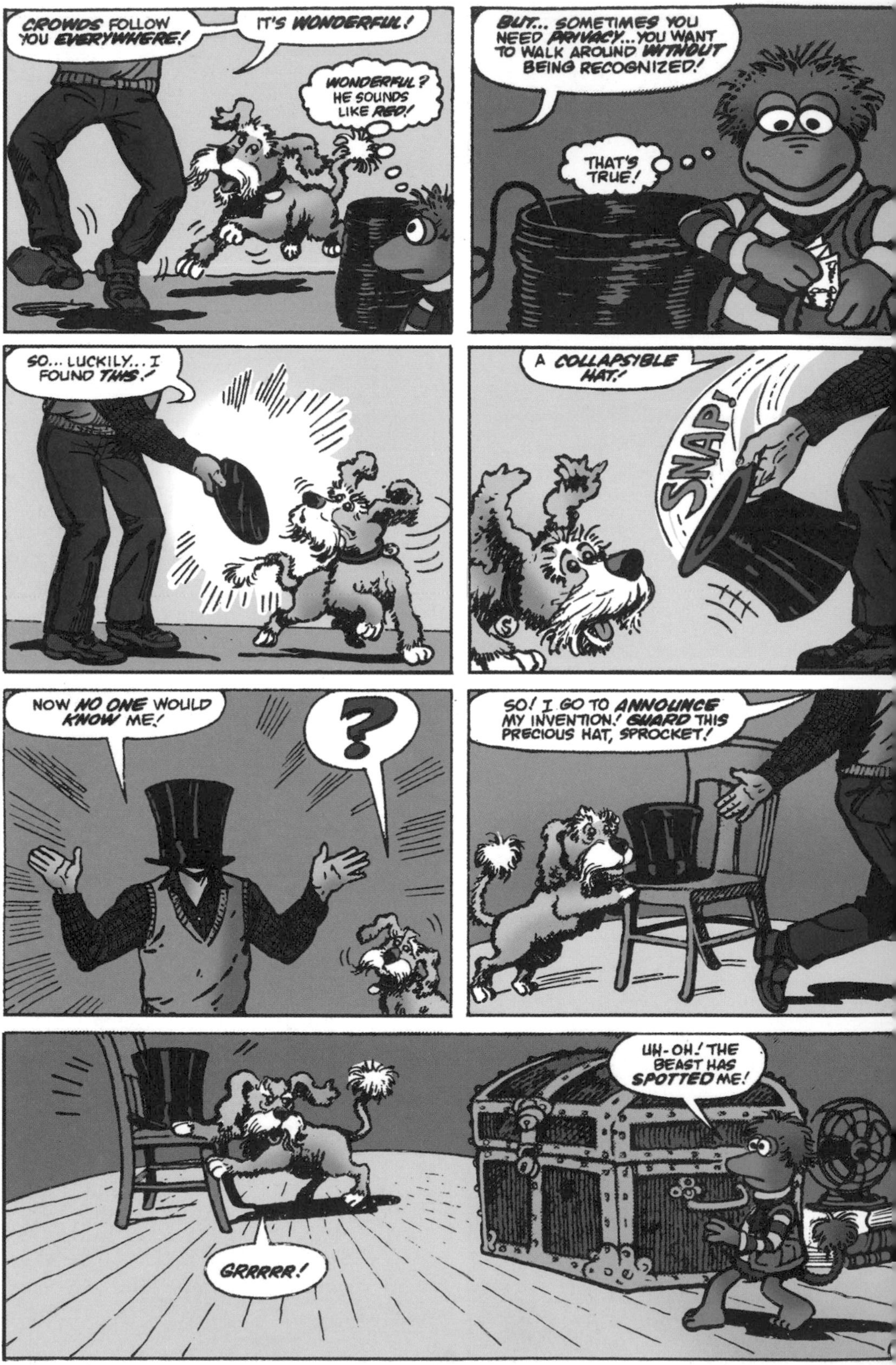
CROWDS FOLLOW YOU EVERYWHERE!
IT'S WONDERFUL!
WONDERFUL? HE SOUNDS LIKE RED!
BUT... SOMETIMES YOU NEED PRIVACY... YOU WANT TO WALK AROUND WITHOUT BEING RECOGNIZED!
THAT'S TRUE!
SO... LUCKILY... I FOUND THIS!
A COLLAPSIBLE HAT!
SNAP!
NOW NO ONE WOULD KNOW ME!
?
SO! I GO TO ANNOUNCE MY INVENTION! GUARD THIS PRECIOUS HAT, SPROCKET!
UH-OH! THE BEAST HAS SPOTTED ME!
GRRRRR!

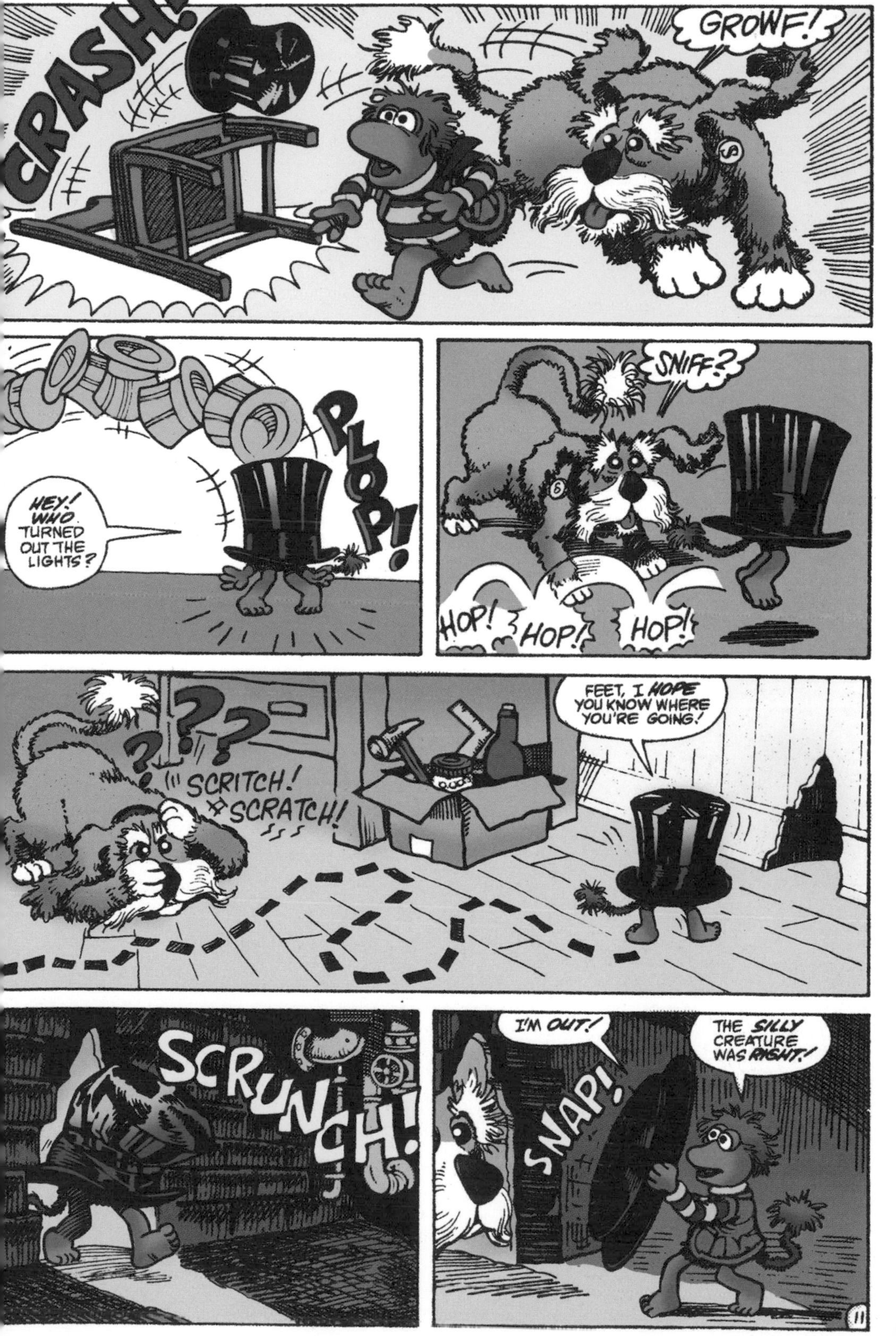
CRASH!
GROWF!
PLOP!
HEY! WHO TURNED OUT THE LIGHTS?
SNIFF?
HOP! HOP! HOP!
SCRITCH! SCRATCH!
FEET, I HOPE YOU KNOW WHERE YOU'RE GOING!
SCRUNCH!
I'M OUT!
SNAP!
THE SILLY CREATURE WAS RIGHT!
11

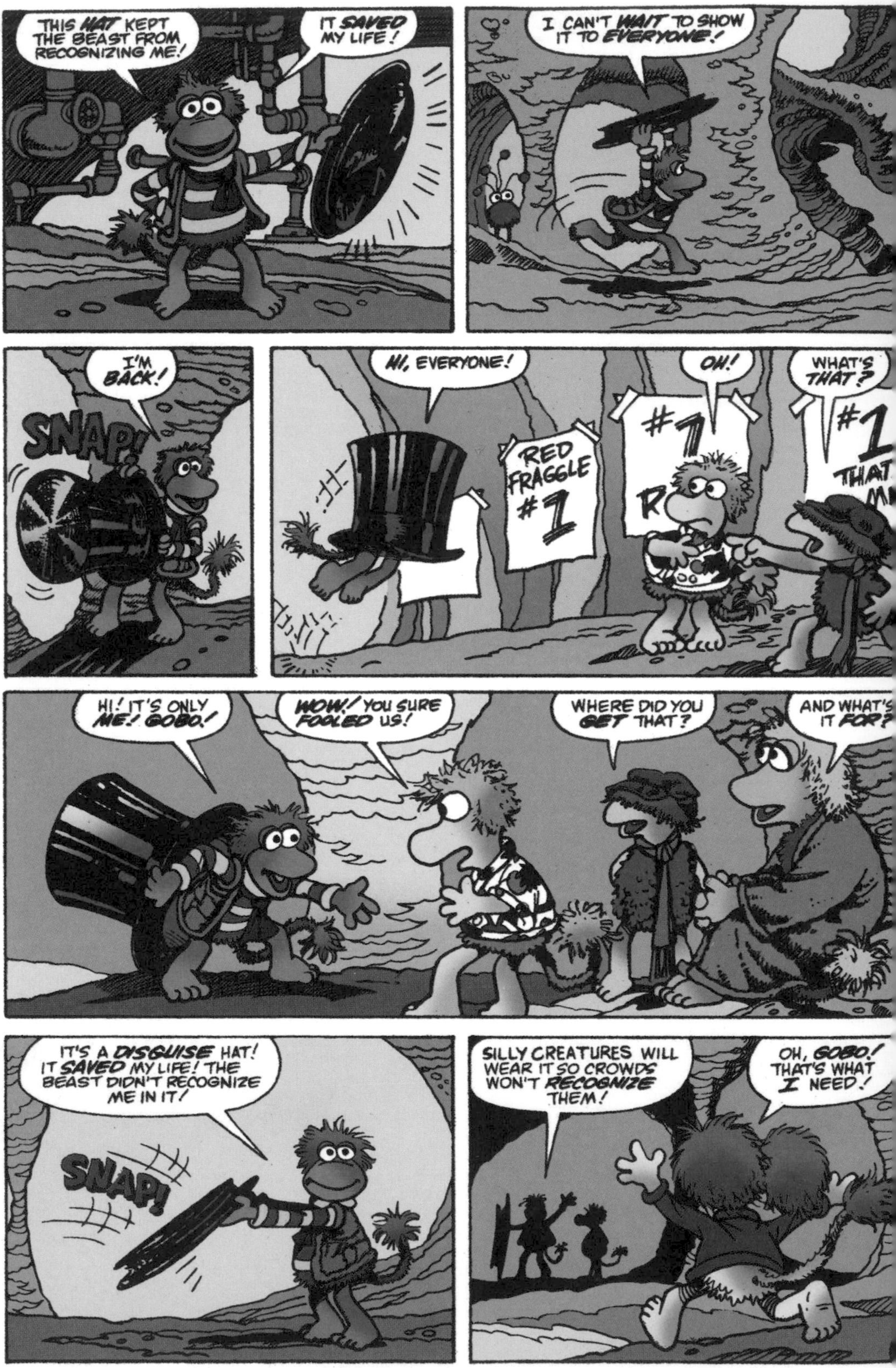
THIS HAT KEPT THE BEAST FROM RECOGNIZING ME!
IT SAVED MY LIFE!
I CAN'T WAIT TO SHOW IT TO EVERYONE!
I'M BACK!
SNAP!
HI, EVERYONE!
RED FRAGGLE #1
OH!
WHAT'S THAT?
HI! IT'S ONLY ME! GOBO!
WOW! YOU SURE FOOLED US!
WHERE DID YOU GET THAT?
AND WHAT'S IT FOR?
IT'S A DISGUISE HAT! IT SAVED MY LIFE! THE BEAST DIDN'T RECOGNIZE ME IN IT!
SNAP!
SILLY CREATURES WILL WEAR IT SO CROWDS WON'T RECOGNIZE THEM!
OH, GOBO! THAT'S WHAT I NEED!

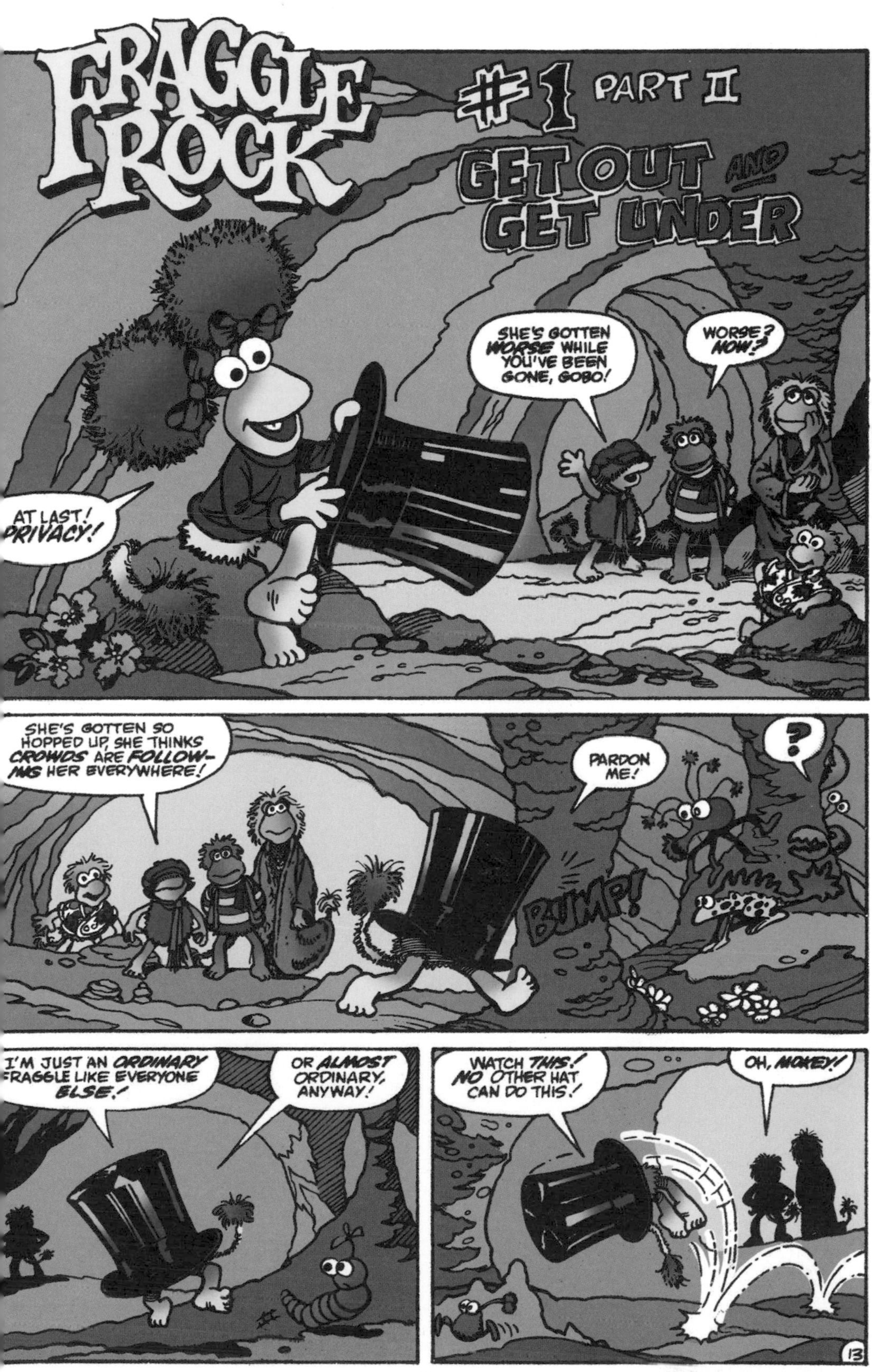
FRAGGLE ROCK
#1 PART II
GET OUT AND GET UNDER
AT LAST! PRIVACY!
SHE'S GOTTEN WORSE WHILE YOU'VE BEEN GONE, GOBO!
WORSE? NOW?
SHE'S GOTTEN SO HOPPED UP, SHE THINKS CROWDS ARE FOLLOWING HER EVERYWHERE!
BUMP!
PARDON ME!
?
I'M JUST AN ORDINARY FRAGGLE LIKE EVERYONE ELSE!
OR ALMOST ORDINARY, ANYWAY!
WATCH THIS! NO OTHER HAT CAN DO THIS!
OH, MOKEY!
13

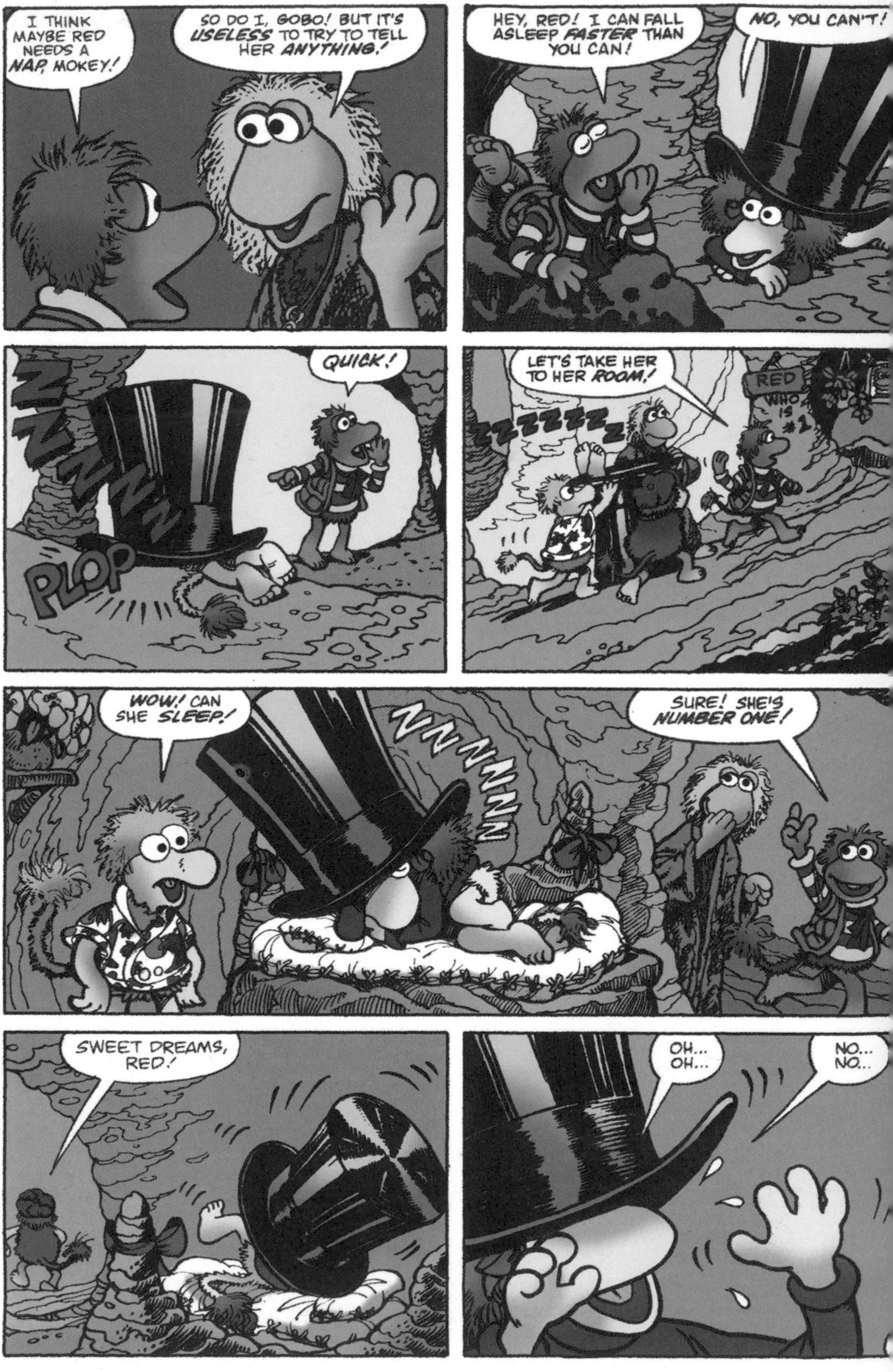
I THINK MAYBE RED NEEDS A NAP, MOKEY!
SO DO I, GOBO! BUT IT'S USELESS TO TRY TO TELL HER ANYTHING!
HEY, RED! I CAN FALL ASLEEP FASTER THAN YOU CAN!
NO, YOU CAN'T!
NNNNNN
PLOP
QUICK!
LET'S TAKE HER TO HER ROOM!
ZZZZZZZ
RED WHO IS #1
WOW! CAN SHE SLEEP!
NNNNNN
SURE! SHE'S NUMBER ONE!
SWEET DREAMS, RED!
OH... OH...
NO... NO...

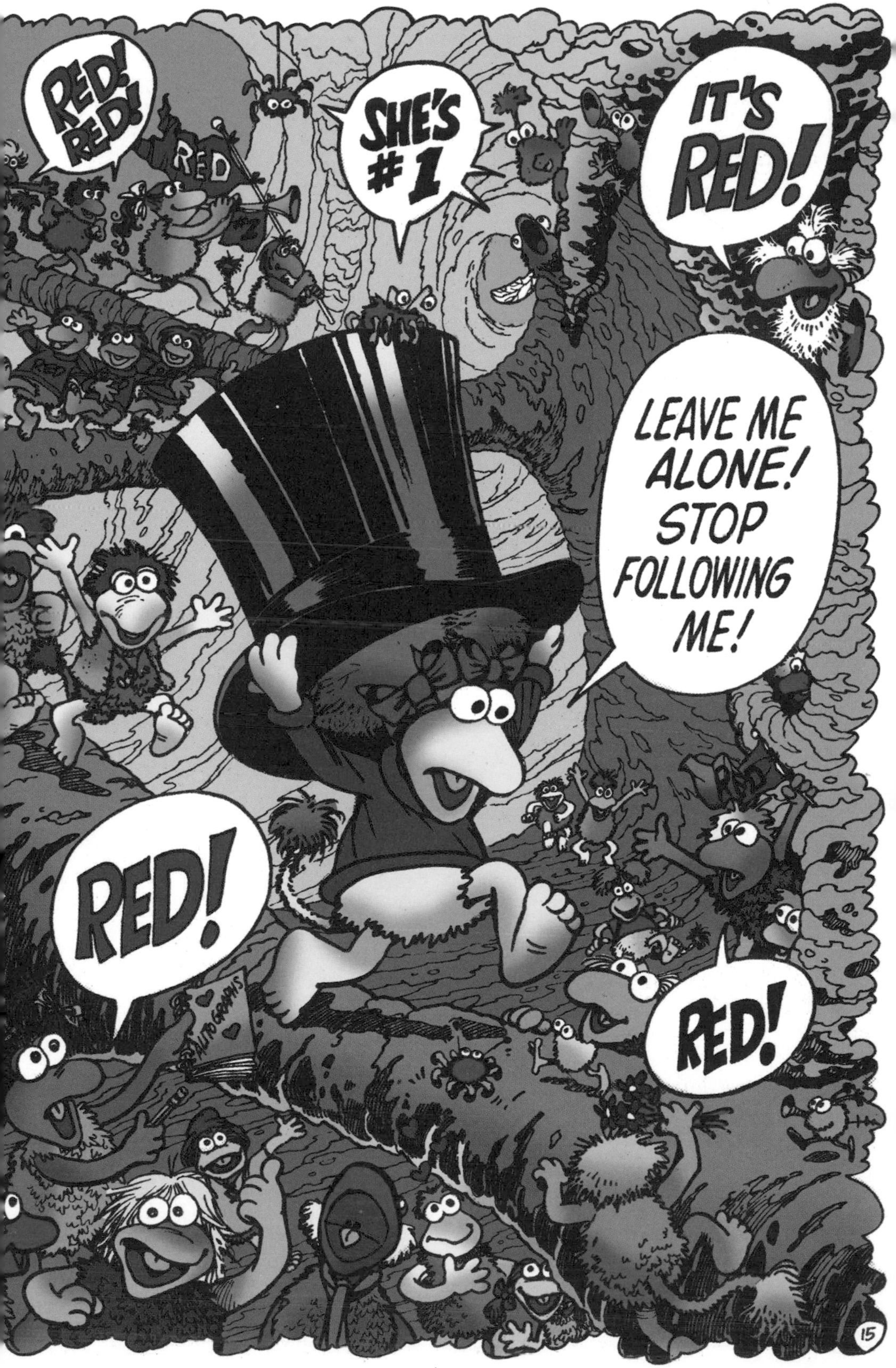
RED! RED!
RED
SHE'S #1
IT'S RED!
LEAVE ME ALONE! STOP FOLLOWING ME!
RED
RED!
AUTOGRAPHS
RED!
15

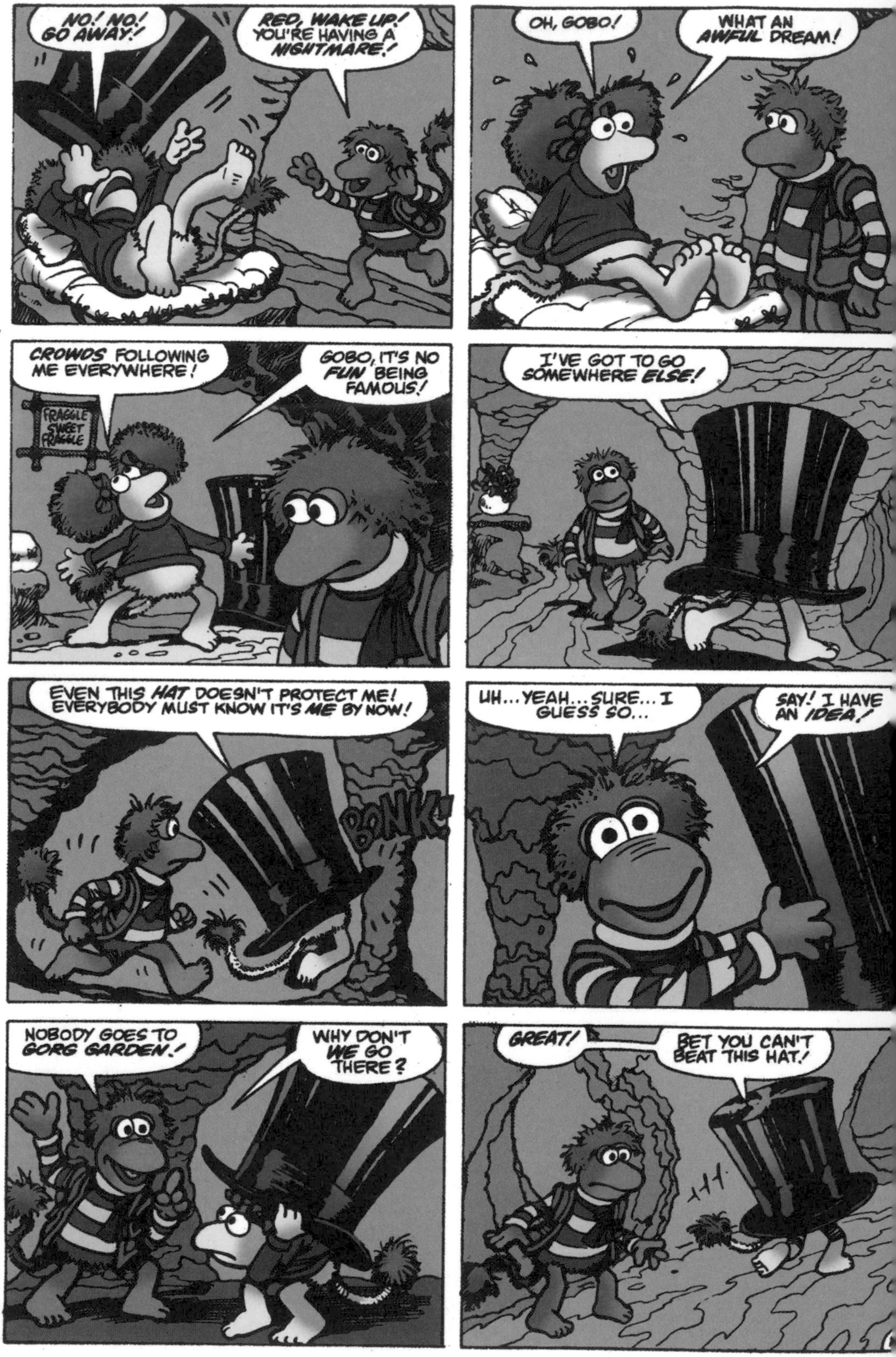
NO! NO! GO AWAY!
RED, WAKE UP! YOU'RE HAVING A NIGHTMARE!
OH, GOBO!
WHAT AN AWFUL DREAM!
CROWDS FOLLOWING ME EVERYWHERE!
FRAGGLE SWEET FRAGGLE
GOBO, IT'S NO FUN BEING FAMOUS!
I'VE GOT TO GO SOMEWHERE ELSE!
EVEN THIS HAT DOESN'T PROTECT ME! EVERYBODY MUST KNOW IT'S ME BY NOW!
BONK!
UH... YEAH... SURE... I GUESS SO...
SAY! I HAVE AN IDEA!
NOBODY GOES TO GORG GARDEN!
WHY DON'T WE GO THERE?
GREAT!
BET YOU CAN'T BEAT THIS HAT!

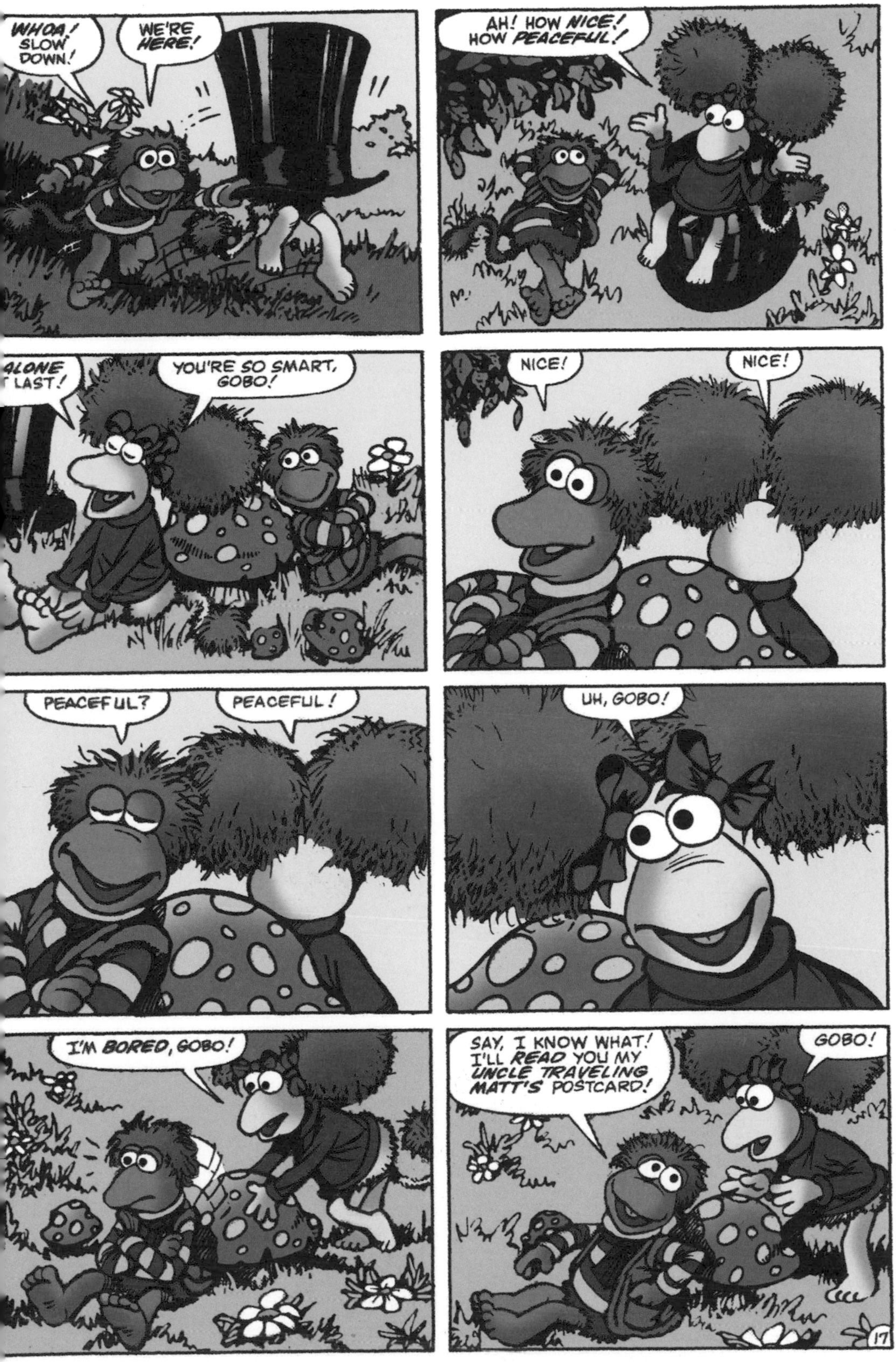
WHOA! SLOW DOWN!
WE'RE HERE!
AH! HOW NICE! HOW PEACEFUL!
ALONE T LAST!
YOU'RE SO SMART, GOBO!
NICE!
NICE!
PEACEFUL?
PEACEFUL!
UH, GOBO!
I'M BORED, GOBO!
SAY, I KNOW WHAT! I'LL READ YOU MY UNCLE TRAVELING MATT'S POSTCARD!
GOBO!
17

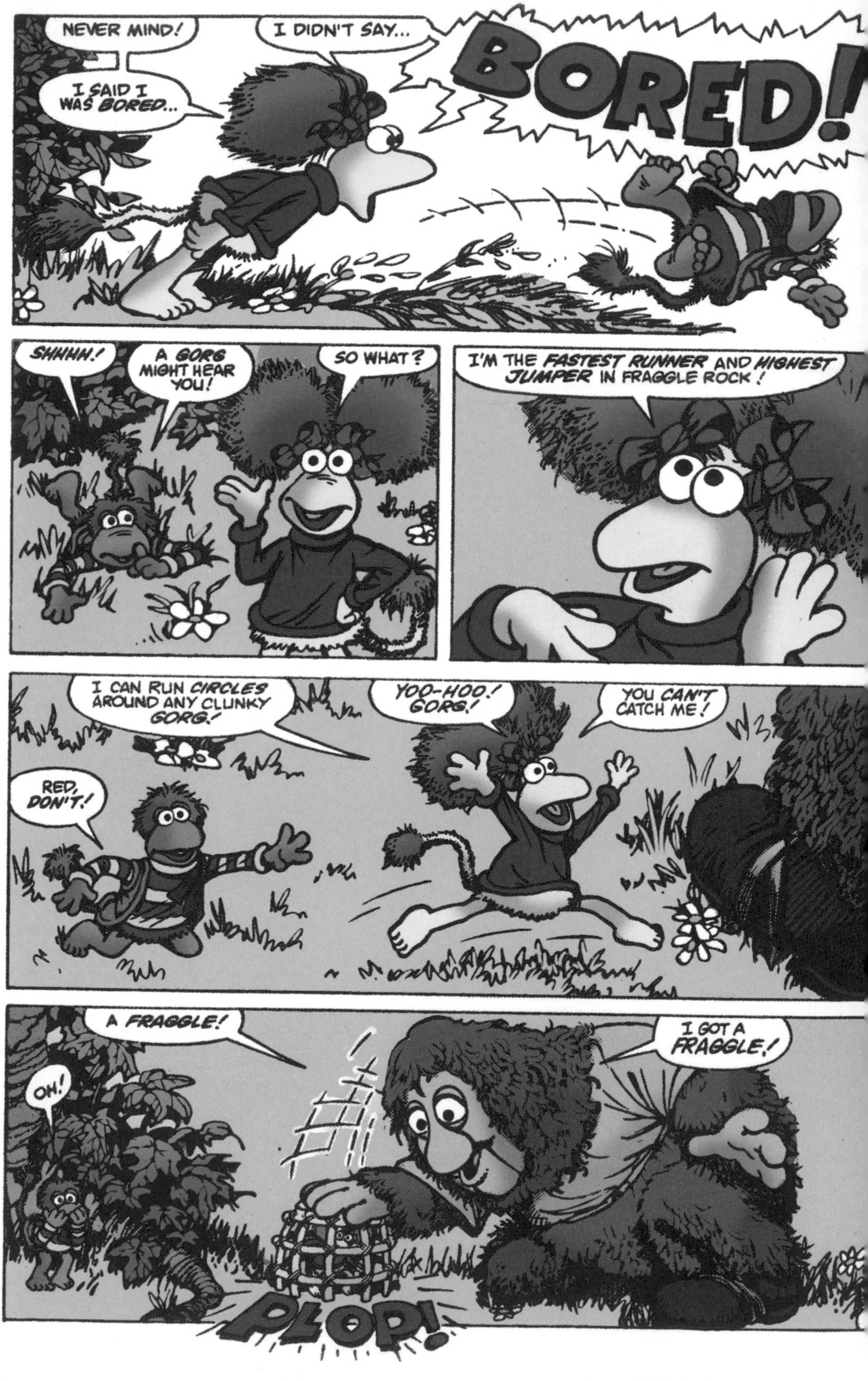
NEVER MIND!
I SAID I WAS BORED...
I DIDN'T SAY...
BORED!
SHHHH!
A GORG MIGHT HEAR YOU!
SO WHAT?
I'M THE FASTEST RUNNER AND HIGHEST JUMPER IN FRAGGLE ROCK!
I CAN RUN CIRCLES AROUND ANY CLUNKY GORG!
RED, DON'T!
YOO-HOO! GORG!
YOU CAN'T CATCH ME!
A FRAGGLE!
OH!
I GOT A FRAGGLE!
PLOP!

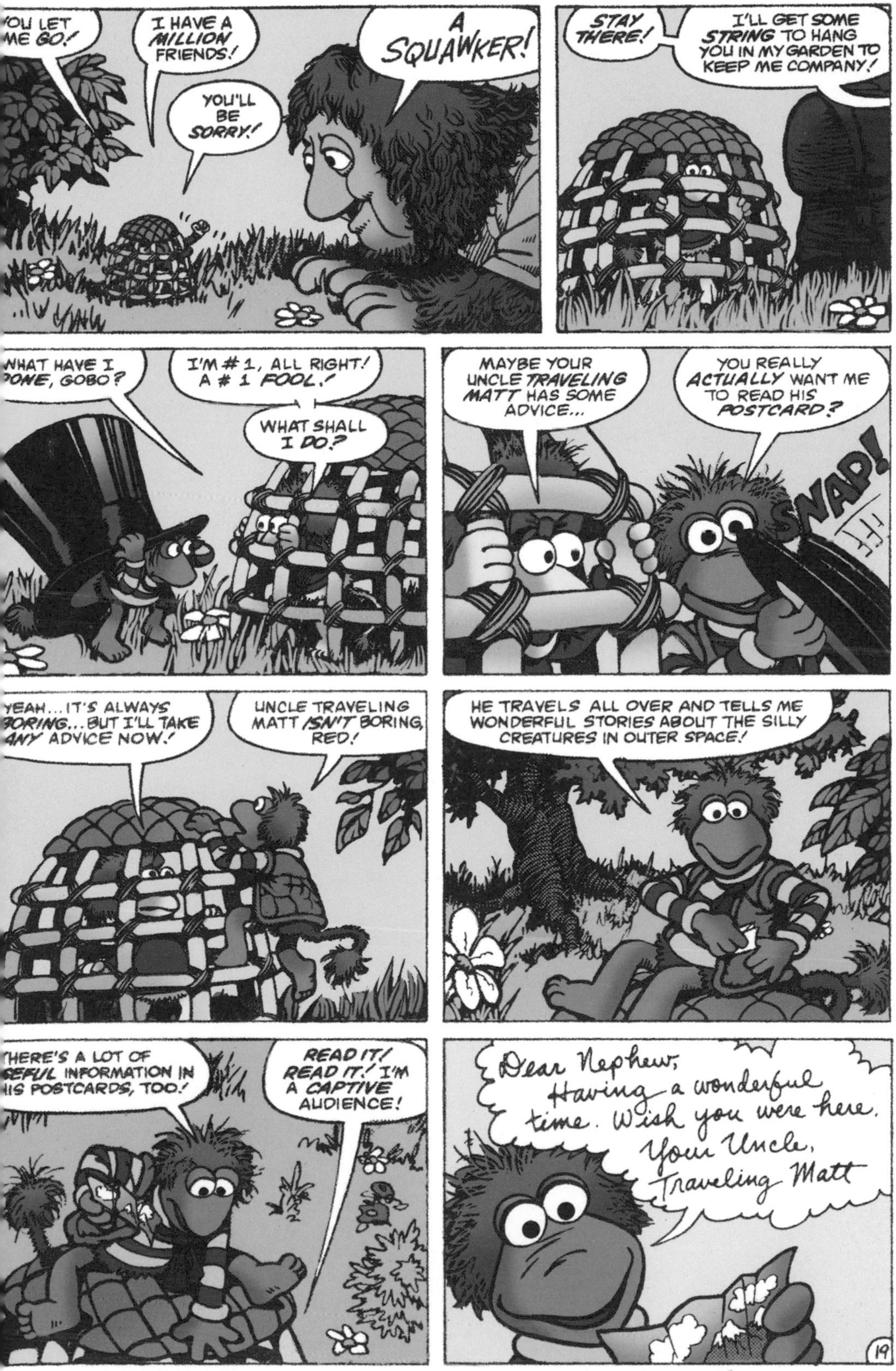
YOU LET ME GO!
I HAVE A MILLION FRIENDS!
YOU'LL BE SORRY!
A SQUAWKER!
STAY THERE!
I'LL GET SOME STRING TO HANG YOU IN MY GARDEN TO KEEP ME COMPANY!
WHAT HAVE I DONE, GOBO?
I'M # 1, ALL RIGHT! A # 1 FOOL!
WHAT SHALL I DO?
MAYBE YOUR UNCLE TRAVELING MATT HAS SOME ADVICE...
YOU REALLY ACTUALLY WANT ME TO READ HIS POSTCARD?
SNAP!
YEAH... IT'S ALWAYS BORING... BUT I'LL TAKE ANY ADVICE NOW!
UNCLE TRAVELING MATT ISN'T BORING, RED!
HE TRAVELS ALL OVER AND TELLS ME WONDERFUL STORIES ABOUT THE SILLY CREATURES IN OUTER SPACE!
THERE'S A LOT OF USEFUL INFORMATION IN HIS POSTCARDS, TOO!
READ IT! READ IT! I'M A CAPTIVE AUDIENCE!
Dear Nephew,
Having a wonderful time. Wish you were here.
Your Uncle,
Traveling Matt
19

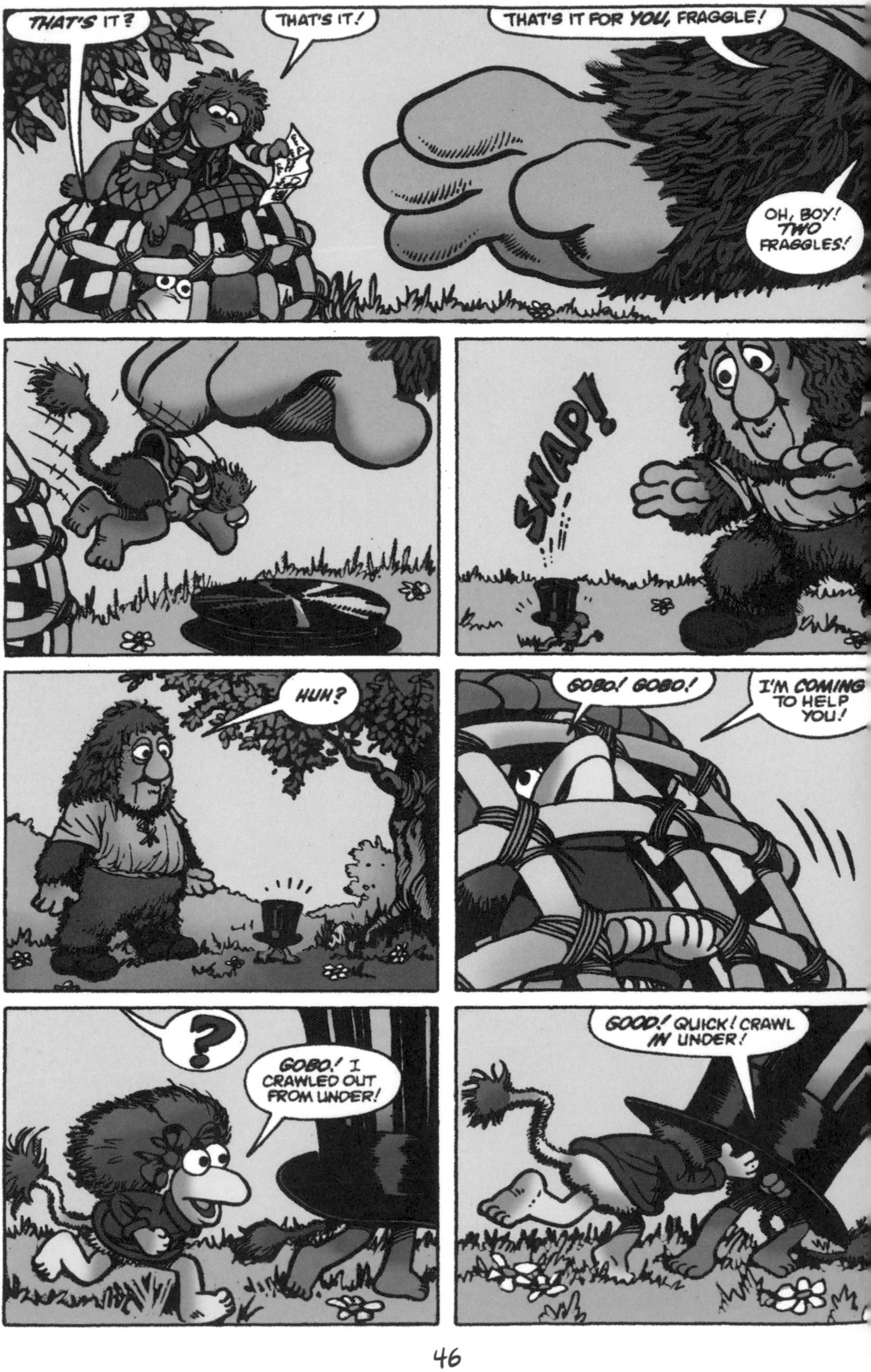
THAT'S IT?
THAT'S IT!
THAT'S IT FOR YOU, FRAGGLE!
OH, BOY! TWO FRAGGLES!
SNAP!
HUH?
GOBO! GOBO!
I'M COMING TO HELP YOU!
?
GOBO! I CRAWLED OUT FROM UNDER!
GOOD! QUICK! CRAWL IN UNDER!

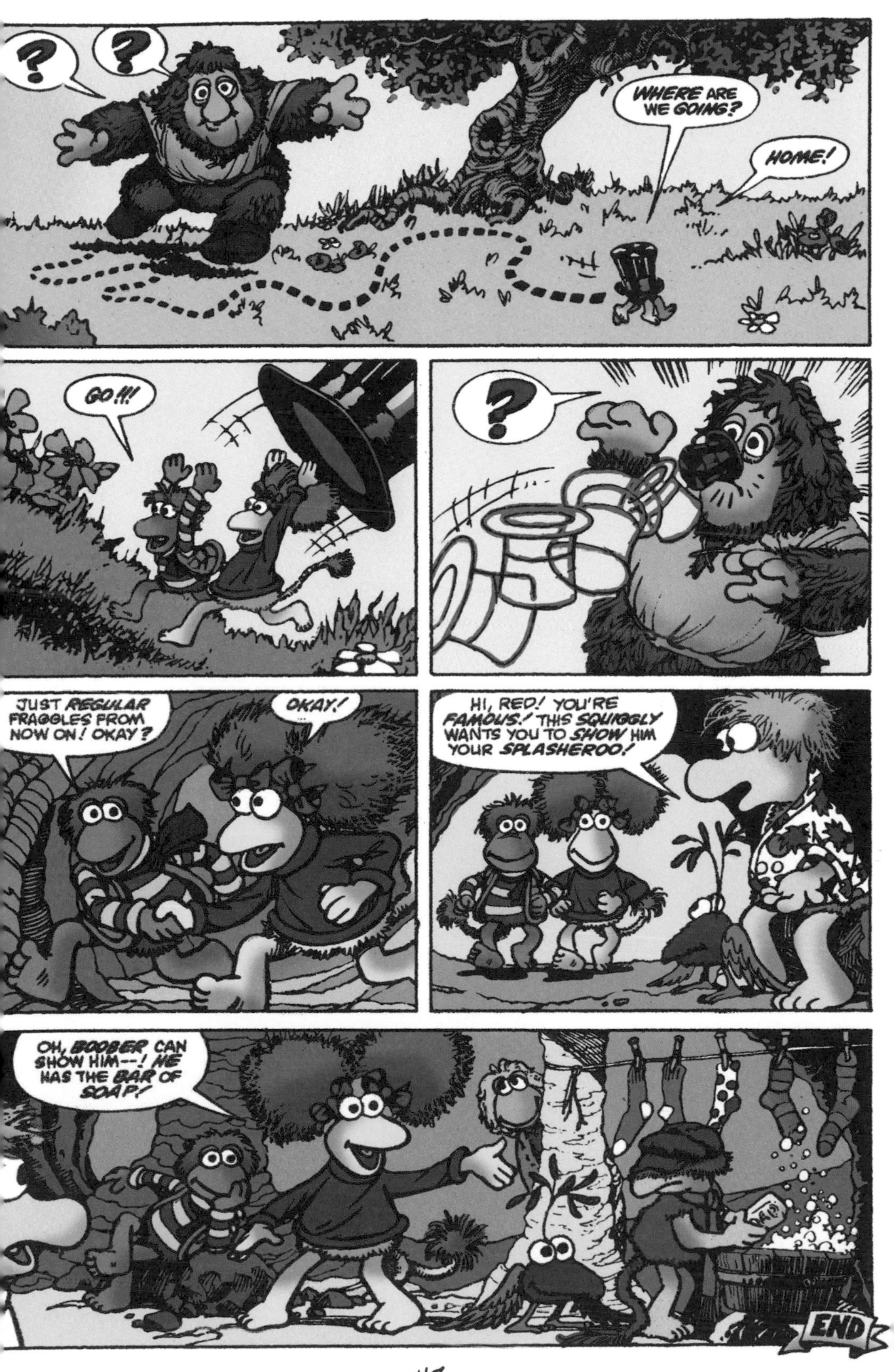
?
?
WHERE ARE WE GOING?
HOME!
GO!!!
?
JUST REGULAR FRAGGLES FROM NOW ON! OKAY?
OKAY!
HI, RED! YOU'RE FAMOUS! THIS SQUIGGLY WANTS YOU TO SHOW HIM YOUR SPLASHEROO!
OH, BOOBER CAN SHOW HIM--! HE HAS THE BAR OF SOAP!
END

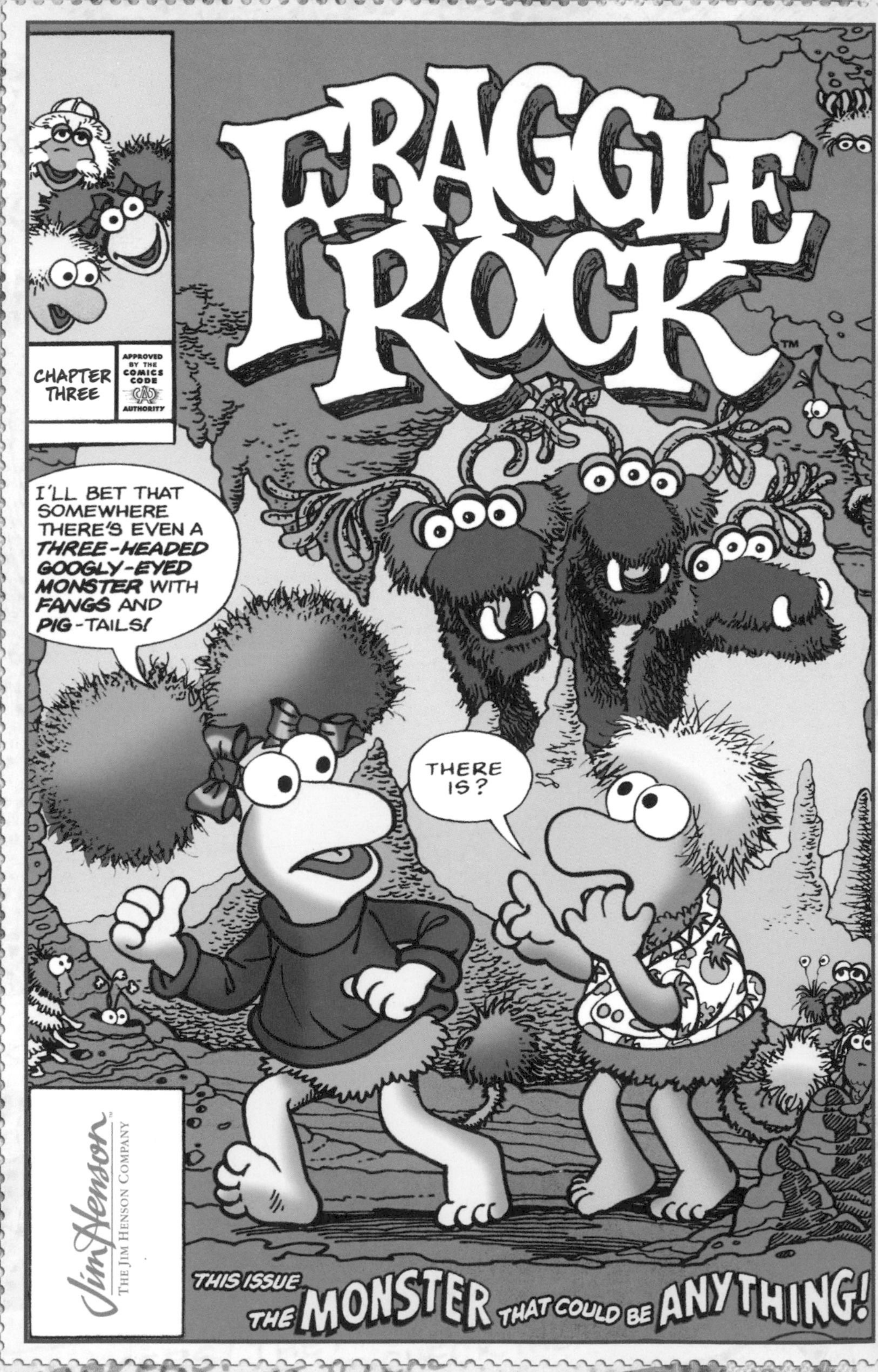
FRAGGLE ROCK™
CHAPTER THREE
APPROVED BY THE COMICS CODE CA AUTHORITY
I'LL BET THAT SOMEWHERE THERE'S EVEN A THREE-HEADED GOOGLY-EYED MONSTER WITH FANGS AND PIG-TAILS!
THERE IS?
Jim Henson™ THE JIM HENSON COMPANY
THIS ISSUE THE MONSTER THAT COULD BE ANYTHING!

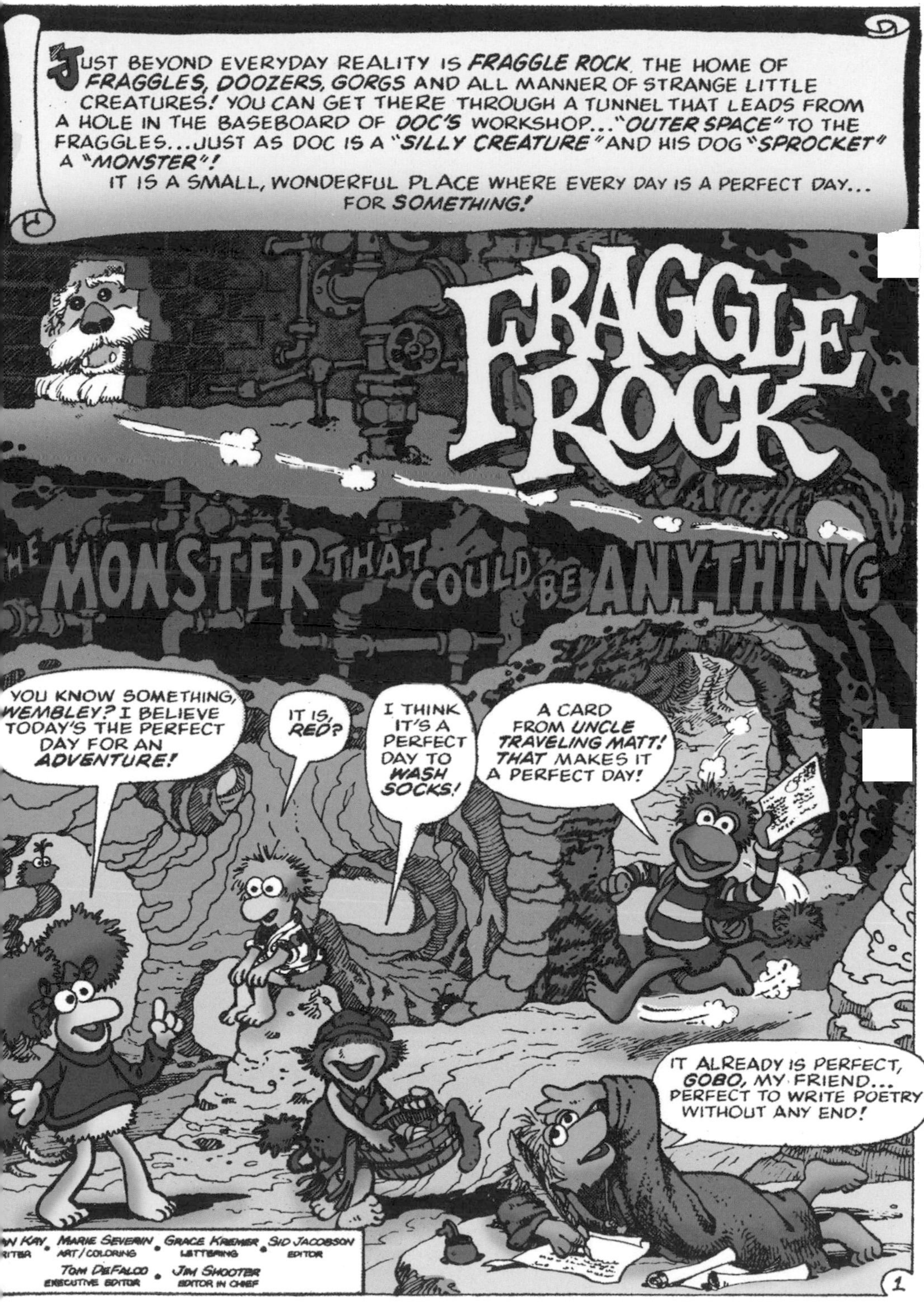
JUST BEYOND EVERYDAY REALITY IS FRAGGLE ROCK, THE HOME OF FRAGGLES, DOOZERS, GORGS AND ALL MANNER OF STRANGE LITTLE CREATURES! YOU CAN GET THERE THROUGH A TUNNEL THAT LEADS FROM A HOLE IN THE BASEBOARD OF DOC'S WORKSHOP..."OUTER SPACE" TO THE FRAGGLES...JUST AS DOC IS A "SILLY CREATURE" AND HIS DOG "SPROCKET" A "MONSTER"!
IT IS A SMALL, WONDERFUL PLACE WHERE EVERY DAY IS A PERFECT DAY... FOR SOMETHING!
FRAGGLE ROCK
MONSTER THAT COULD BE ANYTHING
YOU KNOW SOMETHING, WEMBLEY? I BELIEVE TODAY'S THE PERFECT DAY FOR AN ADVENTURE!
IT IS, RED?
I THINK IT'S A PERFECT DAY TO WASH SOCKS!
A CARD FROM UNCLE TRAVELING MATT! THAT MAKES IT A PERFECT DAY!
IT ALREADY IS PERFECT, GOBO, MY FRIEND... PERFECT TO WRITE POETRY WITHOUT ANY END!
MARIE SEVERIN ART/COLORING
GRACE KREMER LETTERING
SID JACOBSON EDITOR
TOM DEFALCO EXECUTIVE EDITOR
JIM SHOOTER EDITOR IN CHIEF
1

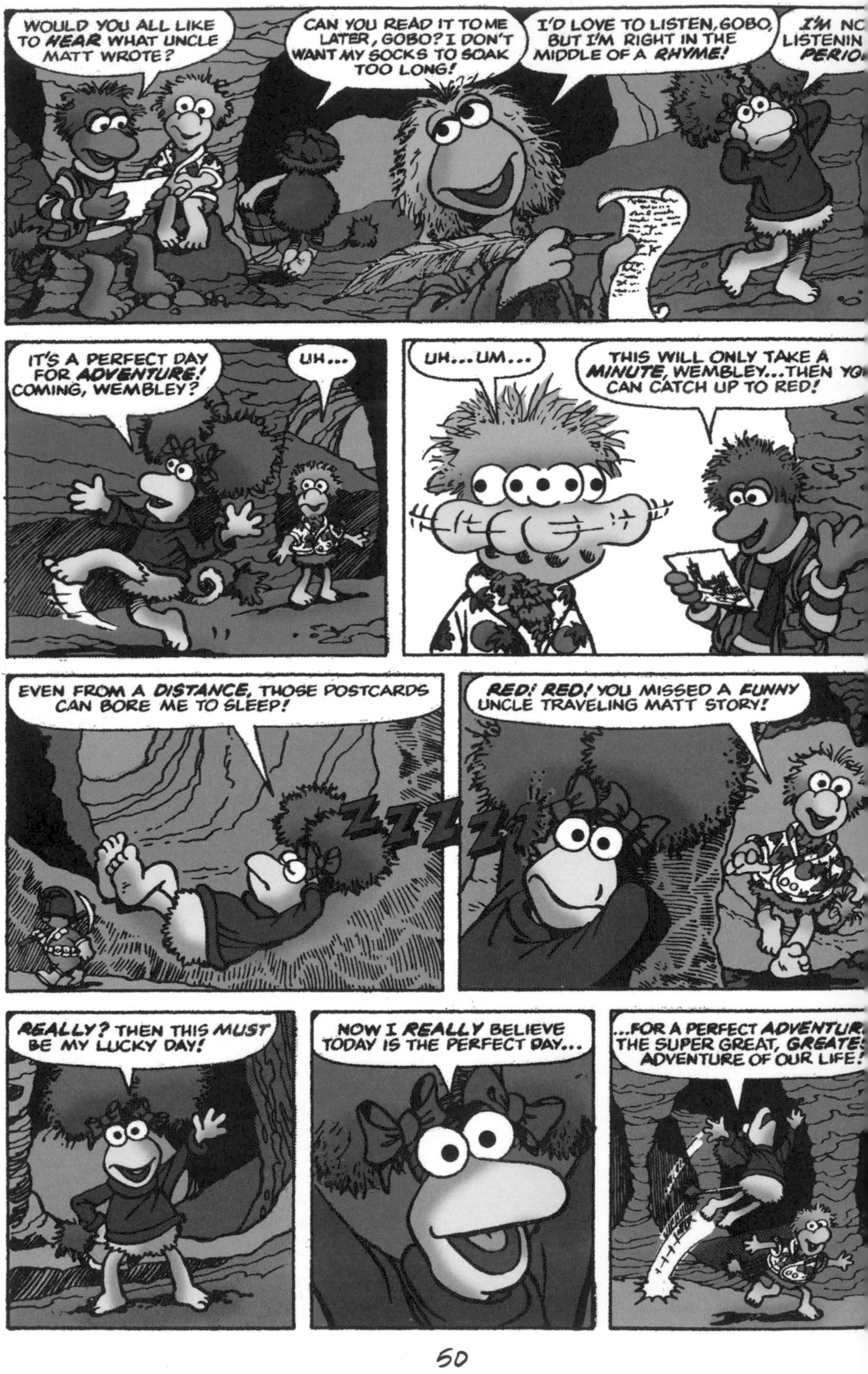

WOULD YOU ALL LIKE TO HEAR WHAT UNCLE MATT WROTE?
CAN YOU READ IT TO ME LATER, GOBO? I DON'T WANT MY SOCKS TO SOAK TOO LONG!
I'D LOVE TO LISTEN, GOBO, BUT I'M RIGHT IN THE MIDDLE OF A RHYME!
I'M NO
LISTENIN
PERIO
IT'S A PERFECT DAY FOR ADVENTURE! COMING, WEMBLEY?
UH...
UH...UM...
THIS WILL ONLY TAKE A MINUTE, WEMBLEY...THEN YO
CAN CATCH UP TO RED!
EVEN FROM A DISTANCE, THOSE POSTCARDS CAN BORE ME TO SLEEP!
RED! RED! YOU MISSED A FUNNY UNCLE TRAVELING MATT STORY!
REALLY? THEN THIS MUST BE MY LUCKY DAY!
NOW I REALLY BELIEVE TODAY IS THE PERFECT DAY...
...FOR A PERFECT ADVENTUR
THE SUPER GREAT, GREATE
ADVENTURE OF OUR LIFE!

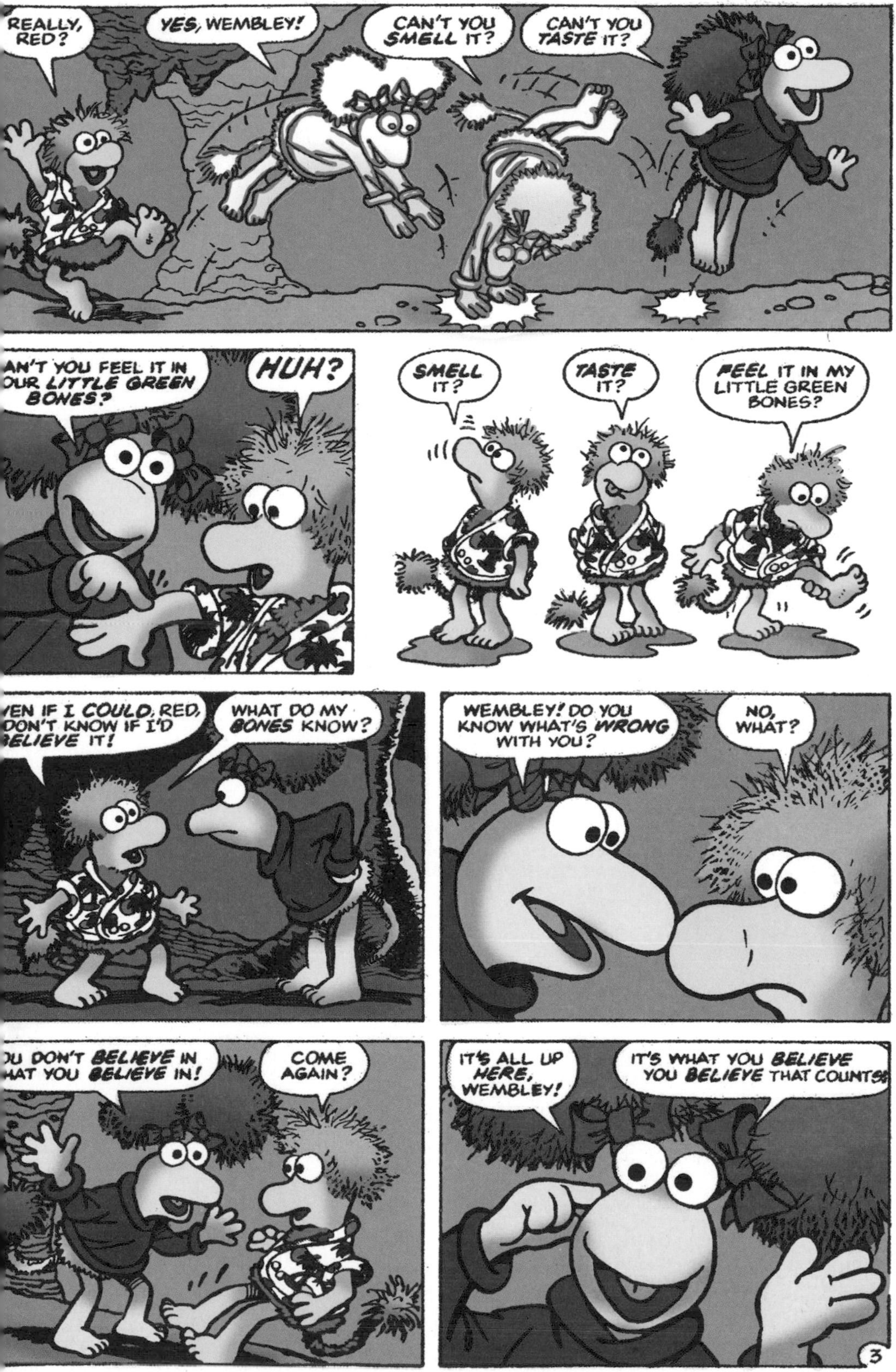
REALLY, RED?
YES, WEMBLEY!
CAN'T YOU SMELL IT?
CAN'T YOU TASTE IT?
AN'T YOU FEEL IT IN OUR LITTLE GREEN BONES?
HUH?
SMELL IT?
TASTE IT?
FEEL IT IN MY LITTLE GREEN BONES?
VEN IF I COULD, RED, DON'T KNOW IF I'D BELIEVE IT!
WHAT DO MY BONES KNOW?
WEMBLEY! DO YOU KNOW WHAT'S WRONG WITH YOU?
NO, WHAT?
OU DON'T BELIEVE IN HAT YOU BELIEVE IN!
COME AGAIN?
IT'S ALL UP HERE, WEMBLEY!
IT'S WHAT YOU BELIEVE YOU BELIEVE THAT COUNTS!
3

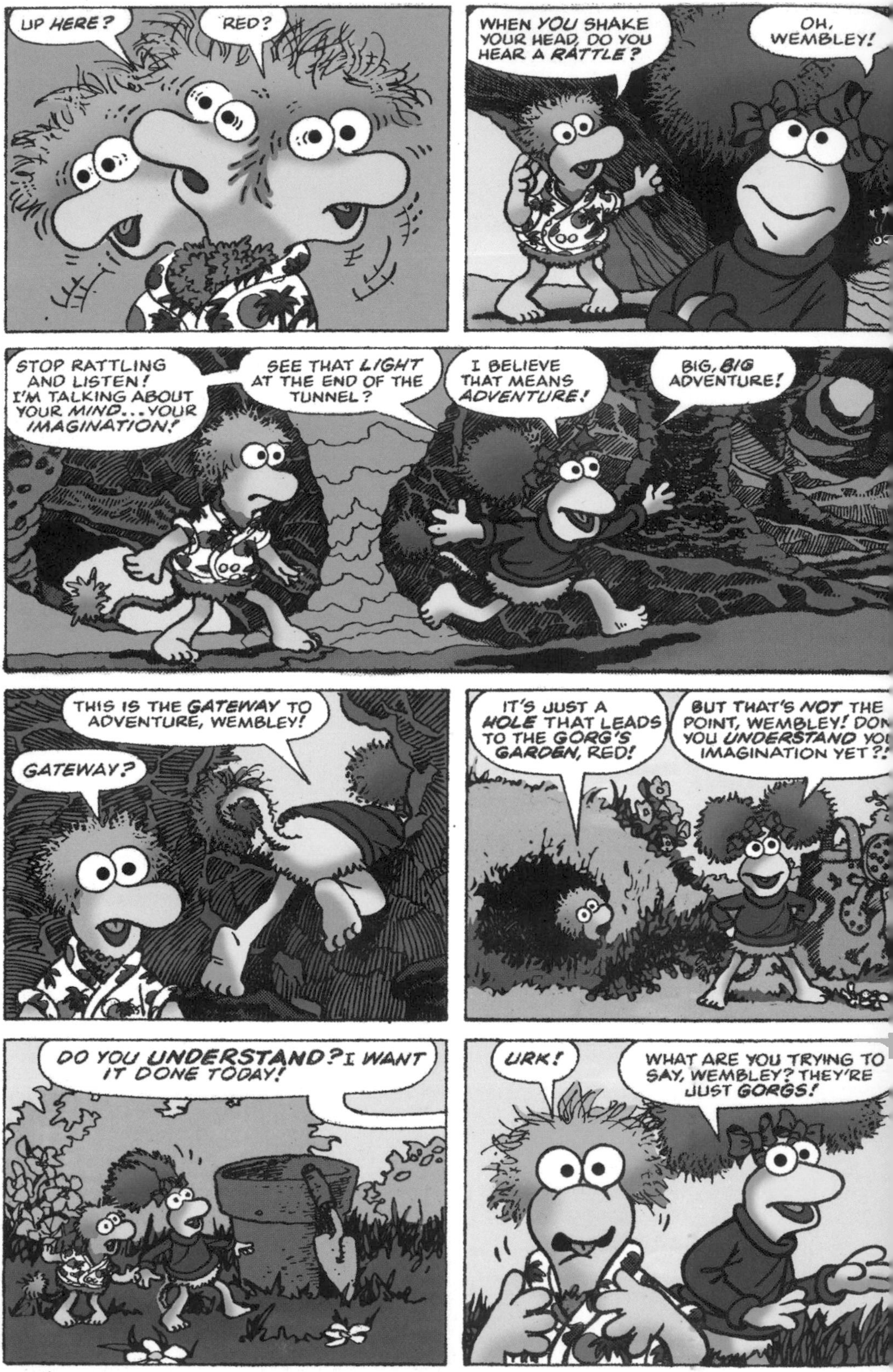

UP HERE?
RED?
WHEN YOU SHAKE YOUR HEAD, DO YOU HEAR A RATTLE?
OH, WEMBLEY!
STOP RATTLING AND LISTEN! I'M TALKING ABOUT YOUR MIND...YOUR IMAGINATION!
SEE THAT LIGHT AT THE END OF THE TUNNEL?
I BELIEVE THAT MEANS ADVENTURE!
BIG, BIG ADVENTURE!
THIS IS THE GATEWAY TO ADVENTURE, WEMBLEY!
GATEWAY?
IT'S JUST A HOLE THAT LEADS TO THE GORG'S GARDEN, RED!
BUT THAT'S NOT THE POINT, WEMBLEY! DON YOU UNDERSTAND YOU IMAGINATION YET?!
DO YOU UNDERSTAND? I WANT IT DONE TODAY!
URK!
WHAT ARE YOU TRYING TO SAY, WEMBLEY? THEY'RE JUST GORGS!

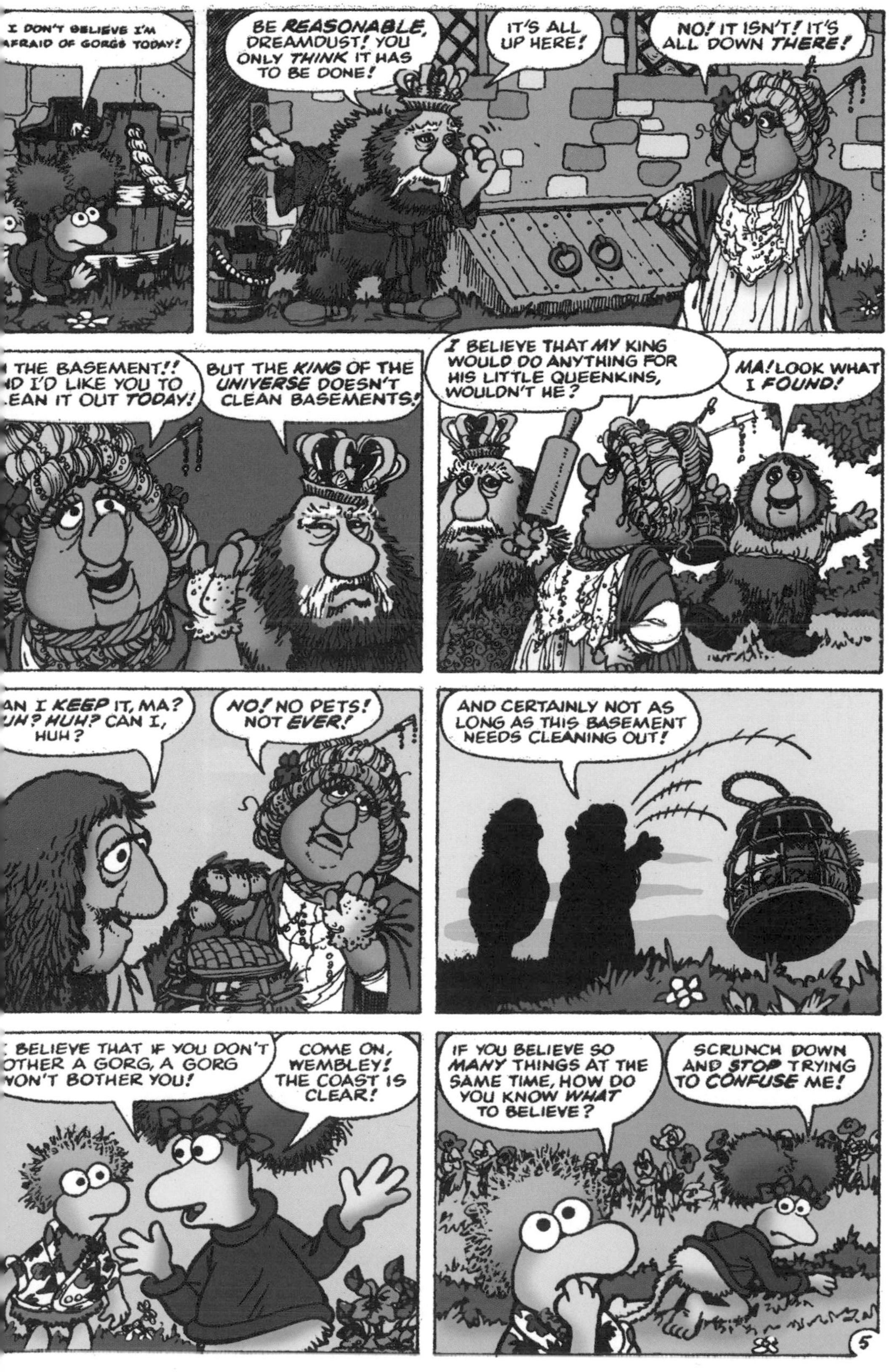
I DON'T BELIEVE I'M
AFRAID OF GORGS TODAY!
BE REASONABLE, DREAMDUST! YOU ONLY THINK IT HAS TO BE DONE!
IT'S ALL UP HERE!
NO! IT ISN'T! IT'S ALL DOWN THERE!
THE BASEMENT!! ID I'D LIKE YOU TO EAN IT OUT TODAY!
BUT THE KING OF THE UNIVERSE DOESN'T CLEAN BASEMENTS!
I BELIEVE THAT MY KING WOULD DO ANYTHING FOR HIS LITTLE QUEENKINS, WOULDN'T HE?
MA! LOOK WHAT I FOUND!
AN I KEEP IT, MA? UH? HUH? CAN I, HUH?
NO! NO PETS! NOT EVER!
AND CERTAINLY NOT AS LONG AS THIS BASEMENT NEEDS CLEANING OUT!
BELIEVE THAT IF YOU DON'T OTHER A GORG, A GORG VON'T BOTHER YOU!
COME ON, WEMBLEY! THE COAST IS CLEAR!
IF YOU BELIEVE SO MANY THINGS AT THE SAME TIME, HOW DO YOU KNOW WHAT TO BELIEVE?
SCRUNCH DOWN AND STOP TRYING TO CONFUSE ME!
5

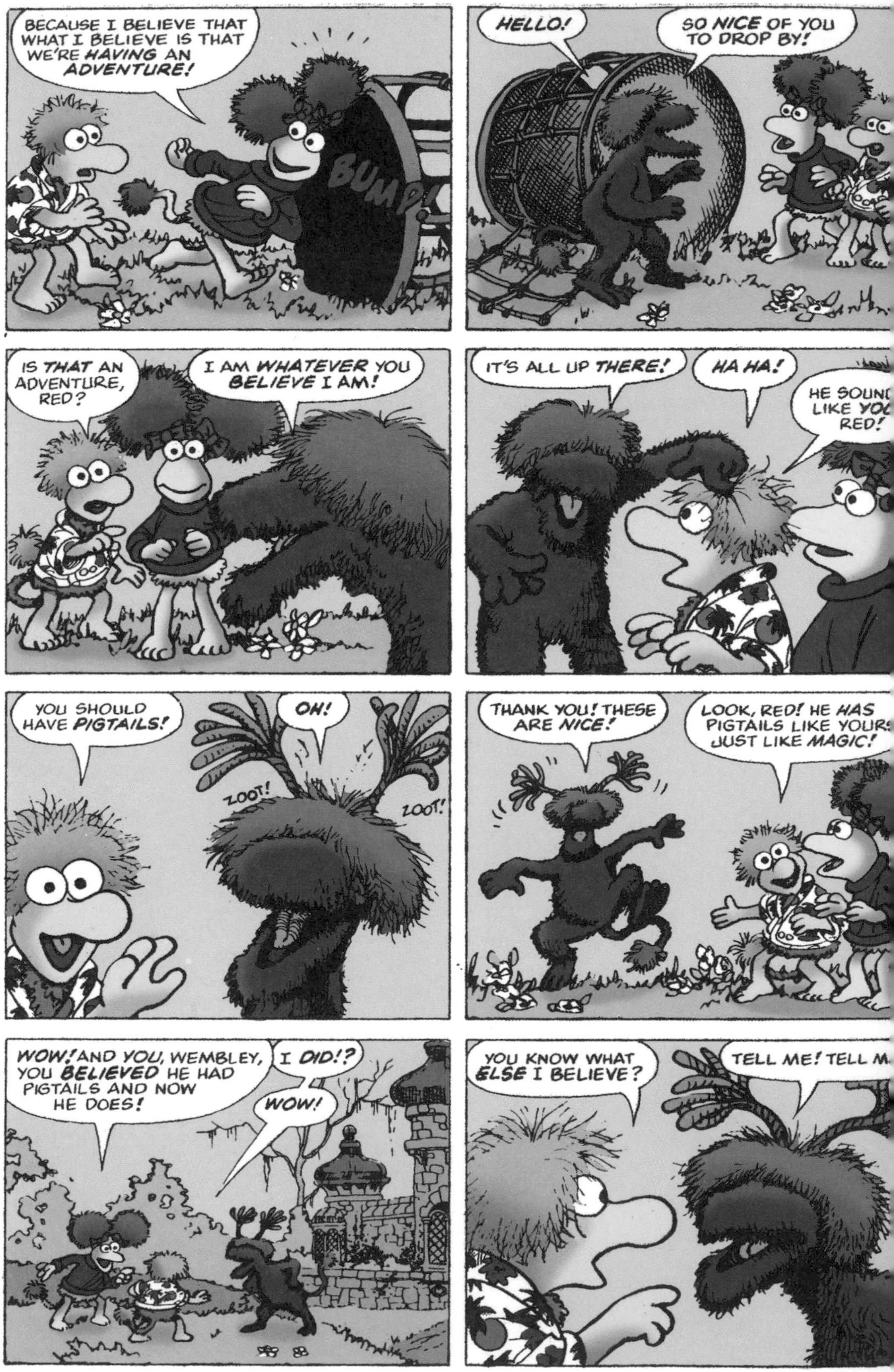
BECAUSE I BELIEVE THAT WHAT I BELIEVE IS THAT WE'RE HAVING AN ADVENTURE!
BUMP!
HELLO!
SO NICE OF YOU TO DROP BY!
IS THAT AN ADVENTURE, RED?
I AM WHATEVER YOU BELIEVE I AM!
IT'S ALL UP THERE!
HA HA!
HE SOUND LIKE YO RED!
YOU SHOULD HAVE PIGTAILS!
OH!
ZOOT!
ZOOT!
THANK YOU! THESE ARE NICE!
LOOK, RED! HE HAS PIGTAILS LIKE YOUR JUST LIKE MAGIC!
WOW! AND YOU, WEMBLEY, YOU BELIEVED HE HAD PIGTAILS AND NOW HE DOES!
I DID!?
WOW!
YOU KNOW WHAT ELSE I BELIEVE?
TELL ME! TELL M

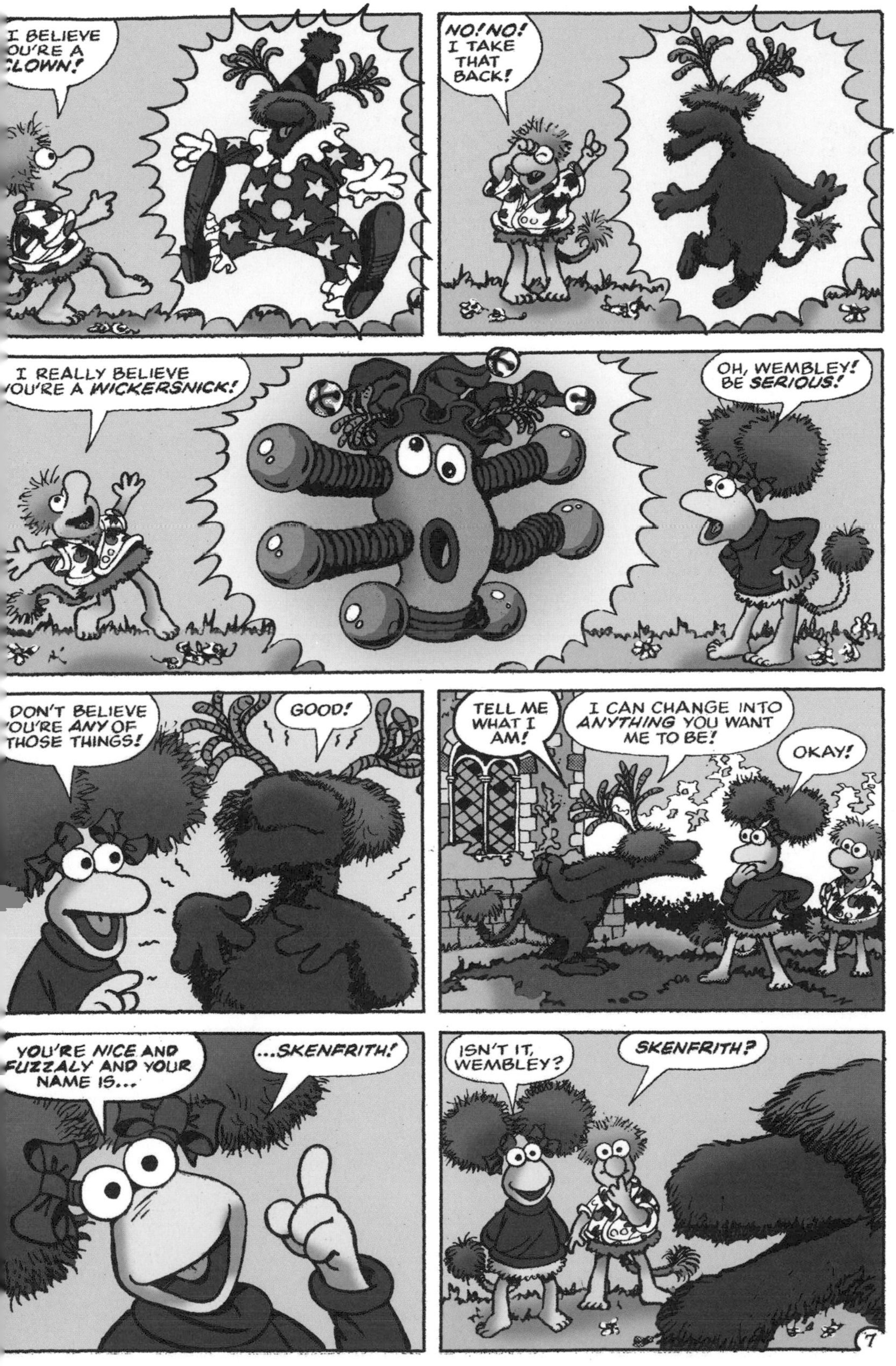
I BELIEVE OU'RE A CLOWN!
NO! NO! I TAKE THAT BACK!
I REALLY BELIEVE OU'RE A WICKERSNICK!
OH, WEMBLEY! BE SERIOUS!
DON'T BELIEVE OU'RE ANY OF THOSE THINGS!
GOOD!
TELL ME WHAT I AM!
I CAN CHANGE INTO ANYTHING YOU WANT ME TO BE!
OKAY!
YOU'RE NICE AND FUZZALY AND YOUR NAME IS...
...SKENFRITH!
ISN'T IT, WEMBLEY?
SKENFRITH?
7

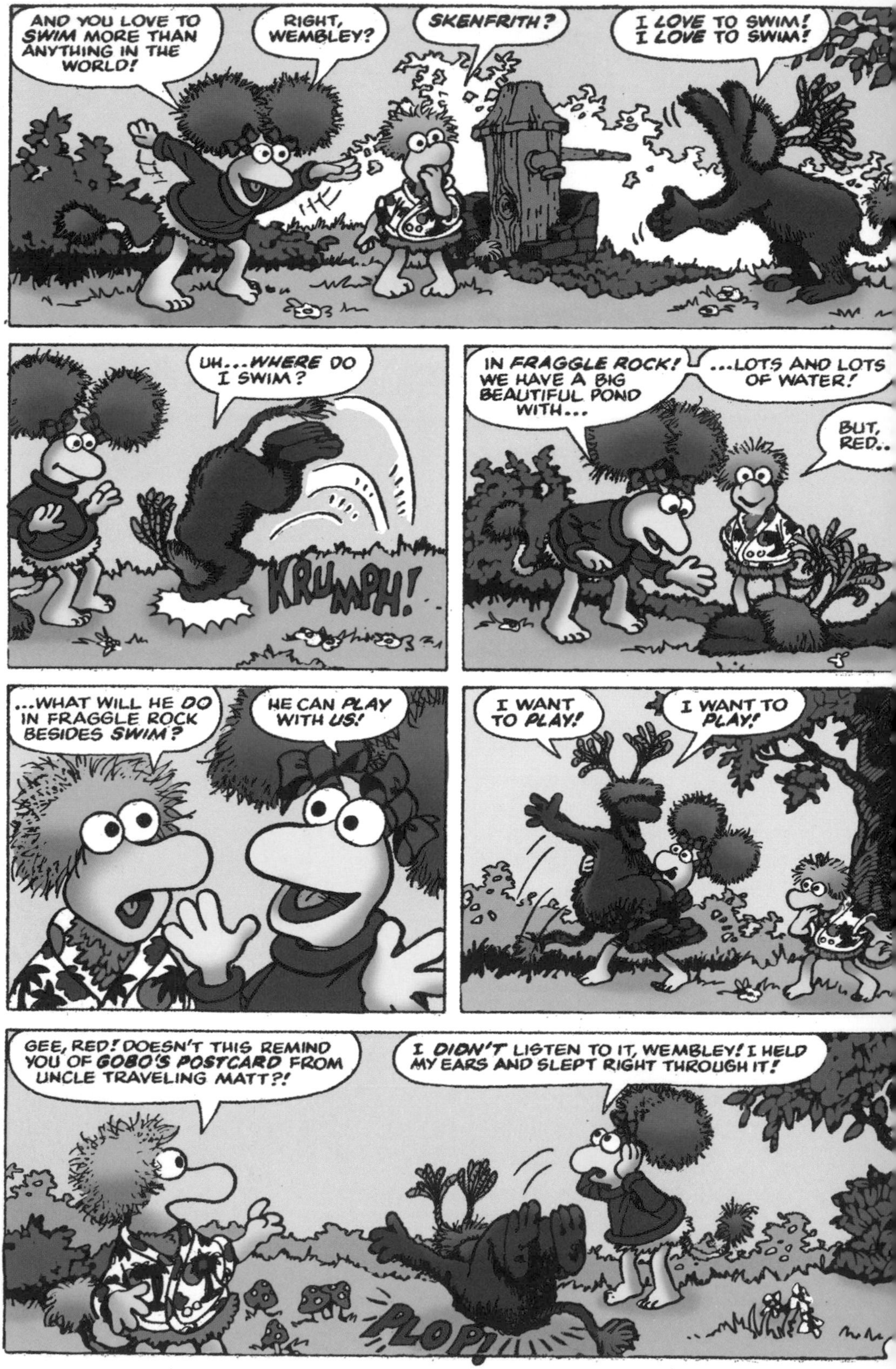
AND YOU LOVE TO SWIM MORE THAN ANYTHING IN THE WORLD!
RIGHT, WEMBLEY?
SKENFRITH?
I LOVE TO SWIM! I LOVE TO SWIM!
UH...WHERE DO I SWIM?
KRUMPH!
IN FRAGGLE ROCK! WE HAVE A BIG BEAUTIFUL POND WITH...
...LOTS AND LOTS OF WATER!
BUT, RED...
...WHAT WILL HE DO IN FRAGGLE ROCK BESIDES SWIM?
HE CAN PLAY WITH US!
I WANT TO PLAY!
I WANT TO PLAY!
GEE, RED! DOESN'T THIS REMIND YOU OF GOBO'S POSTCARD FROM UNCLE TRAVELING MATT?!
I DIDN'T LISTEN TO IT, WEMBLEY! I HELD MY EARS AND SLEPT RIGHT THROUGH IT!
PLOP!

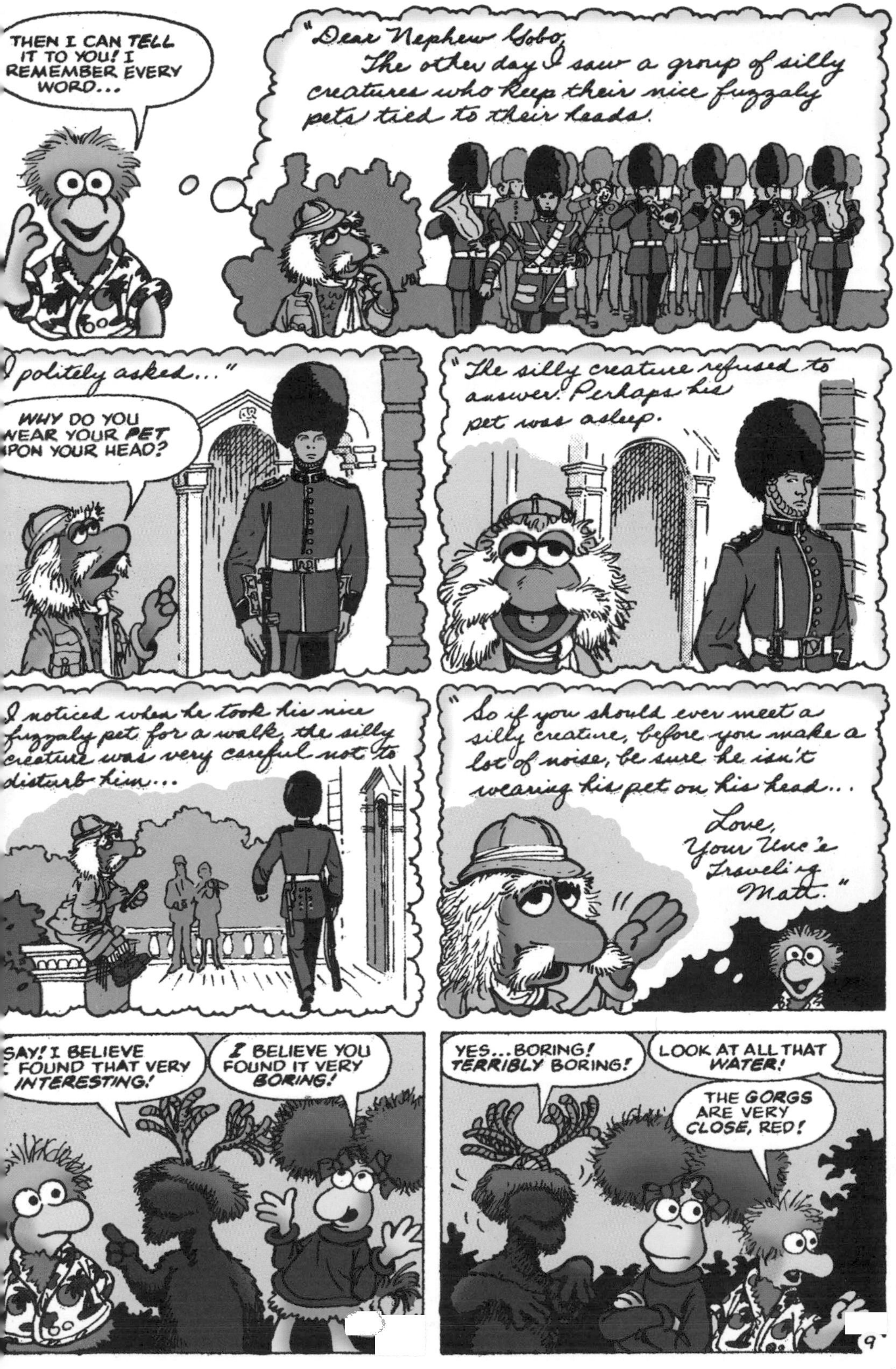
THEN I CAN TELL IT TO YOU! I REMEMBER EVERY WORD...
"Dear Nephew Gobo,
The other day I saw a group of silly creatures who keep their nice fuzzaly pets tied to their heads.
I politely asked..."
WHY DO YOU WEAR YOUR PET PON YOUR HEAD?
"The silly creature refused to answer. Perhaps his pet was asleep.
I noticed when he took his nice fuzzaly pet for a walk, the silly creature was very careful not to disturb him...
"So if you should ever meet a silly creature, before you make a lot of noise, be sure he isn't wearing his pet on his head...
Love,
Your Unc'e Traveli g Matt."
SAY! I BELIEVE FOUND THAT VERY INTERESTING!
I BELIEVE YOU FOUND IT VERY BORING!
YES...BORING! TERRIBLY BORING!
LOOK AT ALL THAT WATER!
THE GORGS ARE VERY CLOSE, RED!

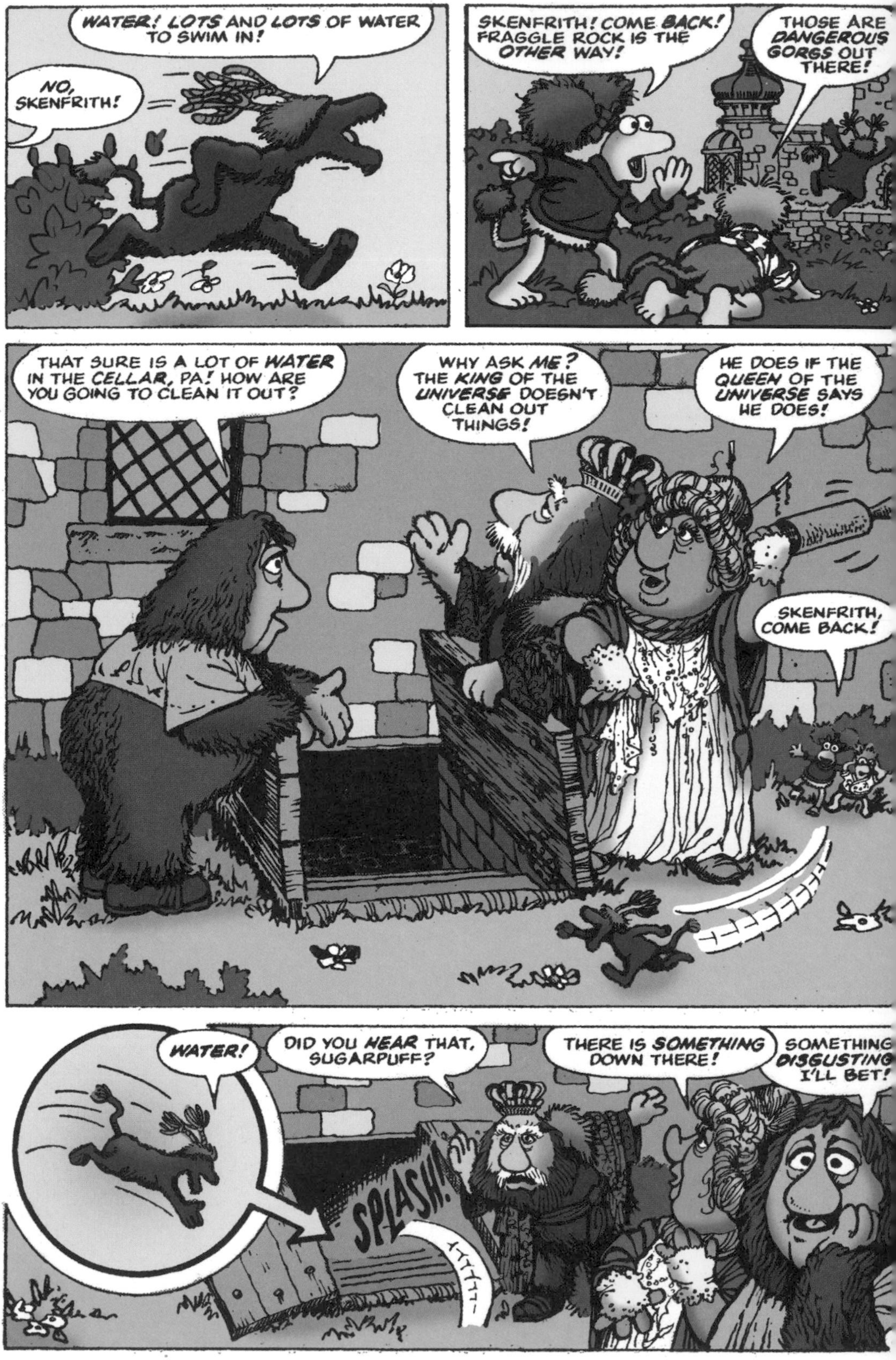

WATER! LOTS AND LOTS OF WATER TO SWIM IN!
NO, SKENFRITH!
SKENFRITH! COME BACK! FRAGGLE ROCK IS THE OTHER WAY!
THOSE ARE DANGEROUS GORGS OUT THERE!
THAT SURE IS A LOT OF WATER IN THE CELLAR, PA! HOW ARE YOU GOING TO CLEAN IT OUT?
WHY ASK ME? THE KING OF THE UNIVERSE DOESN'T CLEAN OUT THINGS!
HE DOES IF THE QUEEN OF THE UNIVERSE SAYS HE DOES!
SKENFRITH, COME BACK!
WATER!
SPLASH!
DID YOU HEAR THAT, SUGARPUFF?
THERE IS SOMETHING DOWN THERE!
SOMETHING DISGUSTING I'LL BET!

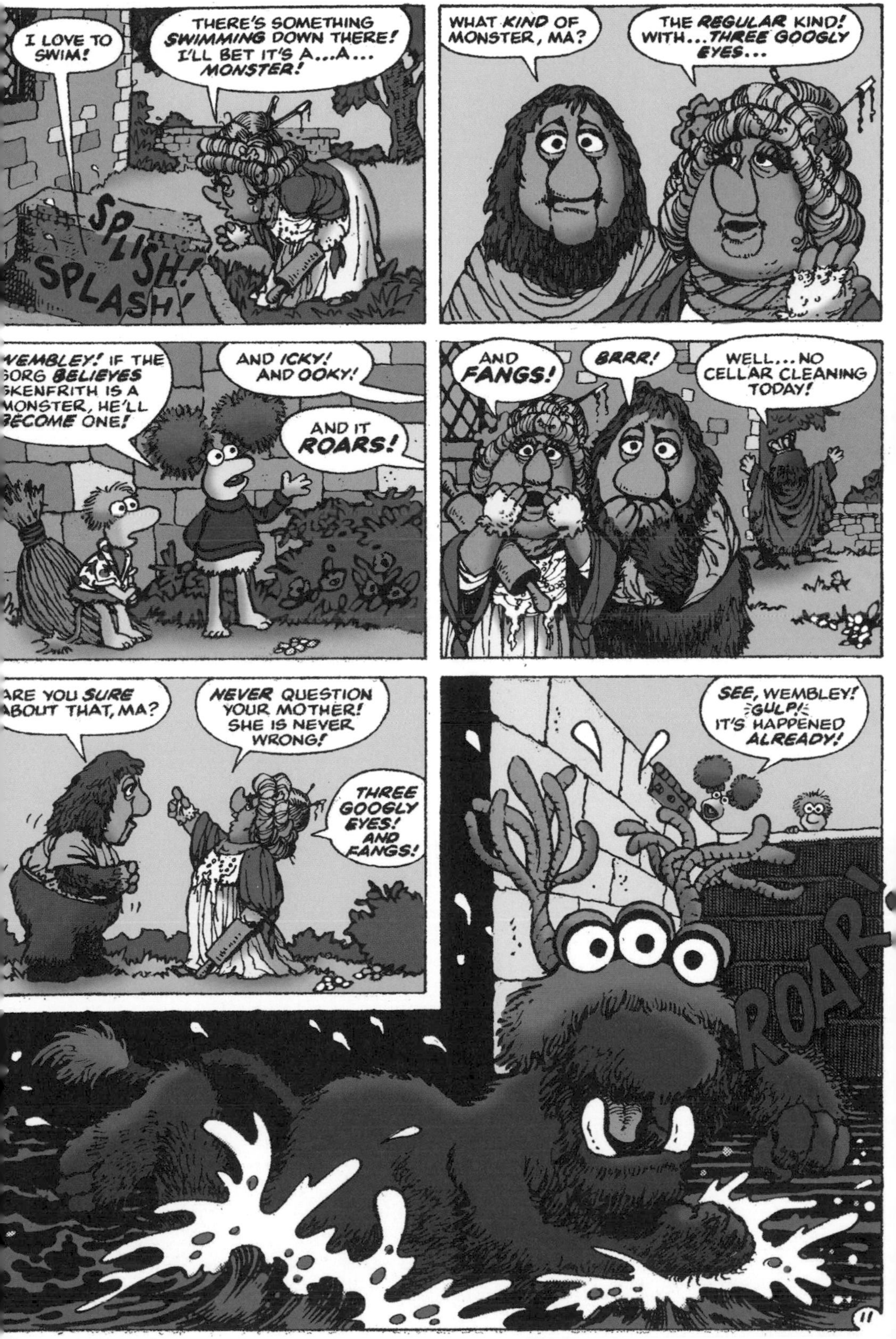
I LOVE TO SWIM!
THERE'S SOMETHING SWIMMING DOWN THERE! I'LL BET IT'S A...A... MONSTER!
SPLISH! SPLASH!
WHAT KIND OF MONSTER, MA?
THE REGULAR KIND! WITH...THREE GOOGLY EYES...
WEMBLEY! IF THE GORG BELIEVES SKENFRITH IS A MONSTER, HE'LL BECOME ONE!
AND ICKY! AND OOKY!
AND IT ROARS!
AND FANGS!
BRRR!
WELL...NO CELLAR CLEANING TODAY!
ARE YOU SURE ABOUT THAT, MA?
NEVER QUESTION YOUR MOTHER! SHE IS NEVER WRONG!
THREE GOOGLY EYES! AND FANGS!
SEE, WEMBLEY! GULP! IT'S HAPPENED ALREADY!
ROAR!
11

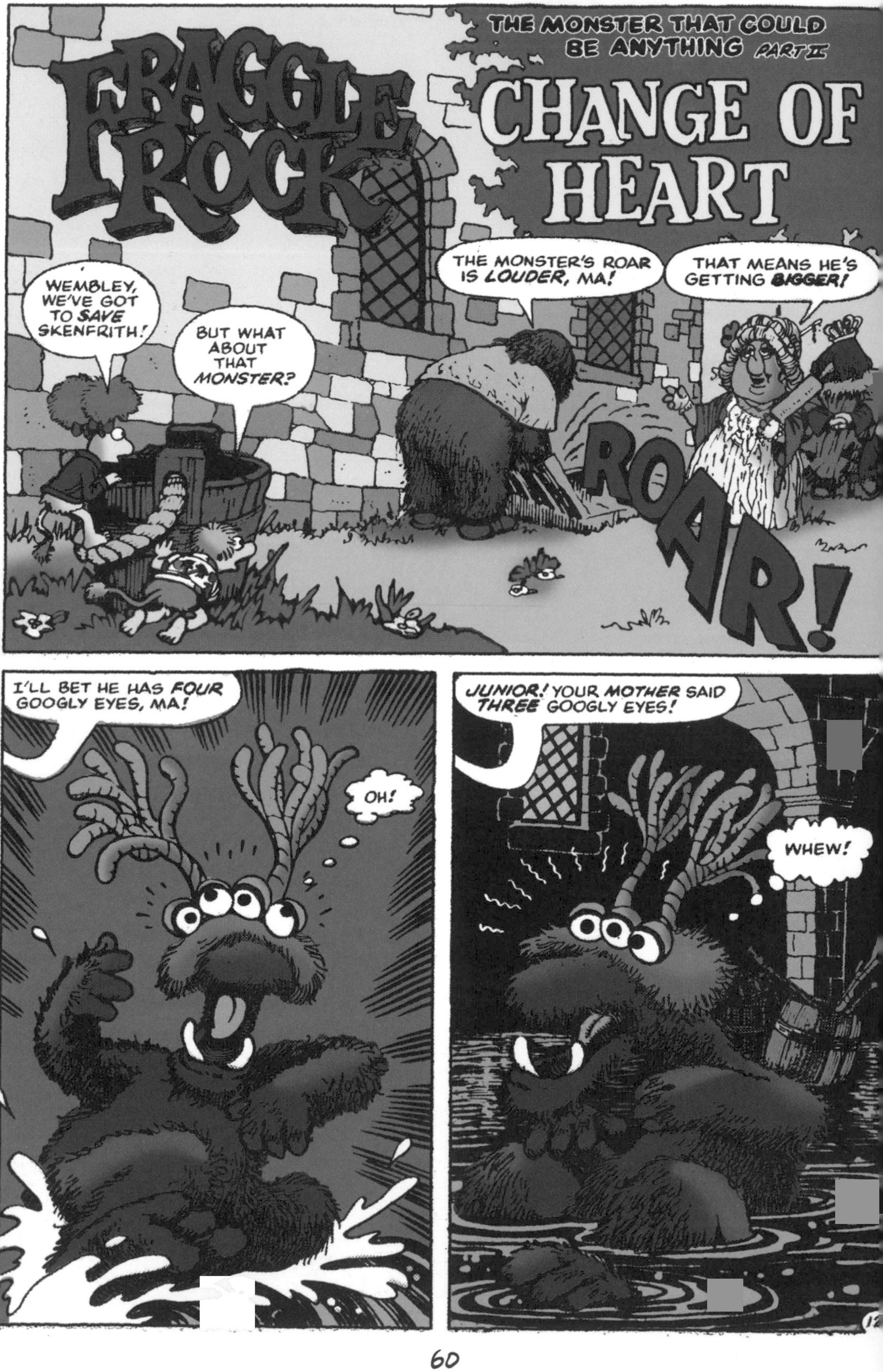
FRAGGLE ROCK
THE MONSTER THAT COULD BE ANYTHING PART II
CHANGE OF HEART
WEMBLEY, WE'VE GOT TO SAVE SKENFRITH!
BUT WHAT ABOUT THAT MONSTER?
THE MONSTER'S ROAR IS LOUDER, MA!
THAT MEANS HE'S GETTING BIGGER!
ROAR!
I'LL BET HE HAS FOUR GOOGLY EYES, MA!
OH!
JUNIOR! YOUR MOTHER SAID THREE GOOGLY EYES!
WHEW!

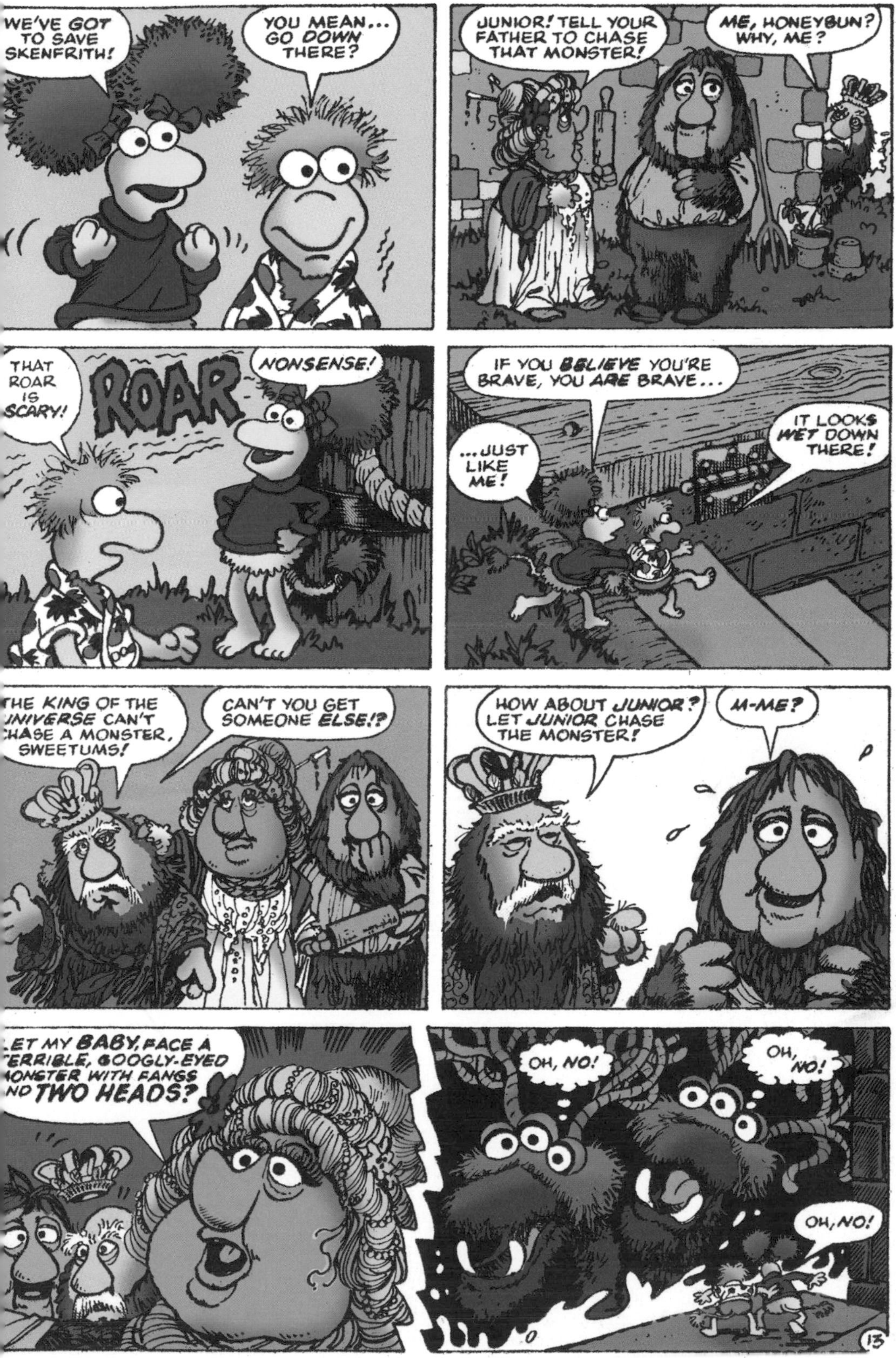

WE'VE GOT TO SAVE SKENFRITH!
YOU MEAN... GO DOWN THERE?
JUNIOR! TELL YOUR FATHER TO CHASE THAT MONSTER!
ME, HONEYBUN? WHY, ME?
THAT ROAR IS SCARY!
ROAR
NONSENSE!
IF YOU BELIEVE YOU'RE BRAVE, YOU ARE BRAVE...
...JUST LIKE ME!
IT LOOKS WET DOWN THERE!
THE KING OF THE UNIVERSE CAN'T CHASE A MONSTER, SWEETUMS!
CAN'T YOU GET SOMEONE ELSE!?
HOW ABOUT JUNIOR? LET JUNIOR CHASE THE MONSTER!
M-ME?
LET MY BABY, FACE A TERRIBLE, GOOGLY-EYED MONSTER WITH FANGS AND TWO HEADS?
OH, NO!
OH, NO!
OH, NO!
13

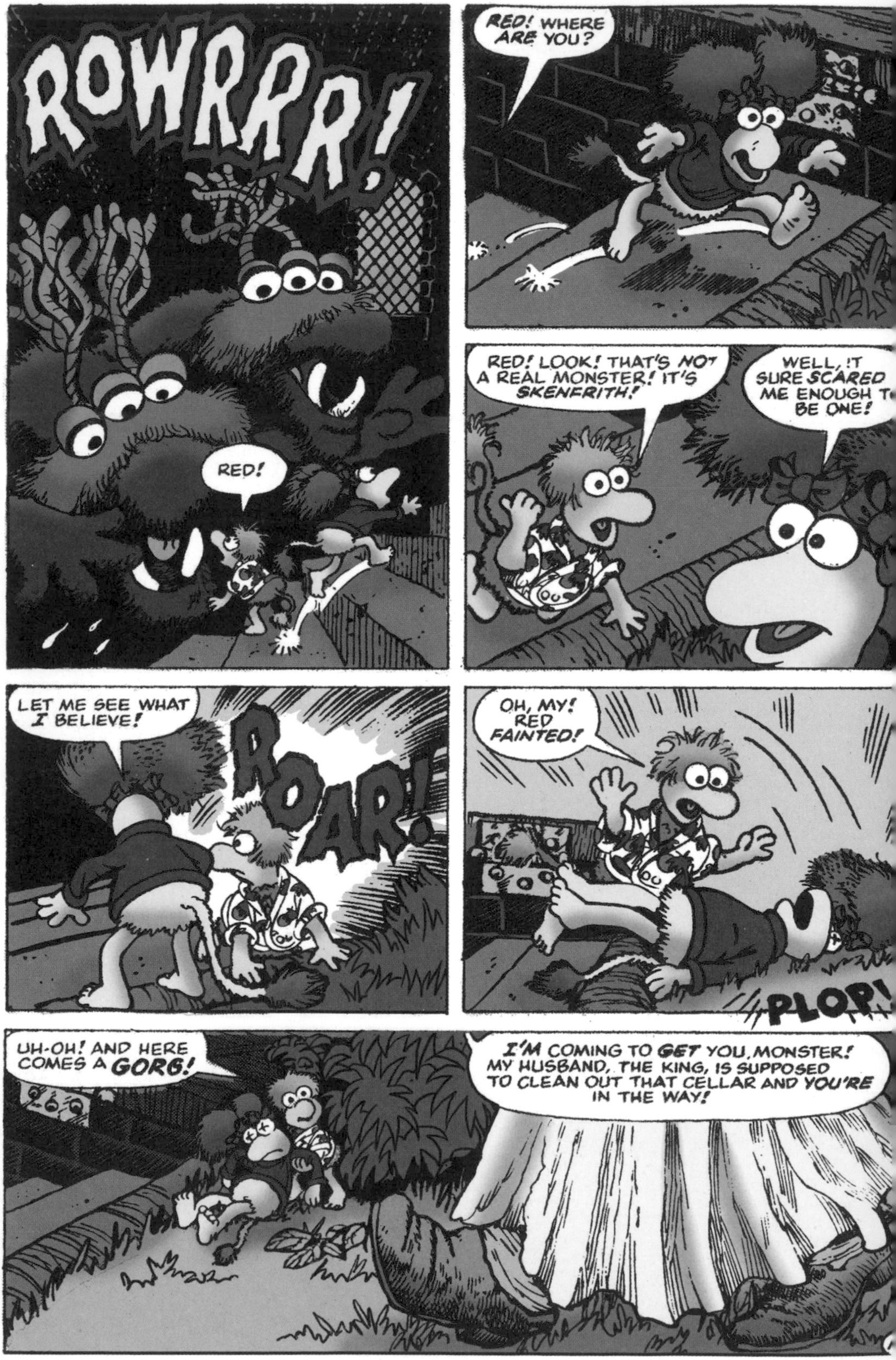
ROWRRR!
RED!
RED! WHERE ARE YOU?
RED! LOOK! THAT'S NOT A REAL MONSTER! IT'S SKENFRITH!
WELL, IT SURE SCARED ME ENOUGH T BE ONE!
LET ME SEE WHAT I BELIEVE!
ROAR!
OH, MY! RED FAINTED!
PLOP!
UH-OH! AND HERE COMES A GORG!
I'M COMING TO GET YOU, MONSTER! MY HUSBAND, THE KING, IS SUPPOSED TO CLEAN OUT THAT CELLAR AND YOU'RE IN THE WAY!

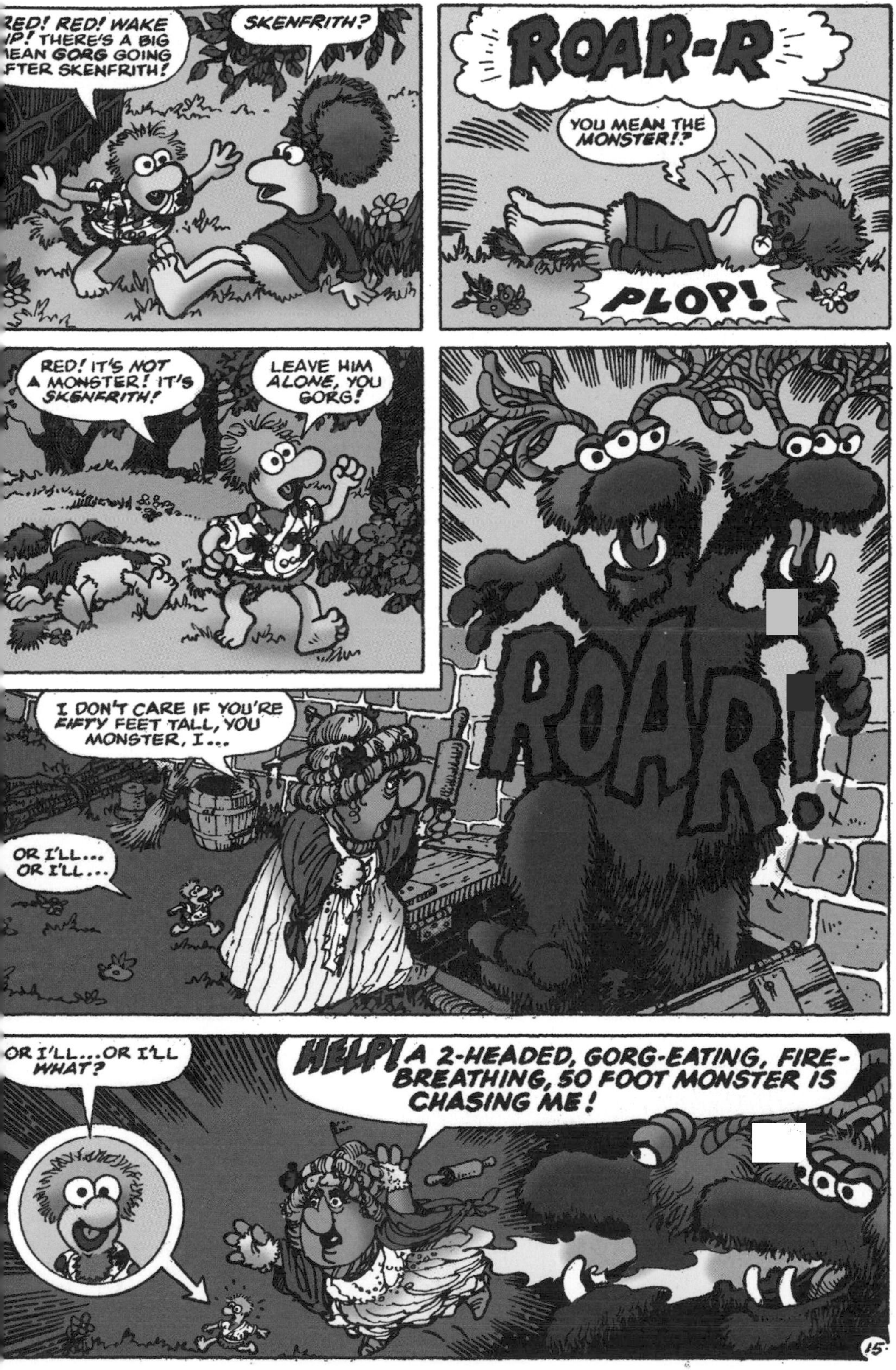

ED! RED! WAKE P! THERE'S A BIG EAN GORG GOING FTER SKENFRITH!
SKENFRITH?
ROAR-R
YOU MEAN THE MONSTER!?
PLOP!
RED! IT'S NOT A MONSTER! IT'S SKENFRITH!
LEAVE HIM ALONE, YOU GORG!
ROAR!
I DON'T CARE IF YOU'RE FIFTY FEET TALL, YOU MONSTER, I...
OR I'LL... OR I'LL...
OR I'LL...OR I'LL WHAT?
HELP! A 2-HEADED, GORG-EATING, FIRE-BREATHING, 50 FOOT MONSTER IS CHASING ME!
15

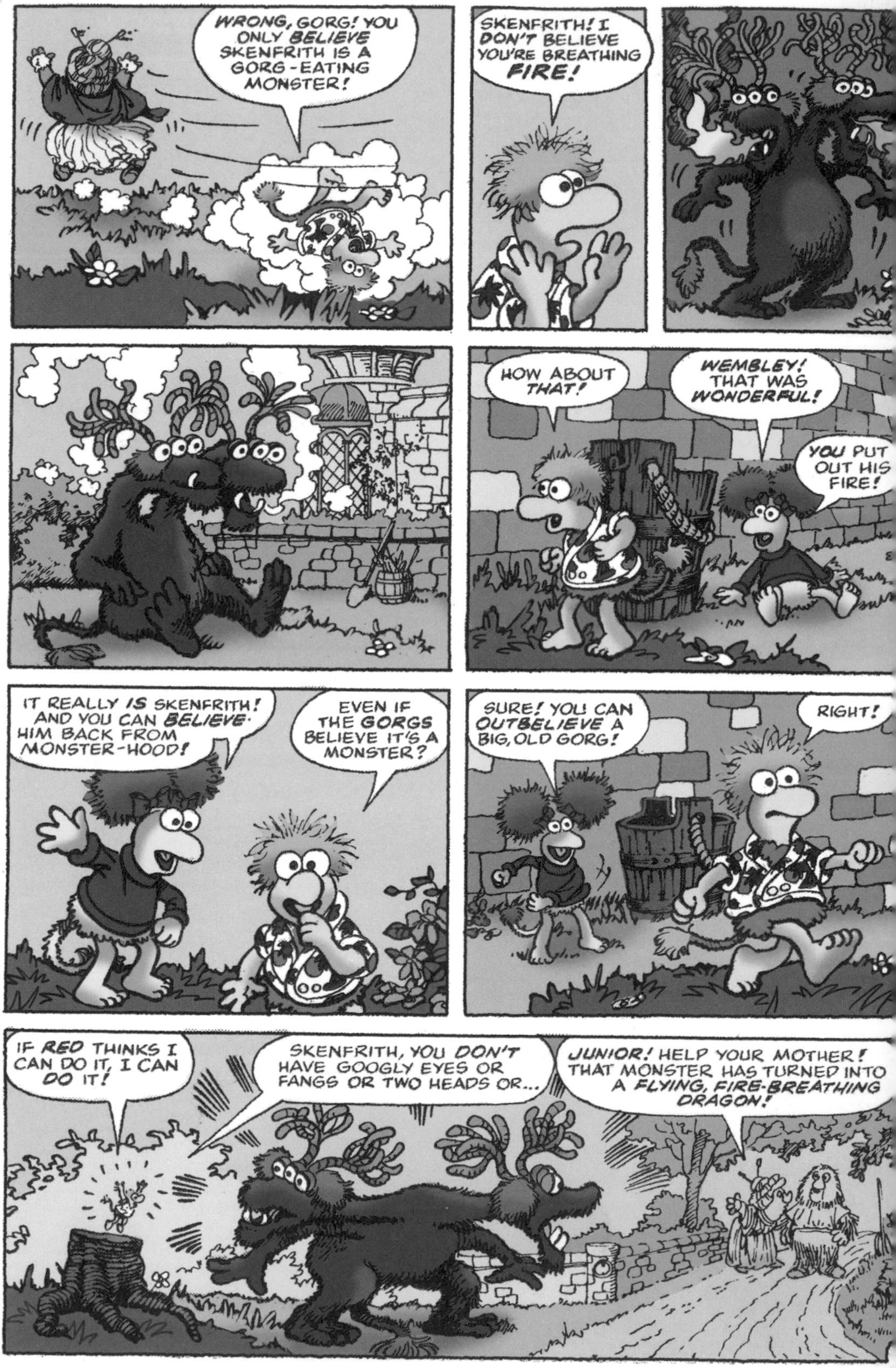
WRONG, GORG! YOU ONLY BELIEVE SKENFRITH IS A GORG-EATING MONSTER!
SKENFRITH! I DON'T BELIEVE YOU'RE BREATHING FIRE!
HOW ABOUT THAT!
WEMBLEY! THAT WAS WONDERFUL!
YOU PUT OUT HIS FIRE!
IT REALLY IS SKENFRITH! AND YOU CAN BELIEVE HIM BACK FROM MONSTER-HOOD!
EVEN IF THE GORGS BELIEVE IT'S A MONSTER?
SURE! YOU CAN OUTBELIEVE A BIG, OLD GORG!
RIGHT!
IF RED THINKS I CAN DO IT, I CAN DO IT!
SKENFRITH, YOU DON'T HAVE GOOGLY EYES OR FANGS OR TWO HEADS OR...
JUNIOR! HELP YOUR MOTHER! THAT MONSTER HAS TURNED INTO A FLYING, FIRE-BREATHING DRAGON!

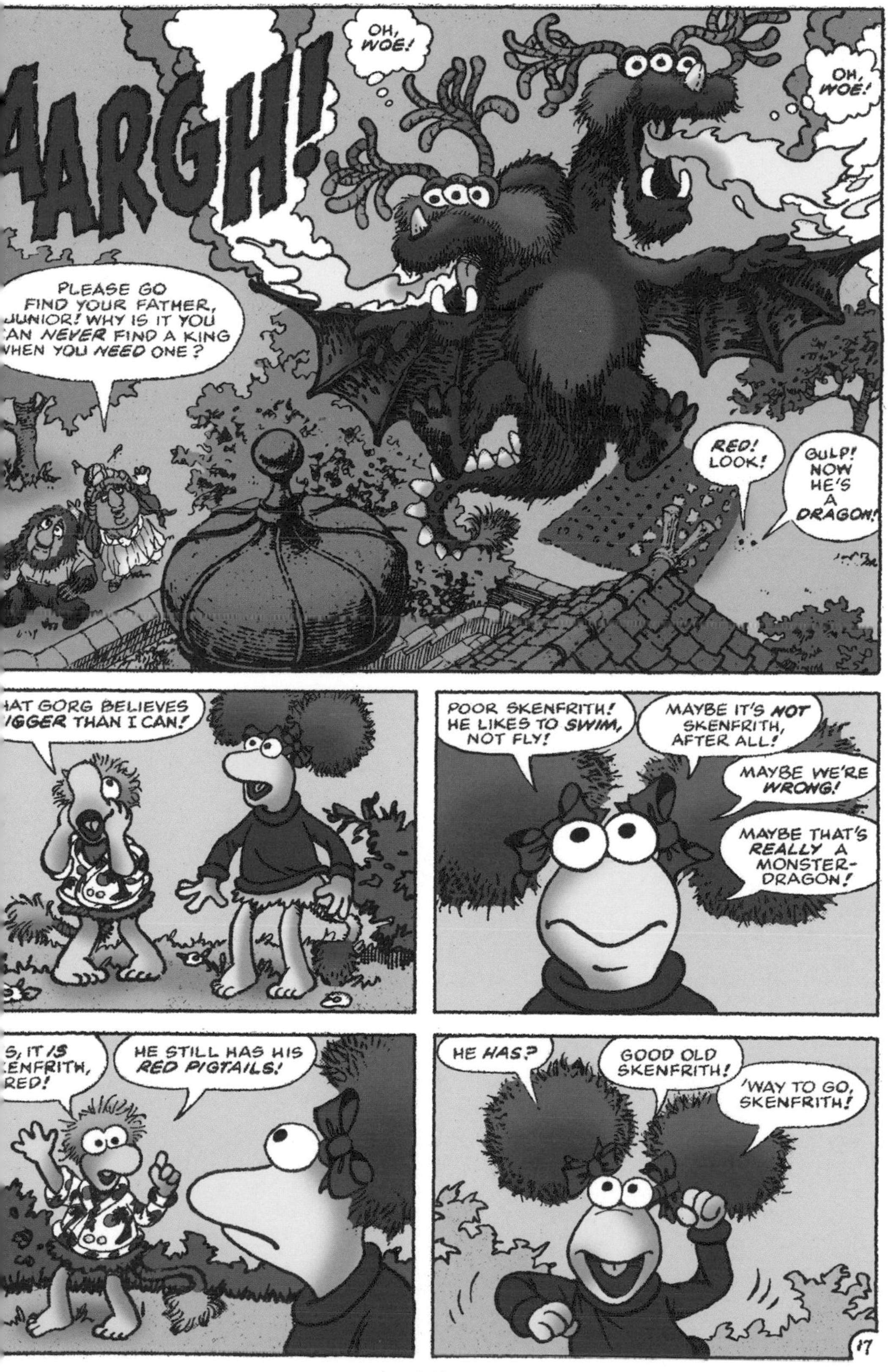
AARGH!
OH, WOE!
OH, WOE!
PLEASE GO FIND YOUR FATHER, JUNIOR! WHY IS IT YOU CAN NEVER FIND A KING WHEN YOU NEED ONE?
RED! LOOK!
GULP! NOW HE'S A DRAGON!
HAT GORG BELIEVES IGGER THAN I CAN!
POOR SKENFRITH! HE LIKES TO SWIM, NOT FLY!
MAYBE IT'S NOT SKENFRITH, AFTER ALL!
MAYBE WE'RE WRONG!
MAYBE THAT'S REALLY A MONSTER-DRAGON!
S, IT IS ENFRITH, RED!
HE STILL HAS HIS RED PIGTAILS!
HE HAS?
GOOD OLD SKENFRITH!
'WAY TO GO, SKENFRITH!
17

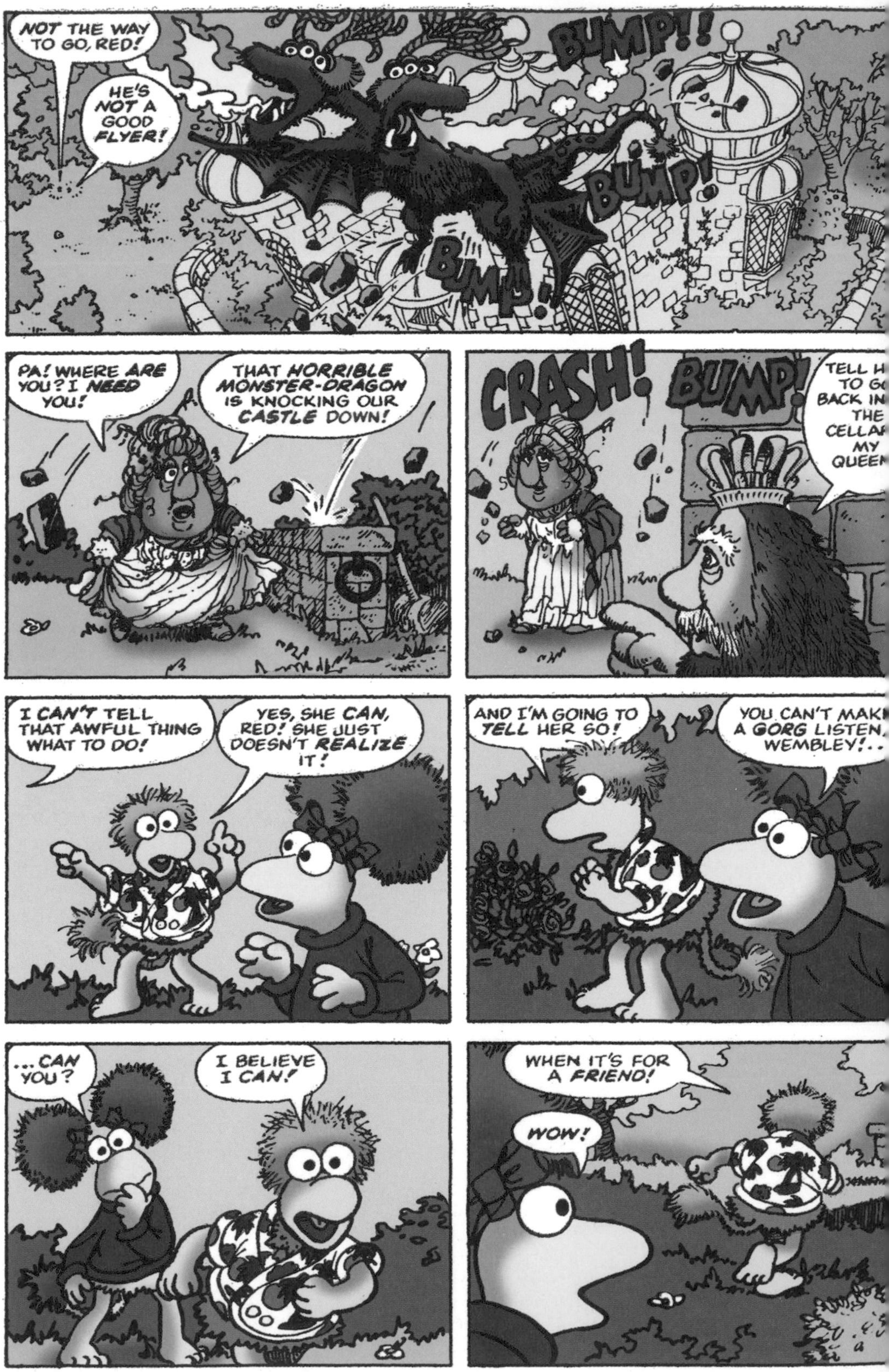
NOT THE WAY TO GO, RED!
HE'S NOT A GOOD FLYER!
BUMP!!
BUMP!
BUMP!
PA! WHERE ARE YOU? I NEED YOU!
THAT HORRIBLE MONSTER-DRAGON IS KNOCKING OUR CASTLE DOWN!
CRASH!
BUMP!
I CAN'T TELL THAT AWFUL THING WHAT TO DO!
YES, SHE CAN, RED! SHE JUST DOESN'T REALIZE IT!
AND I'M GOING TO TELL HER SO!
...CAN YOU?
I BELIEVE I CAN!
WHEN IT'S FOR A FRIEND!
WOW!

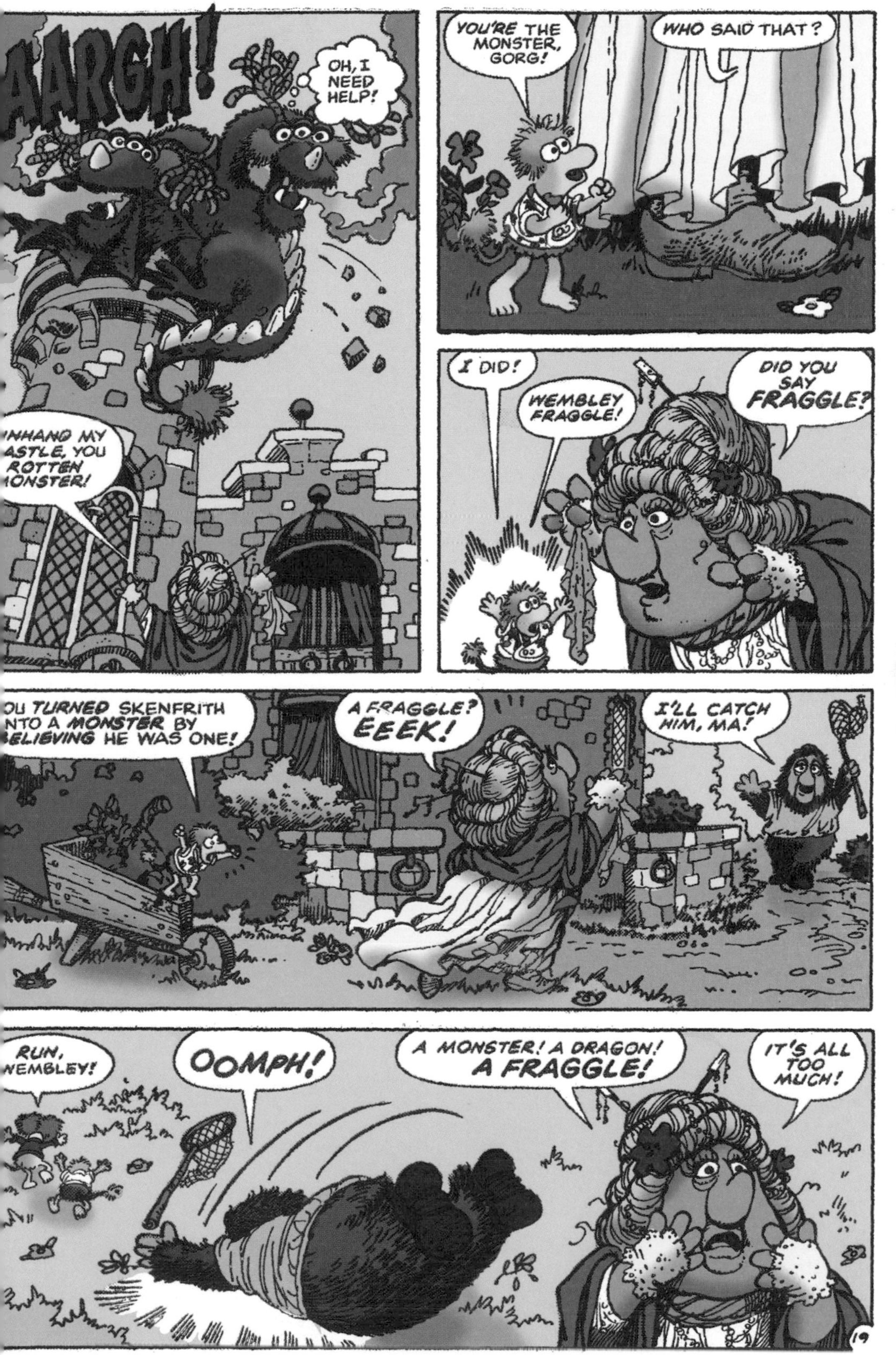
AARGH!
OH, I NEED HELP!
UNHAND MY CASTLE, YOU ROTTEN MONSTER!
YOU'RE THE MONSTER, GORG!
WHO SAID THAT?
I DID!
WEMBLEY FRAGGLE!
DID YOU SAY FRAGGLE?
OU TURNED SKENFRITH NTO A MONSTER BY ELIEVING HE WAS ONE!
A FRAGGLE? EEEK!
I'LL CATCH HIM, MA!
RUN, WEMBLEY!
OOMPH!
A MONSTER! A DRAGON! A FRAGGLE!
IT'S ALL TOO MUCH!
19

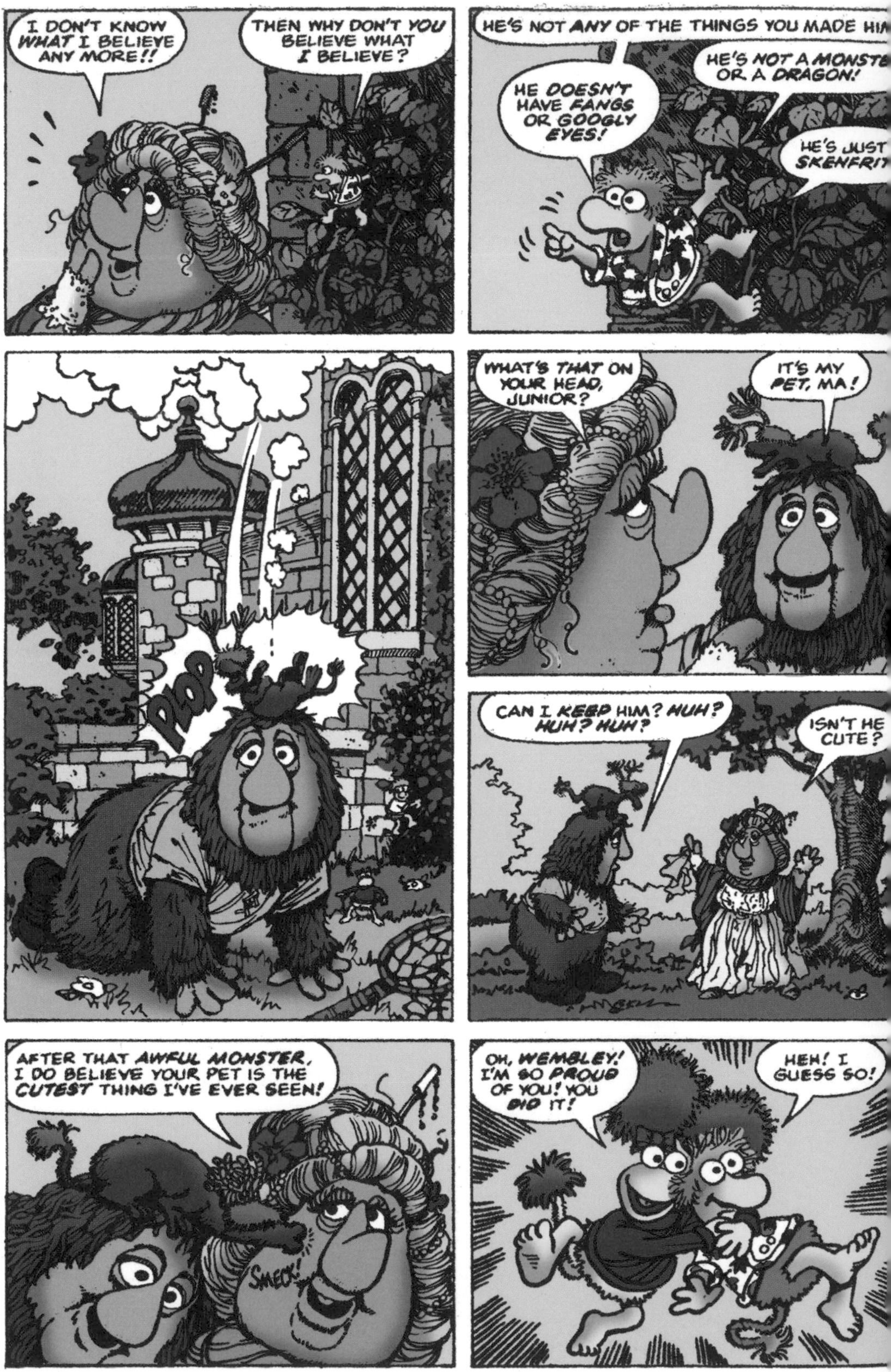
I DON'T KNOW WHAT I BELIEVE ANY MORE!!
THEN WHY DON'T YOU BELIEVE WHAT I BELIEVE?
HE'S NOT ANY OF THE THINGS YOU MADE HI
HE DOESN'T HAVE FANGS OR GOOGLY EYES!
HE'S NOT A MONSTE OR A DRAGON!
HE'S JUST SKENFRIT
PLOP
WHAT'S THAT ON YOUR HEAD, JUNIOR?
IT'S MY PET, MA!
CAN I KEEP HIM? HUH? HUH? HUH?
ISN'T HE CUTE?
AFTER THAT AWFUL MONSTER, I DO BELIEVE YOUR PET IS THE CUTEST THING I'VE EVER SEEN!
SMECK!
OH, WEMBLEY! I'M SO PROUD OF YOU! YOU DID IT!
HEH! I GUESS SO!

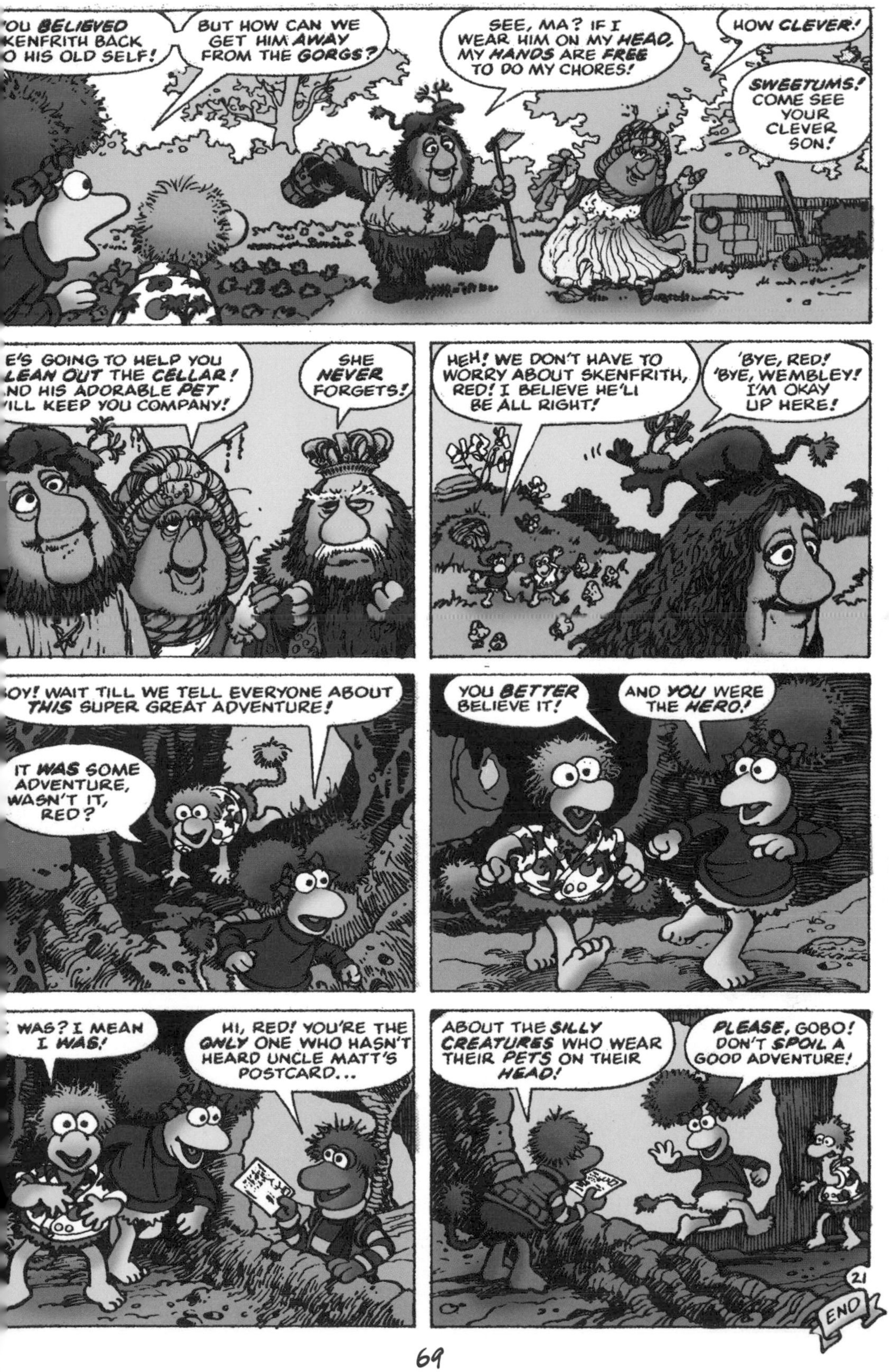

OU BELIEVED KENFRITH BACK O HIS OLD SELF!
BUT HOW CAN WE GET HIM AWAY FROM THE GORGS?
SEE, MA? IF I WEAR HIM ON MY HEAD, MY HANDS ARE FREE TO DO MY CHORES!
HOW CLEVER!
SWEETUMS! COME SEE YOUR CLEVER SON!
E'S GOING TO HELP YOU LEAN OUT THE CELLAR! ND HIS ADORABLE PET ILL KEEP YOU COMPANY!
SHE NEVER FORGETS!
HEH! WE DON'T HAVE TO WORRY ABOUT SKENFRITH, RED! I BELIEVE HE'LI BE ALL RIGHT!
'BYE, RED! 'BYE, WEMBLEY! I'M OKAY UP HERE!
OY! WAIT TILL WE TELL EVERYONE ABOUT THIS SUPER GREAT ADVENTURE!
IT WAS SOME ADVENTURE, WASN'T IT, RED?
YOU BETTER BELIEVE IT!
AND YOU WERE THE HERO!
WAS? I MEAN I WAS!
HI, RED! YOU'RE THE ONLY ONE WHO HASN'T HEARD UNCLE MATT'S POSTCARD...
ABOUT THE SILLY CREATURES WHO WEAR THEIR PETS ON THEIR HEAD!
PLEASE, GOBO! DON'T SPOIL A GOOD ADVENTURE!
21
END

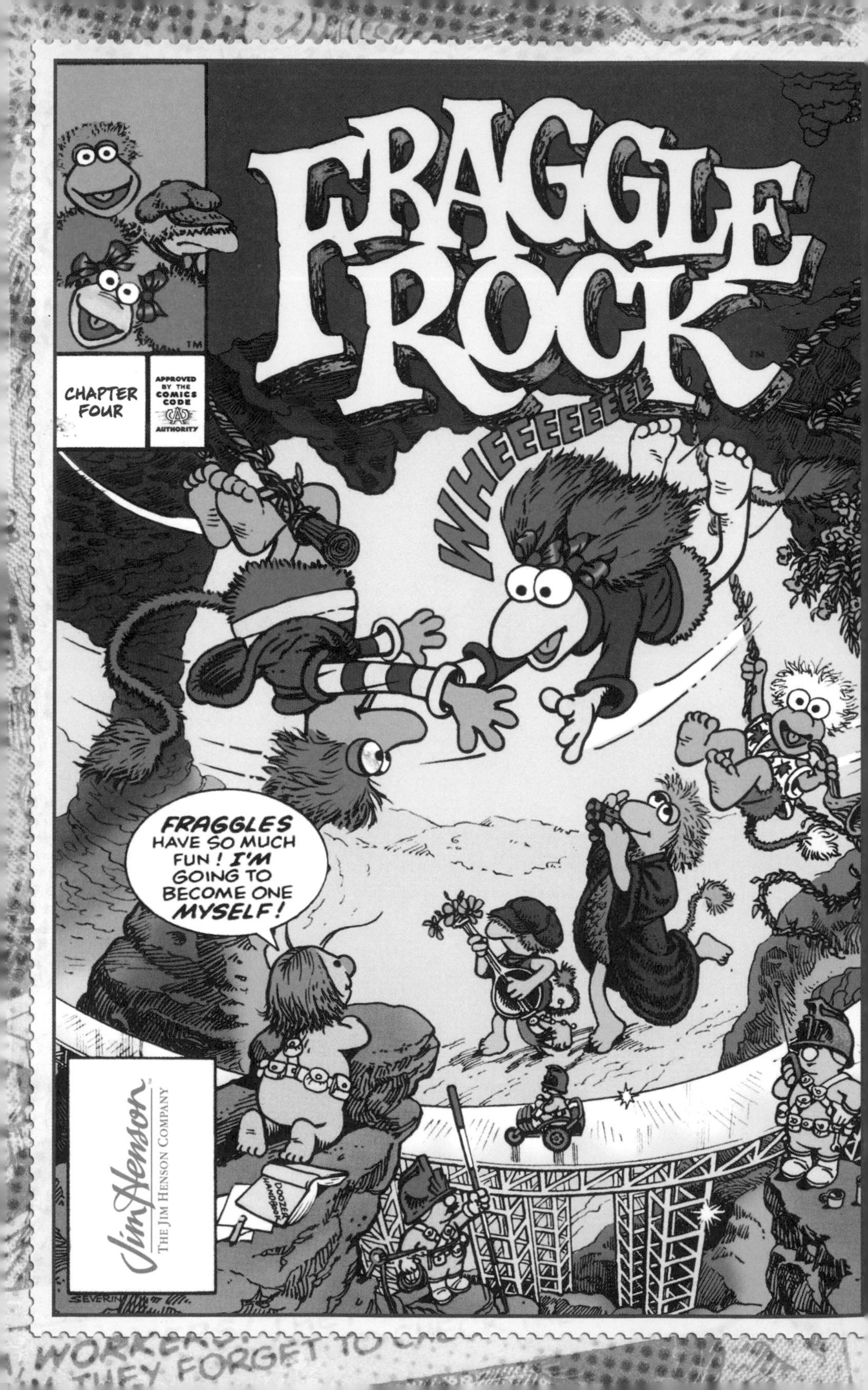
FRAGGLE ROCK
CHAPTER FOUR
APPROVED BY THE COMICS CODE AUTHORITY
WHEEEEEEEE
FRAGGLES HAVE SO MUCH FUN! I'M GOING TO BECOME ONE MYSELF!
DOOZER HANDBOOK
Jim Henson
THE JIM HENSON COMPANY
SEVERIN
THEY FORGET TO

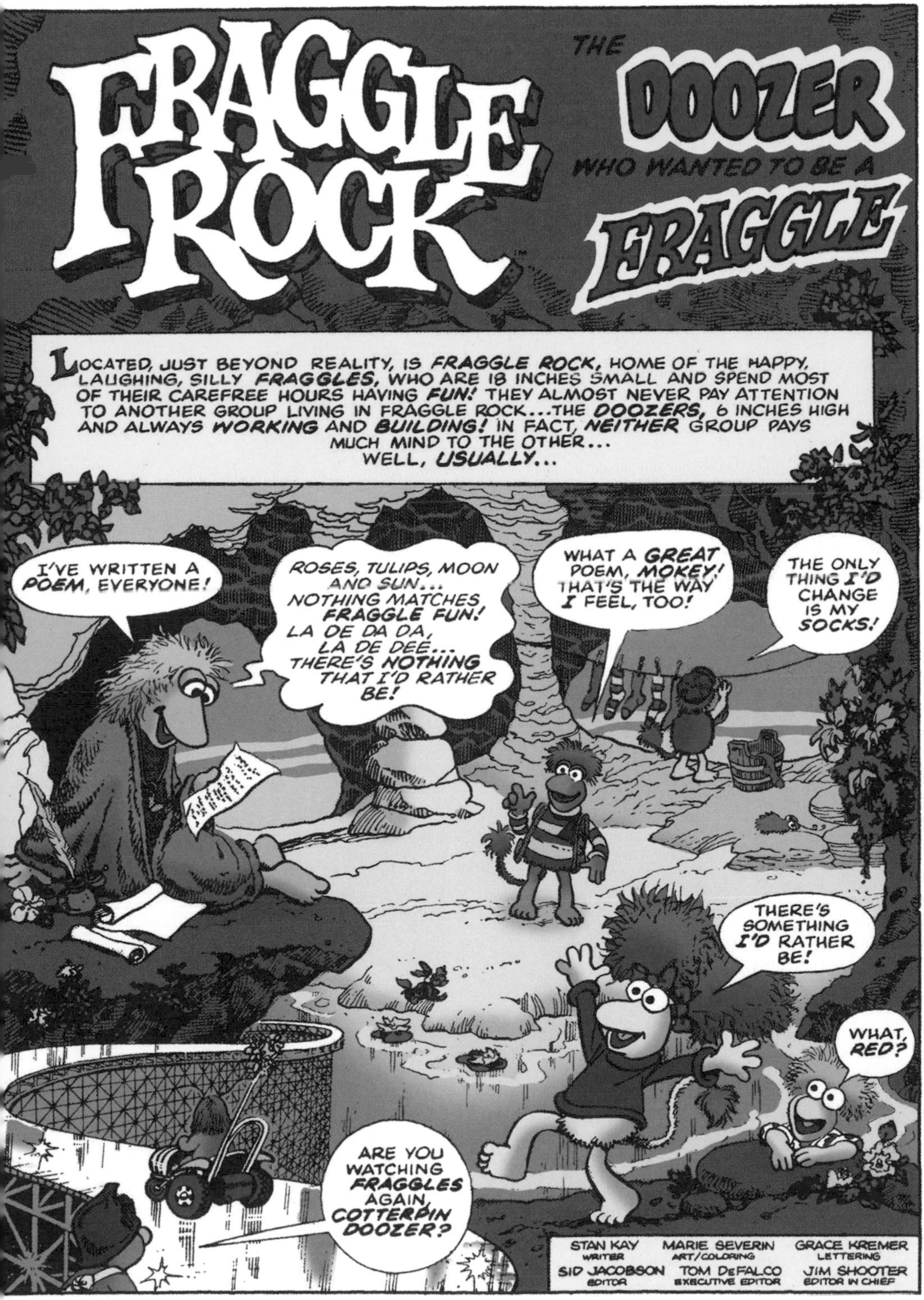
FRAGGLE ROCK
THE DOOZER WHO WANTED TO BE A FRAGGLE
LOCATED, JUST BEYOND REALITY, IS FRAGGLE ROCK, HOME OF THE HAPPY, LAUGHING, SILLY FRAGGLES, WHO ARE 18 INCHES SMALL AND SPEND MOST OF THEIR CAREFREE HOURS HAVING FUN! THEY ALMOST NEVER PAY ATTENTION TO ANOTHER GROUP LIVING IN FRAGGLE ROCK...THE DOOZERS, 6 INCHES HIGH AND ALWAYS WORKING AND BUILDING! IN FACT, NEITHER GROUP PAYS MUCH MIND TO THE OTHER... WELL, USUALLY...
I'VE WRITTEN A POEM, EVERYONE!
ROSES, TULIPS, MOON AND SUN... NOTHING MATCHES FRAGGLE FUN! LA DE DA DA, LA DE DEE... THERE'S NOTHING THAT I'D RATHER BE!
WHAT A GREAT POEM, MOKEY! THAT'S THE WAY I FEEL, TOO!
THE ONLY THING I'D CHANGE IS MY SOCKS!
THERE'S SOMETHING I'D RATHER BE!
WHAT, RED?
ARE YOU WATCHING FRAGGLES AGAIN, COTTERPIN DOOZER?
STAN KAY WRITER
MARIE SEVERIN ART/COLORING
GRACE KREMER LETTERING
SID JACOBSON EDITOR
TOM DeFALCO EXECUTIVE EDITOR
JIM SHOOTER EDITOR IN CHIEF

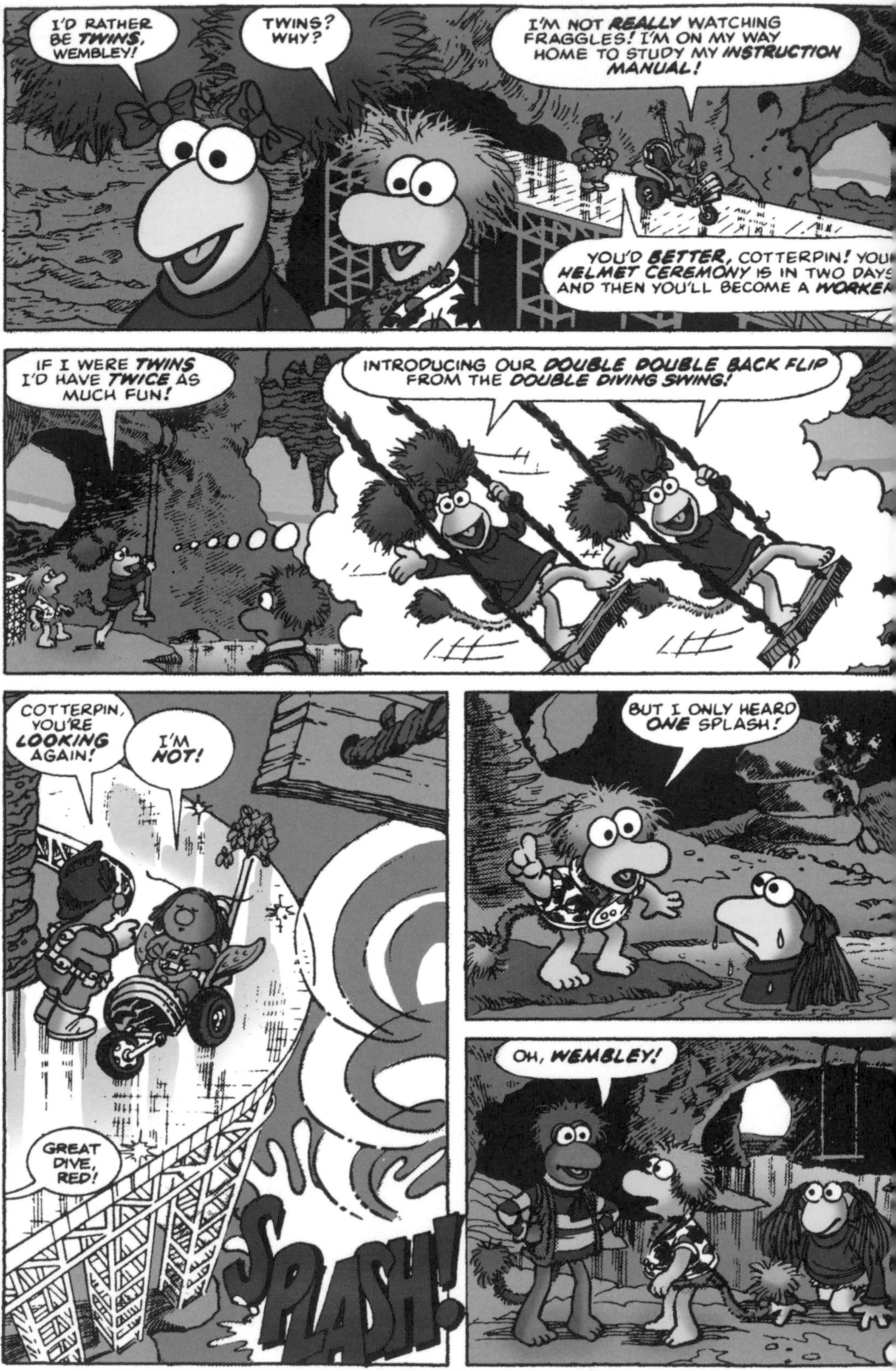

I'D RATHER BE TWINS, WEMBLEY!
TWINS? WHY?
I'M NOT REALLY WATCHING FRAGGLES! I'M ON MY WAY HOME TO STUDY MY INSTRUCTION MANUAL!
YOU'D BETTER, COTTERPIN! YOUR HELMET CEREMONY IS IN TWO DAYS AND THEN YOU'LL BECOME A WORKER
IF I WERE TWINS I'D HAVE TWICE AS MUCH FUN!
INTRODUCING OUR DOUBLE DOUBLE BACK FLIP FROM THE DOUBLE DIVING SWING!
COTTERPIN, YOU'RE LOOKING AGAIN!
I'M NOT!
GREAT DIVE, RED!
SPLASH!
BUT I ONLY HEARD ONE SPLASH!
OH, WEMBLEY!

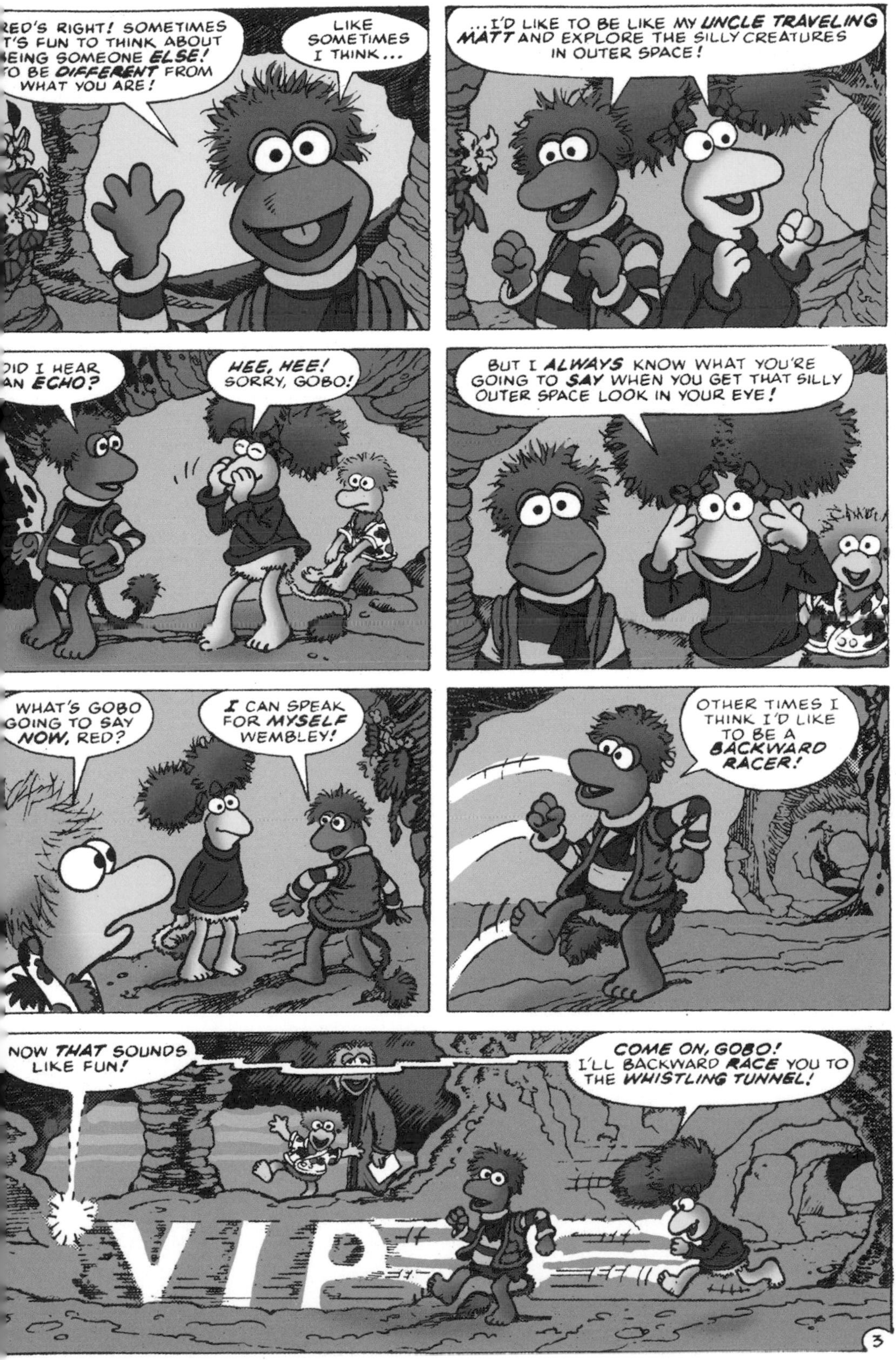

RED'S RIGHT! SOMETIMES IT'S FUN TO THINK ABOUT BEING SOMEONE ELSE! TO BE DIFFERENT FROM WHAT YOU ARE!
LIKE SOMETIMES I THINK...
...I'D LIKE TO BE LIKE MY UNCLE TRAVELING MATT AND EXPLORE THE SILLY CREATURES IN OUTER SPACE!
DID I HEAR AN ECHO?
HEE, HEE! SORRY, GOBO!
BUT I ALWAYS KNOW WHAT YOU'RE GOING TO SAY WHEN YOU GET THAT SILLY OUTER SPACE LOOK IN YOUR EYE!
WHAT'S GOBO GOING TO SAY NOW, RED?
I CAN SPEAK FOR MYSELF WEMBLEY!
OTHER TIMES I THINK I'D LIKE TO BE A BACKWARD RACER!
NOW THAT SOUNDS LIKE FUN!
COME ON, GOBO! I'LL BACKWARD RACE YOU TO THE WHISTLING TUNNEL!
VIP
3

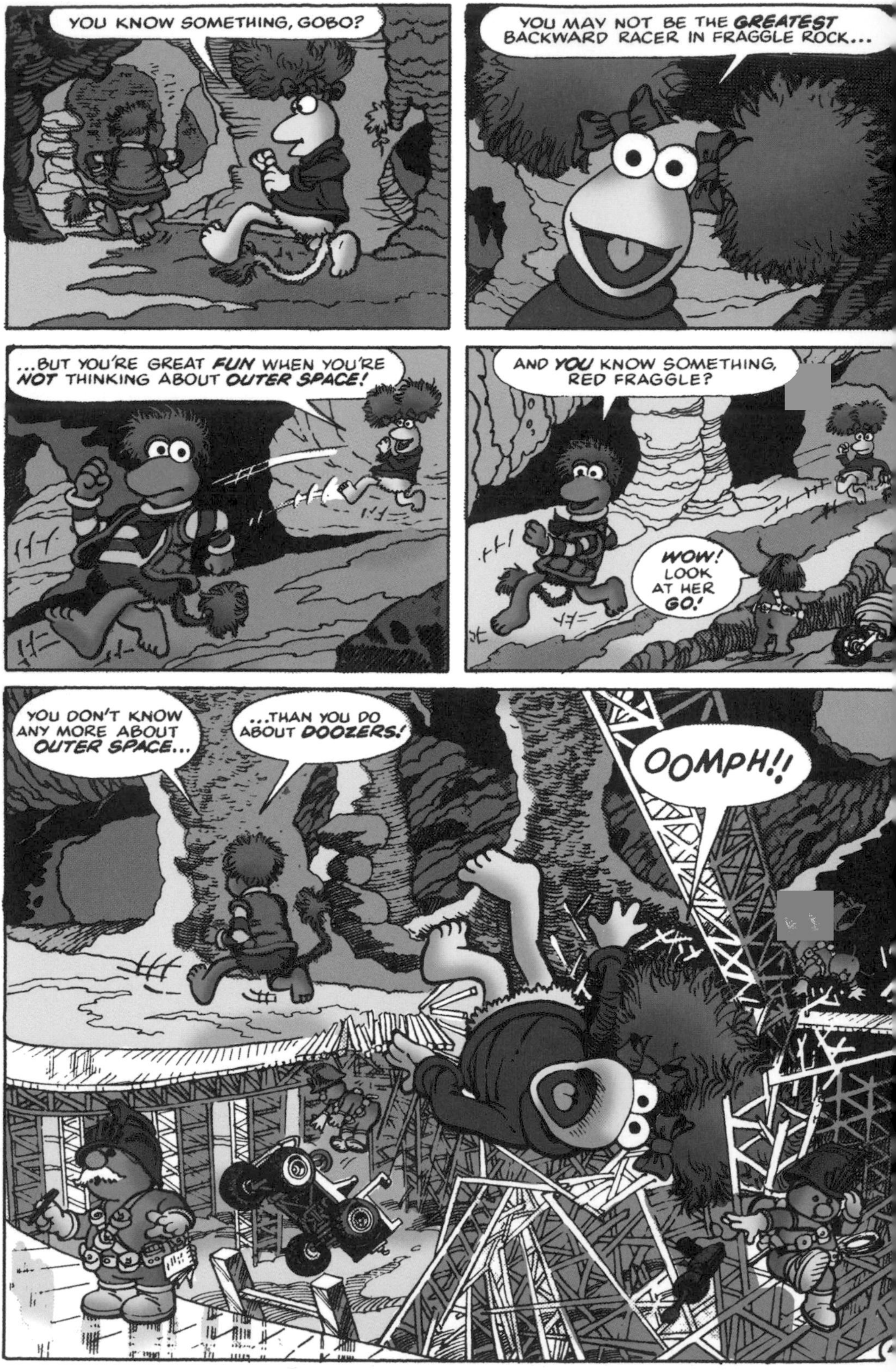
YOU KNOW SOMETHING, GOBO?
YOU MAY NOT BE THE GREATEST BACKWARD RACER IN FRAGGLE ROCK...
...BUT YOU'RE GREAT FUN WHEN YOU'RE NOT THINKING ABOUT OUTER SPACE!
AND YOU KNOW SOMETHING, RED FRAGGLE?
WOW! LOOK AT HER GO!
YOU DON'T KNOW ANY MORE ABOUT OUTER SPACE...
...THAN YOU DO ABOUT DOOZERS!
OOMPH!!

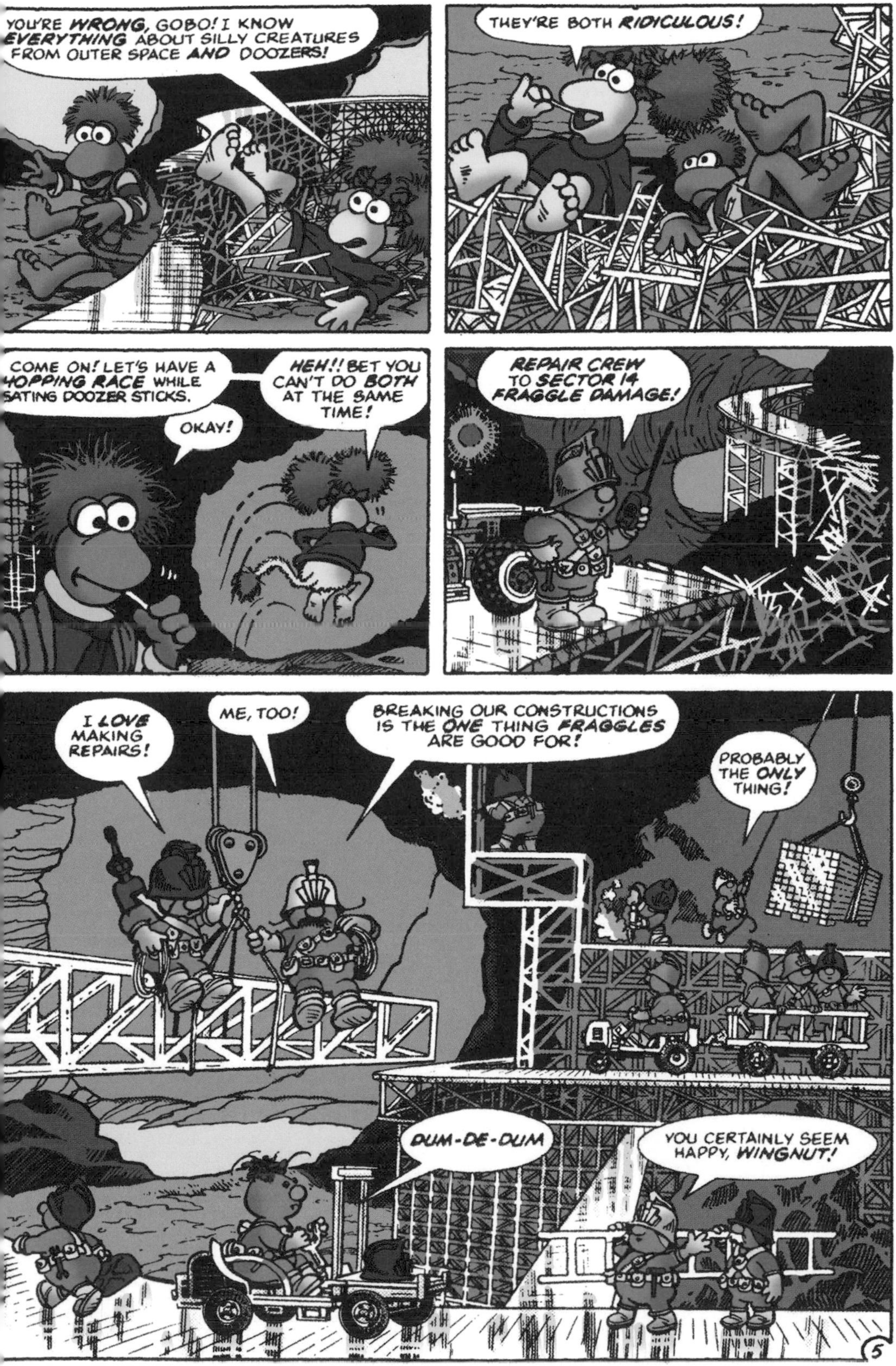
YOU'RE WRONG, GOBO! I KNOW EVERYTHING ABOUT SILLY CREATURES FROM OUTER SPACE AND DOOZERS!
THEY'RE BOTH RIDICULOUS!
COME ON! LET'S HAVE A HOPPING RACE WHILE EATING DOOZER STICKS.
HEH!! BET YOU CAN'T DO BOTH AT THE SAME TIME!
OKAY!
REPAIR CREW TO SECTOR 14 FRAGGLE DAMAGE!
I LOVE MAKING REPAIRS!
ME, TOO!
BREAKING OUR CONSTRUCTIONS IS THE ONE THING FRAGGLES ARE GOOD FOR!
PROBABLY THE ONLY THING!
DUM-DE-DUM
YOU CERTAINLY SEEM HAPPY, WINGNUT!
5

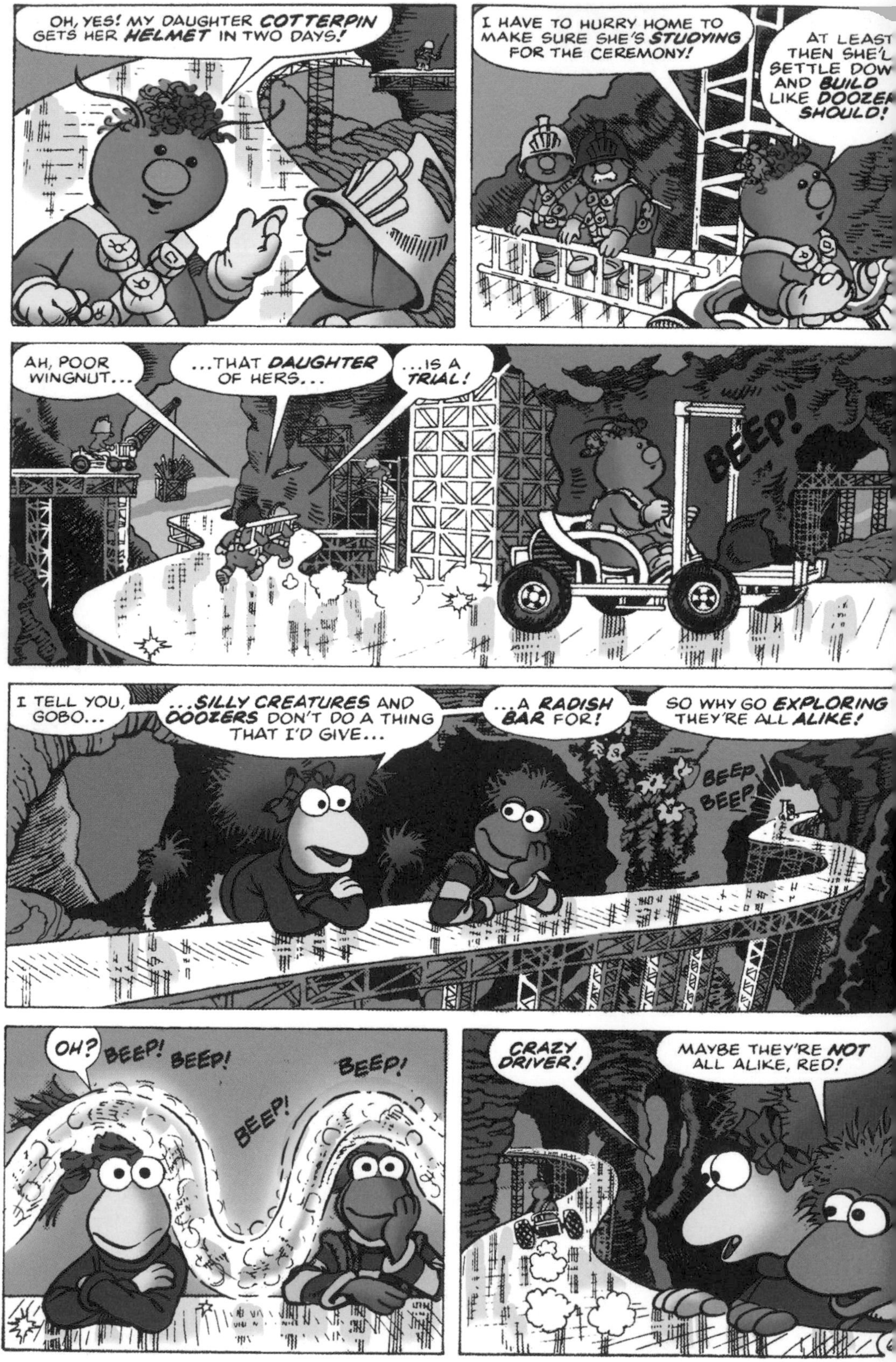
OH, YES! MY DAUGHTER COTTERPIN GETS HER HELMET IN TWO DAYS!
I HAVE TO HURRY HOME TO MAKE SURE SHE'S STUDYING FOR THE CEREMONY!
AT LEAST THEN SHE'L SETTLE DOW AND BUILD LIKE DOOZER SHOULD!
AH, POOR WINGNUT...
...THAT DAUGHTER OF HERS...
...IS A TRIAL!
BEEP!
I TELL YOU, GOBO...
...SILLY CREATURES AND DOOZERS DON'T DO A THING THAT I'D GIVE...
...A RADISH BAR FOR!
SO WHY GO EXPLORING THEY'RE ALL ALIKE!
BEEP BEEP
OH?
BEEP! BEEP! BEEP! BEEP!
CRAZY DRIVER!
MAYBE THEY'RE NOT ALL ALIKE, RED!

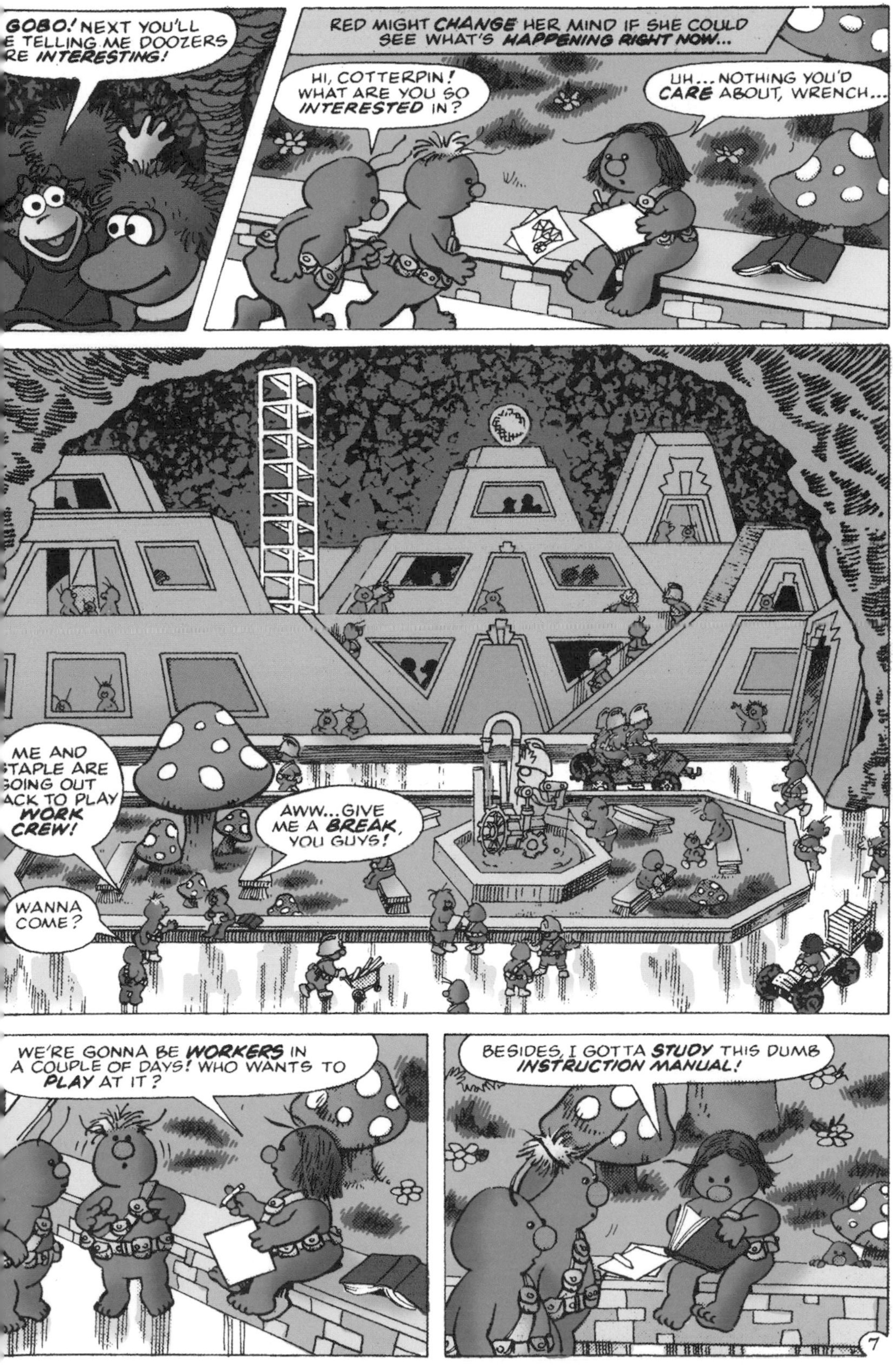
GOBO! NEXT YOU'LL
E TELLING ME DOOZERS
RE INTERESTING!
RED MIGHT CHANGE HER MIND IF SHE COULD SEE WHAT'S HAPPENING RIGHT NOW...
HI, COTTERPIN! WHAT ARE YOU SO INTERESTED IN?
UH... NOTHING YOU'D CARE ABOUT, WRENCH...
ME AND
TAPLE ARE
OING OUT
ACK TO PLAY
WORK
CREW!
WANNA COME?
AWW...GIVE ME A BREAK, YOU GUYS!
WE'RE GONNA BE WORKERS IN A COUPLE OF DAYS! WHO WANTS TO PLAY AT IT?
BESIDES, I GOTTA STUDY THIS DUMB INSTRUCTION MANUAL!
7

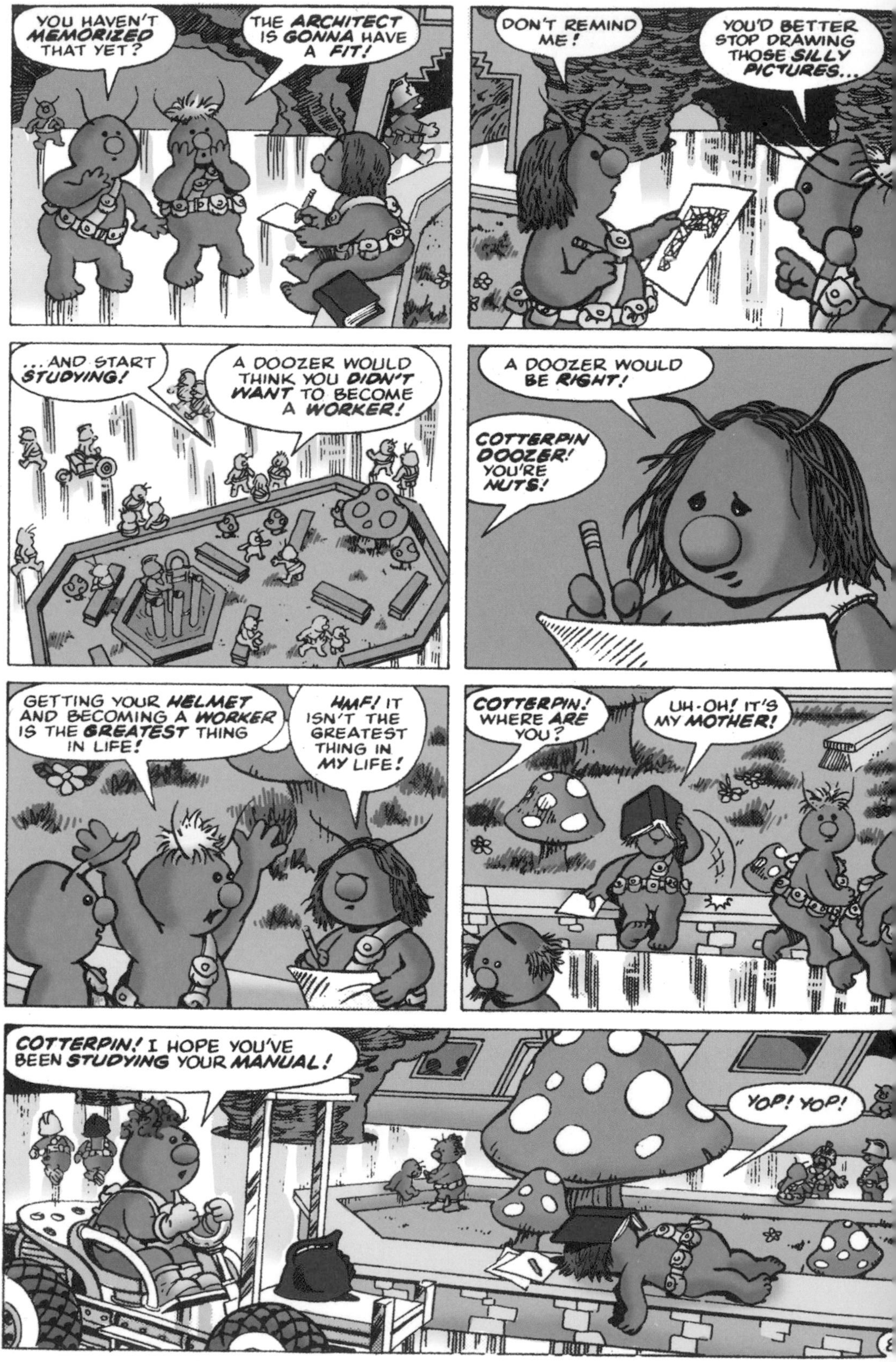
YOU HAVEN'T MEMORIZED THAT YET?
THE ARCHITECT IS GONNA HAVE A FIT!
DON'T REMIND ME!
YOU'D BETTER STOP DRAWING THOSE SILLY PICTURES...
...AND START STUDYING!
A DOOZER WOULD THINK YOU DIDN'T WANT TO BECOME A WORKER!
A DOOZER WOULD BE RIGHT!
COTTERPIN DOOZER! YOU'RE NUTS!
GETTING YOUR HELMET AND BECOMING A WORKER IS THE GREATEST THING IN LIFE!
HMF! IT ISN'T THE GREATEST THING IN MY LIFE!
COTTERPIN! WHERE ARE YOU?
UH-OH! IT'S MY MOTHER!
COTTERPIN! I HOPE YOU'VE BEEN STUDYING YOUR MANUAL!
YOP! YOP!

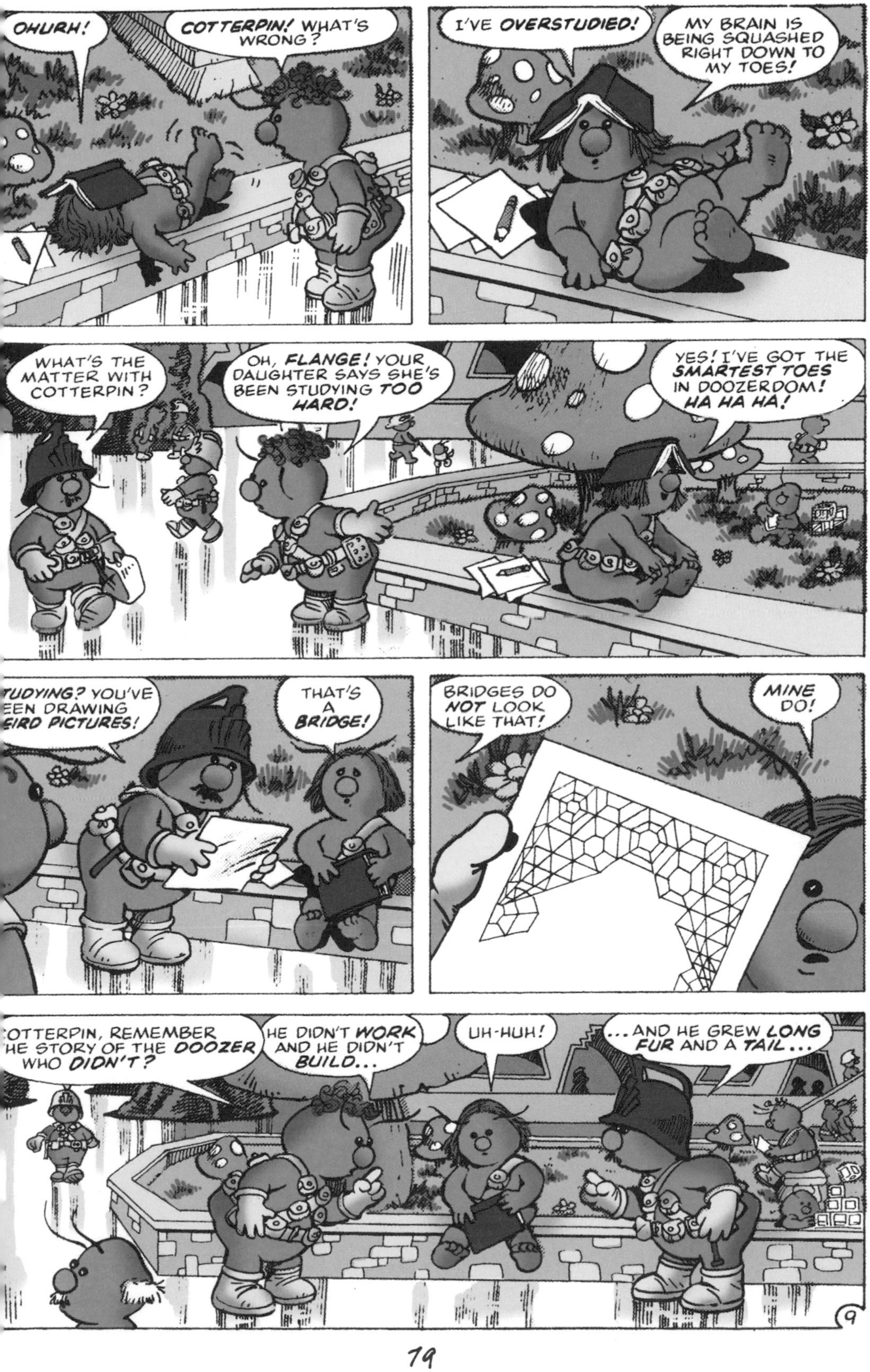
OHURH!
COTTERPIN! WHAT'S WRONG?
I'VE OVERSTUDIED!
MY BRAIN IS BEING SQUASHED RIGHT DOWN TO MY TOES!
WHAT'S THE MATTER WITH COTTERPIN?
OH, FLANGE! YOUR DAUGHTER SAYS SHE'S BEEN STUDYING TOO HARD!
YES! I'VE GOT THE SMARTEST TOES IN DOOZERDOM! HA HA HA!
TUDYING? YOU'VE EEN DRAWING EIRD PICTURES!
THAT'S A BRIDGE!
BRIDGES DO NOT LOOK LIKE THAT!
MINE DO!
OTTERPIN, REMEMBER HE STORY OF THE DOOZER WHO DIDN'T?
HE DIDN'T WORK AND HE DIDN'T BUILD...
UH-HUH!
...AND HE GREW LONG FUR AND A TAIL...
9

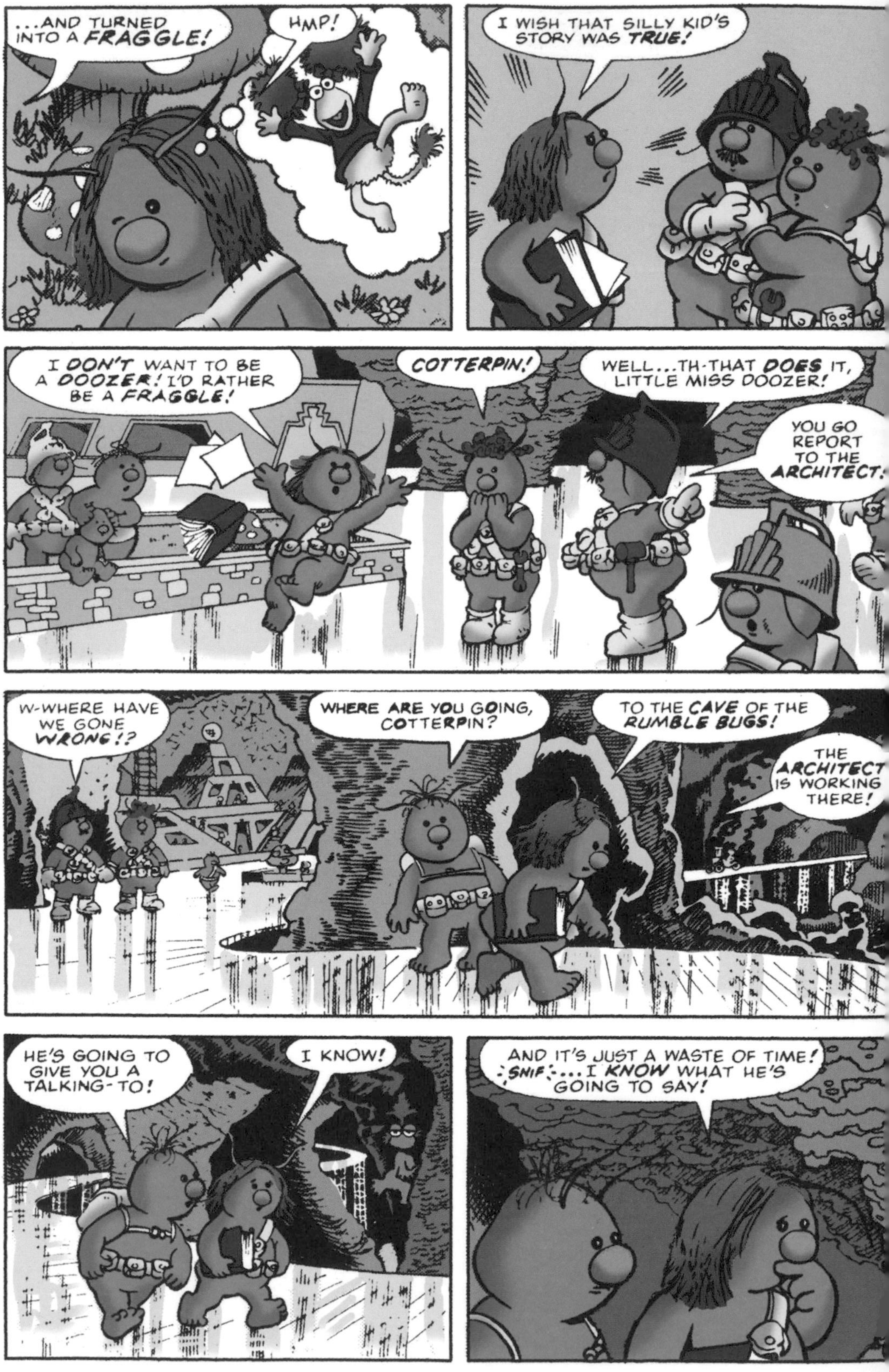
...AND TURNED INTO A FRAGGLE!
HMP!
I WISH THAT SILLY KID'S STORY WAS TRUE!
I DON'T WANT TO BE A DOOZER! I'D RATHER BE A FRAGGLE!
COTTERPIN!
WELL...TH-THAT DOES IT, LITTLE MISS DOOZER!
YOU GO REPORT TO THE ARCHITECT!
W-WHERE HAVE WE GONE WRONG!?
WHERE ARE YOU GOING, COTTERPIN?
TO THE CAVE OF THE RUMBLE BUGS!
THE ARCHITECT IS WORKING THERE!
HE'S GOING TO GIVE YOU A TALKING-TO!
I KNOW!
AND IT'S JUST A WASTE OF TIME! SNIF ...I KNOW WHAT HE'S GOING TO SAY!

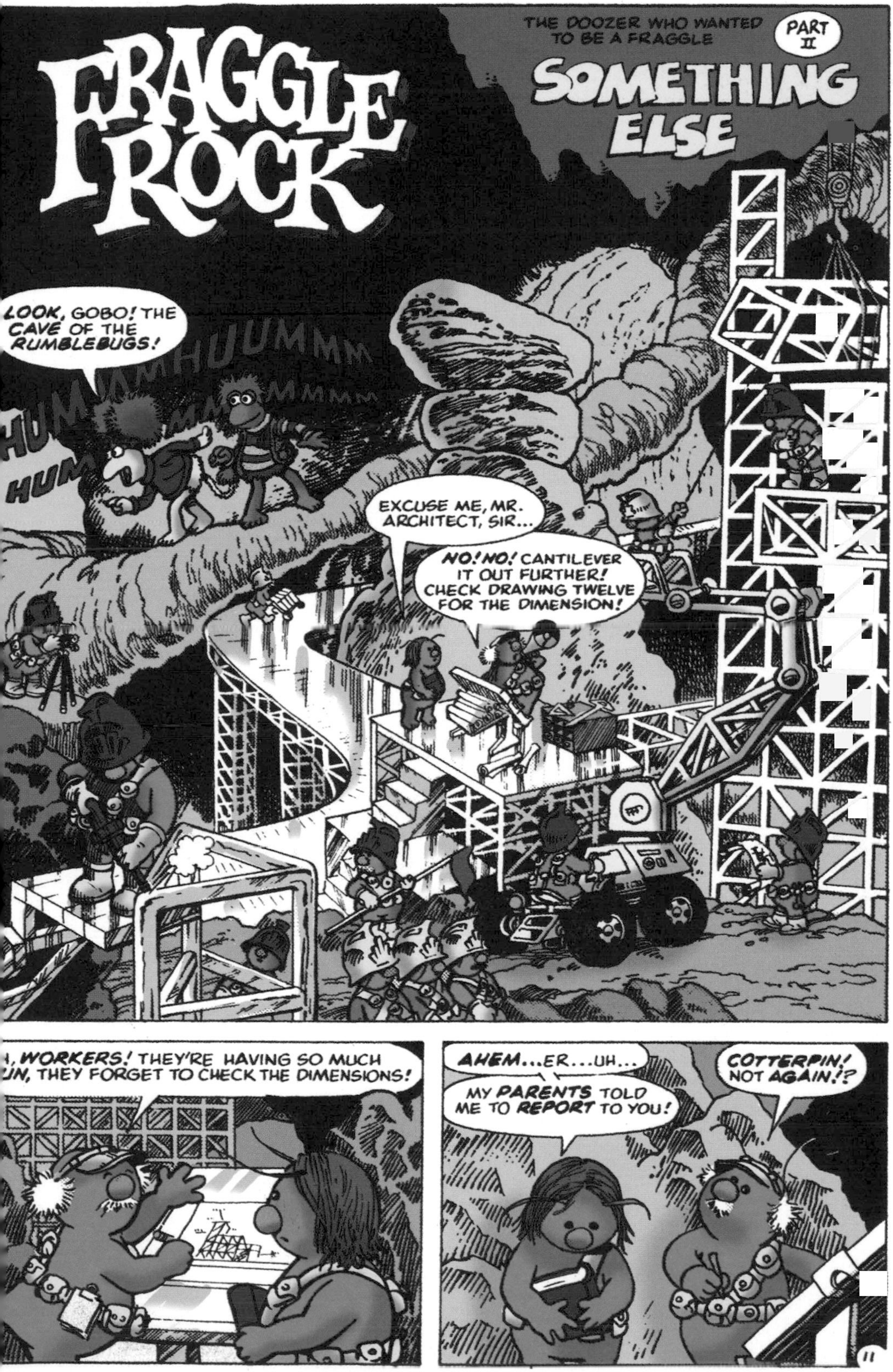
FRAGGLE ROCK
THE DOOZER WHO WANTED TO BE A FRAGGLE
PART II
SOMETHING ELSE
LOOK, GOBO! THE CAVE OF THE RUMBLEBUGS!
HUMMMHUUMMM
HUM
HUM
EXCUSE ME, MR. ARCHITECT, SIR...
NO! NO! CANTILEVER IT OUT FURTHER! CHECK DRAWING TWELVE FOR THE DIMENSION!
, WORKERS! THEY'RE HAVING SO MUCH
UN, THEY FORGET TO CHECK THE DIMENSIONS!
AHEM...ER...UH...
MY PARENTS TOLD ME TO REPORT TO YOU!
COTTERPIN! NOT AGAIN!?
11

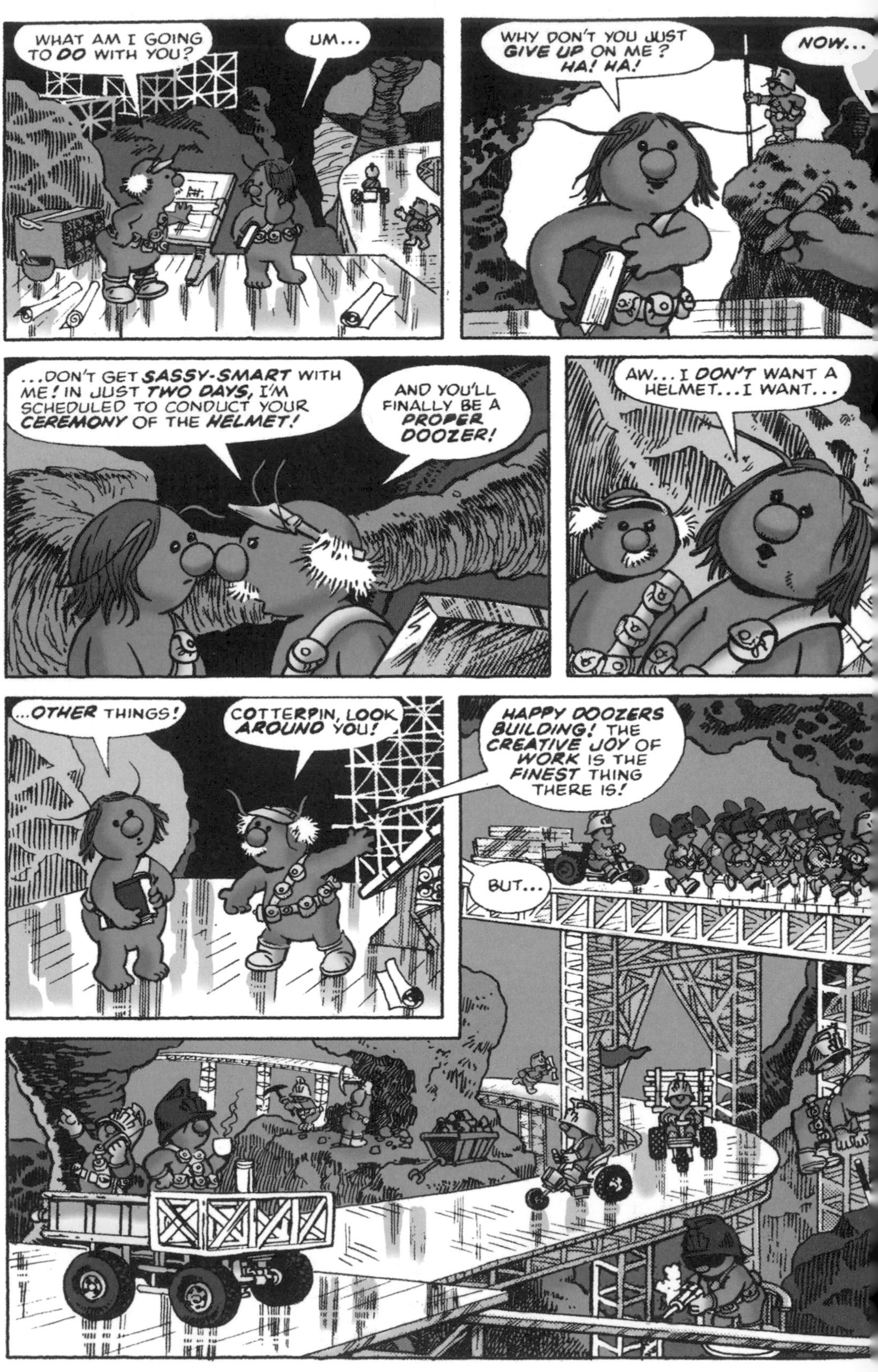
WHAT AM I GOING TO DO WITH YOU?
UM...
WHY DON'T YOU JUST GIVE UP ON ME? HA! HA!
NOW...
...DON'T GET SASSY-SMART WITH ME! IN JUST TWO DAYS, I'M SCHEDULED TO CONDUCT YOUR CEREMONY OF THE HELMET!
AND YOU'LL FINALLY BE A PROPER DOOZER!
AW... I DON'T WANT A HELMET... I WANT...
...OTHER THINGS!
COTTERPIN, LOOK AROUND YOU!
HAPPY DOOZERS BUILDING! THE CREATIVE JOY OF WORK IS THE FINEST THING THERE IS!
BUT...

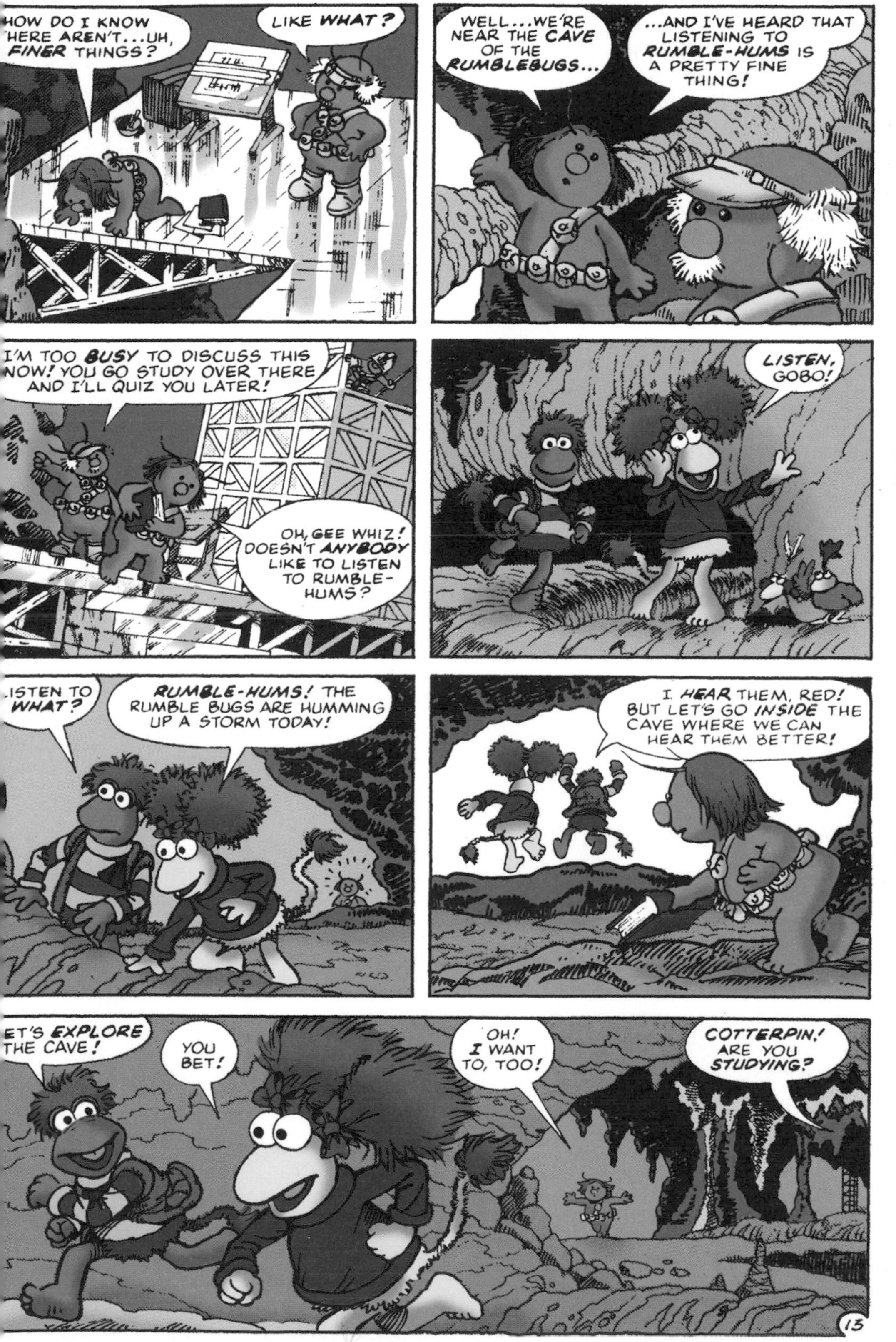
HOW DO I KNOW
THERE AREN'T...UH, FINER THINGS?
LIKE WHAT?
WELL...WE'RE NEAR THE CAVE OF THE RUMBLEBUGS...
...AND I'VE HEARD THAT LISTENING TO RUMBLE-HUMS IS A PRETTY FINE THING!
I'M TOO BUSY TO DISCUSS THIS NOW! YOU GO STUDY OVER THERE AND I'LL QUIZ YOU LATER!
OH, GEE WHIZ! DOESN'T ANYBODY LIKE TO LISTEN TO RUMBLE-HUMS?
LISTEN, GOBO!
LISTEN TO WHAT?
RUMBLE-HUMS! THE RUMBLE BUGS ARE HUMMING UP A STORM TODAY!
I. HEAR THEM, RED! BUT LET'S GO INSIDE THE CAVE WHERE WE CAN HEAR THEM BETTER!
LET'S EXPLORE THE CAVE!
YOU BET!
OH! I WANT TO, TOO!
COTTERPIN! ARE YOU STUDYING?
13

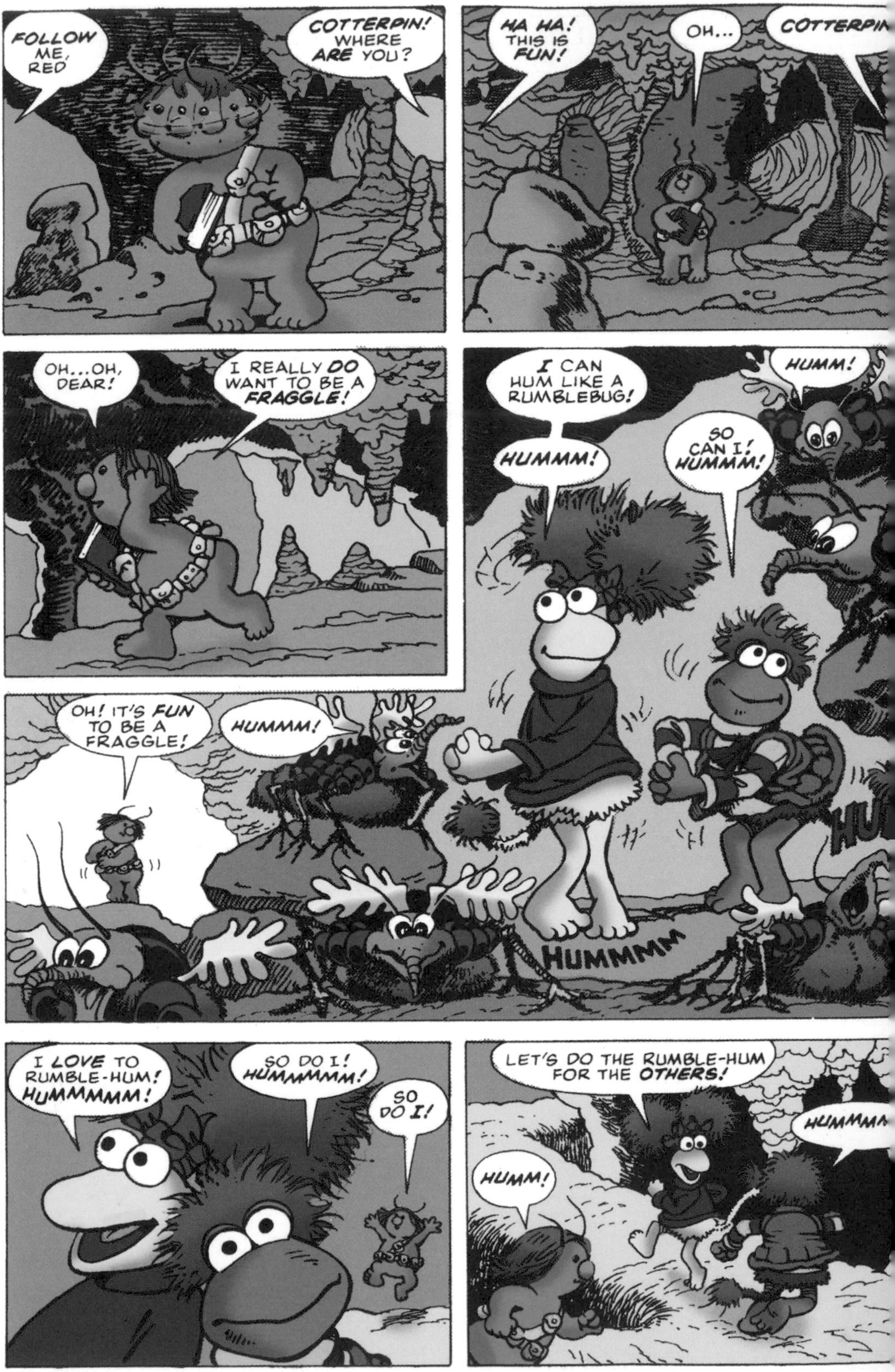
FOLLOW ME, RED
COTTERPIN! WHERE ARE YOU?
HA HA! THIS IS FUN!
OH...
COTTERPIN
OH...OH, DEAR!
I REALLY DO WANT TO BE A FRAGGLE!
I CAN HUM LIKE A RUMBLEBUG!
HUMMM!
SO CAN I! HUMMM!
HUMM!
OH! IT'S FUN TO BE A FRAGGLE!
HUMMM!
HUMMMM
I LOVE TO RUMBLE-HUM! HUMMMMM!
SO DO I! HUMMMMM!
SO DO I!
LET'S DO THE RUMBLE-HUM FOR THE OTHERS!
HUMM!
HUMMMM

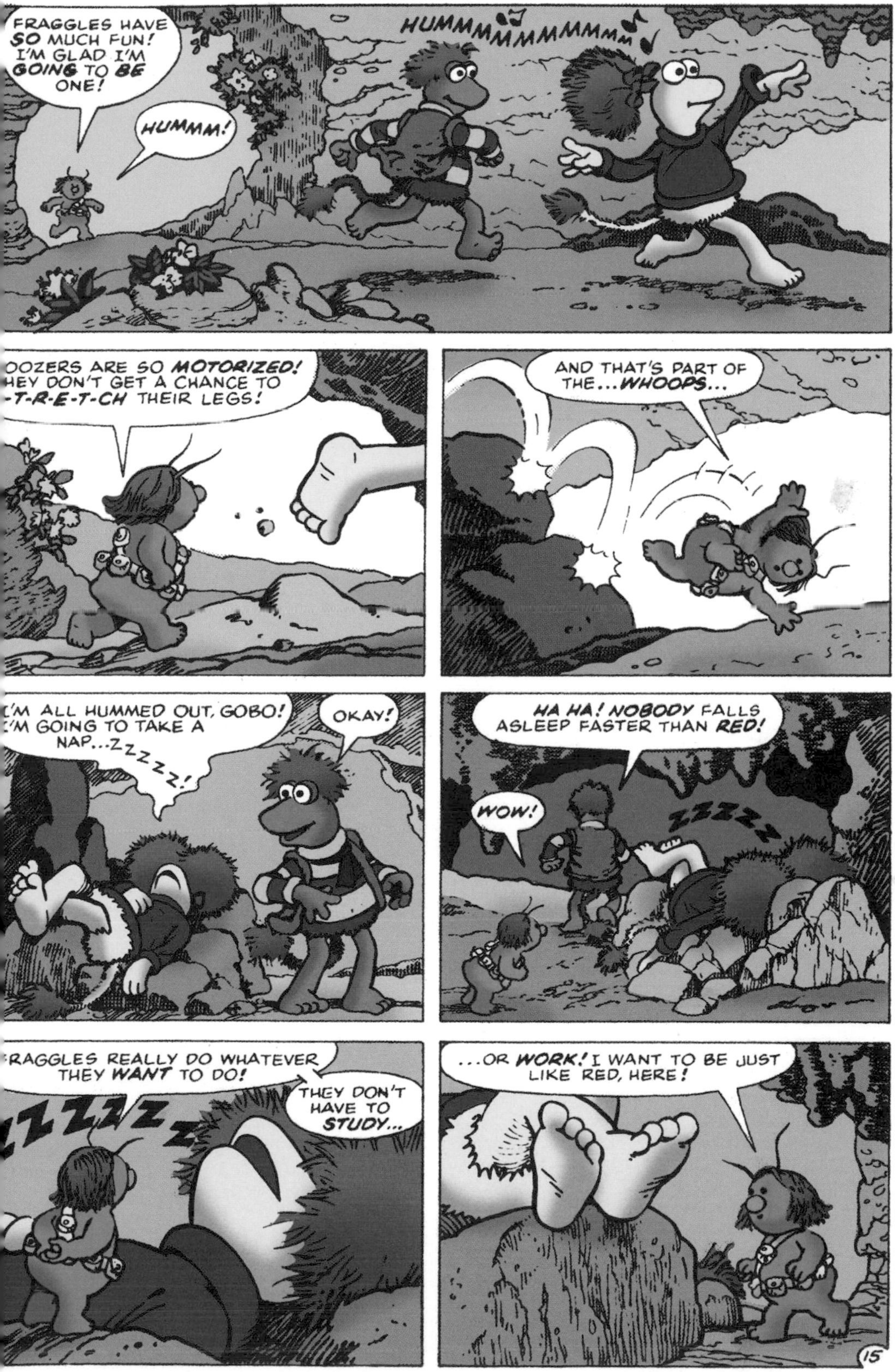
FRAGGLES HAVE SO MUCH FUN! I'M GLAD I'M GOING TO BE ONE!
HUMMM!
HUMMMMMMMMMMM
OOZERS ARE SO MOTORIZED! HEY DON'T GET A CHANCE TO -T-R-E-T-CH THEIR LEGS!
AND THAT'S PART OF THE...WHOOPS...
'M ALL HUMMED OUT, GOBO! 'M GOING TO TAKE A NAP...ZZZZZ!
OKAY!
HA HA! NOBODY FALLS ASLEEP FASTER THAN RED!
WOW!
ZZZZZ
RAGGLES REALLY DO WHATEVER THEY WANT TO DO!
ZZZZZZ
THEY DON'T HAVE TO STUDY...
...OR WORK! I WANT TO BE JUST LIKE RED, HERE!
15

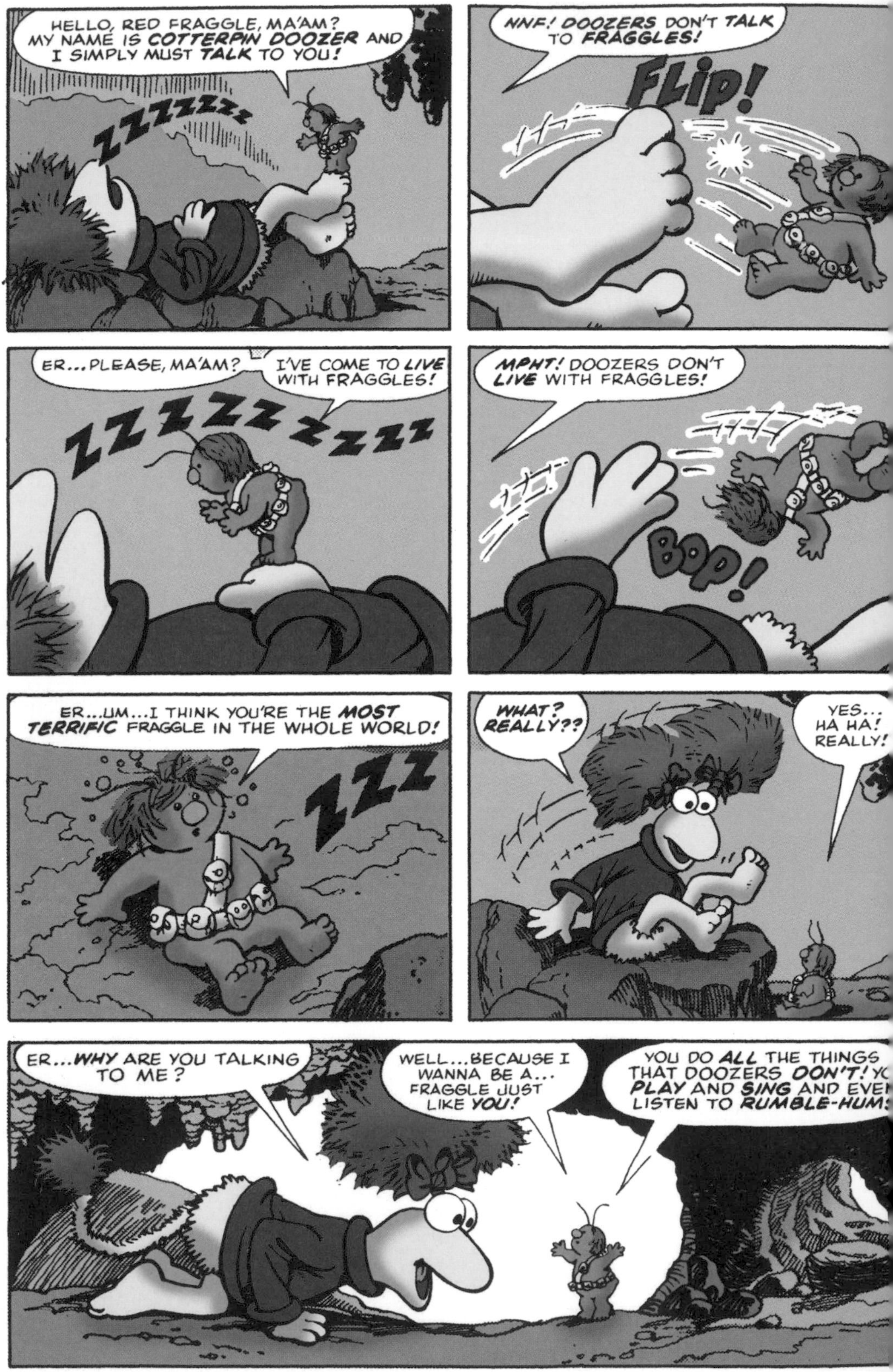

HELLO, RED FRAGGLE, MA'AM? MY NAME IS COTTERPIN DOOZER AND I SIMPLY MUST TALK TO YOU!
ZZZZZZzz
NNF! DOOZERS DON'T TALK TO FRAGGLES!
FLIP!
ER...PLEASE, MA'AM?
I'VE COME TO LIVE WITH FRAGGLES!
ZZZZZZzzzz
MPHT! DOOZERS DON'T LIVE WITH FRAGGLES!
BOP!
ER...UM...I THINK YOU'RE THE MOST TERRIFIC FRAGGLE IN THE WHOLE WORLD!
ZZZ
WHAT? REALLY??
YES... HA HA! REALLY!
ER...WHY ARE YOU TALKING TO ME?
WELL...BECAUSE I WANNA BE A... FRAGGLE JUST LIKE YOU!
YOU DO ALL THE THINGS THAT DOOZERS DON'T! YO PLAY AND SING AND EVE LISTEN TO RUMBLE-HUM

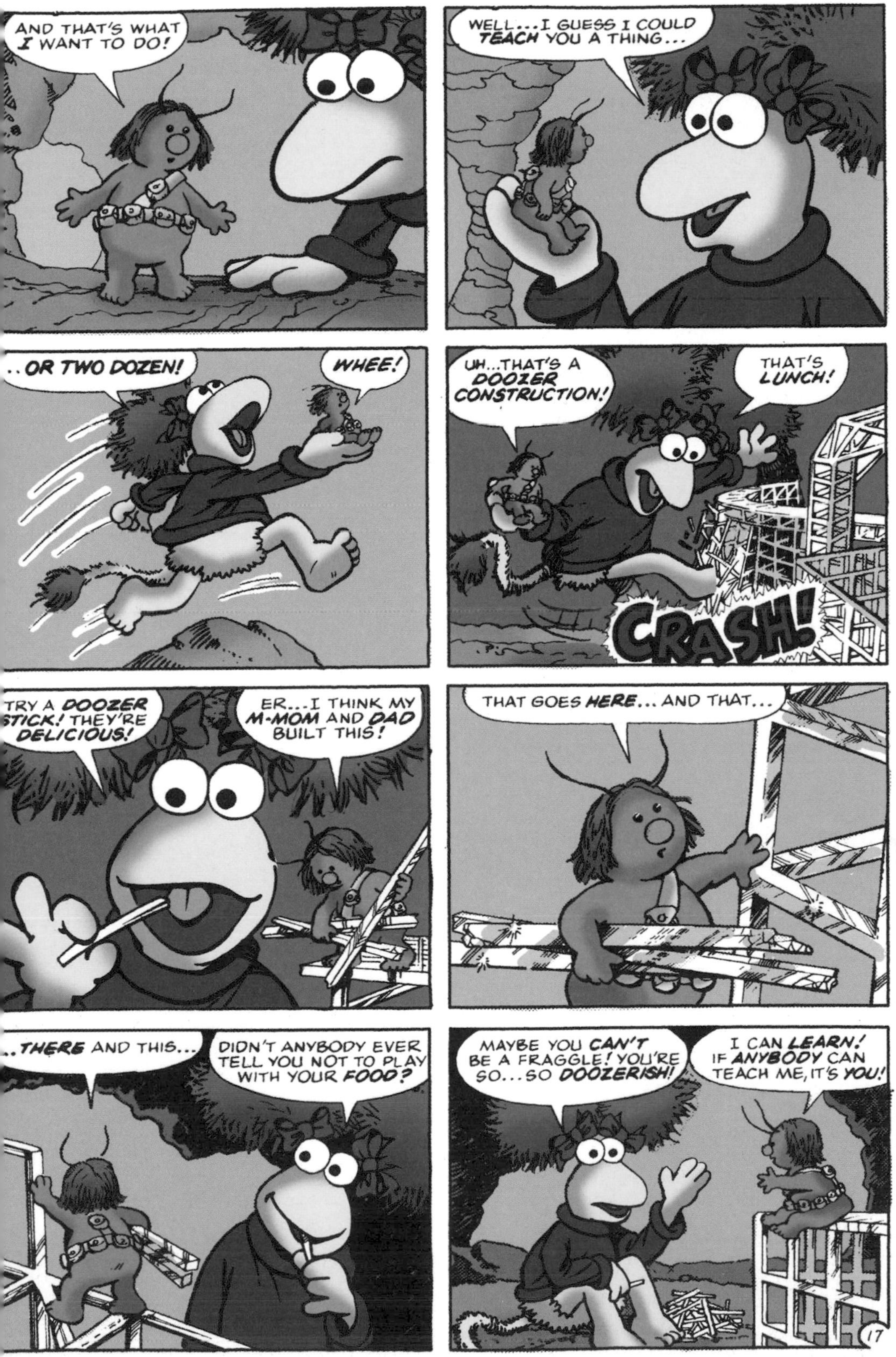
AND THAT'S WHAT I WANT TO DO!
WELL... I GUESS I COULD TEACH YOU A THING...
..OR TWO DOZEN!
WHEE!
UH...THAT'S A DOOZER CONSTRUCTION!
THAT'S LUNCH!
CRASH!
TRY A DOOZER STICK! THEY'RE DELICIOUS!
ER... I THINK MY M-MOM AND DAD BUILT THIS!
THAT GOES HERE... AND THAT...
..THERE AND THIS...
DIDN'T ANYBODY EVER TELL YOU NOT TO PLAY WITH YOUR FOOD?
MAYBE YOU CAN'T BE A FRAGGLE! YOU'RE SO... SO DOOZERISH!
I CAN LEARN! IF ANYBODY CAN TEACH ME, IT'S YOU!
17

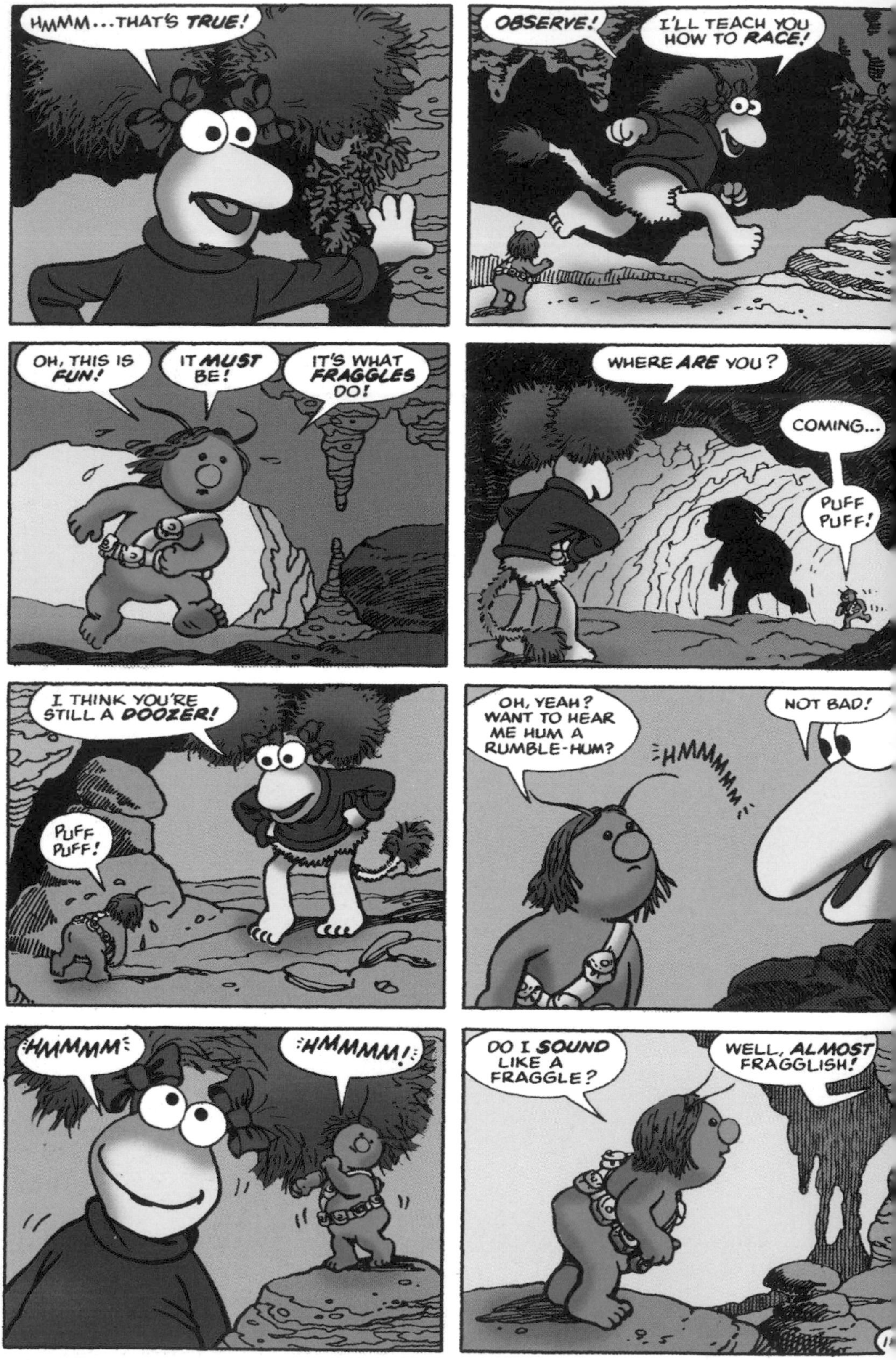
HMMM...THAT'S TRUE!
OBSERVE!
I'LL TEACH YOU HOW TO RACE!
OH, THIS IS FUN!
IT MUST BE!
IT'S WHAT FRAGGLES DO!
WHERE ARE YOU?
COMING...
PUFF PUFF!
I THINK YOU'RE STILL A DOOZER!
PUFF PUFF!
OH, YEAH? WANT TO HEAR ME HUM A RUMBLE-HUM?
HMMMMM
NOT BAD!
HMMMM
HMMMM!
DO I SOUND LIKE A FRAGGLE?
WELL, ALMOST FRAGGLISH!

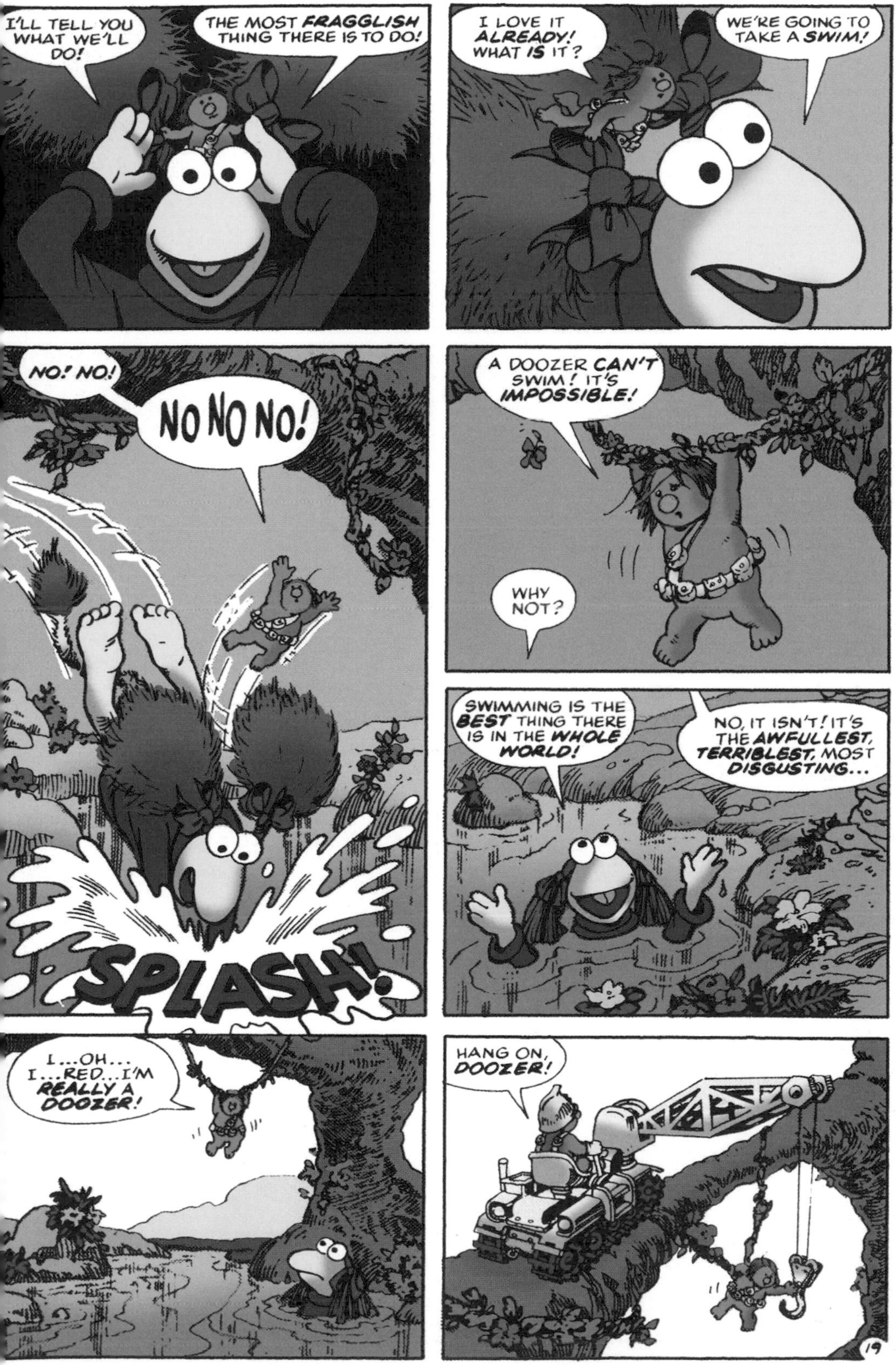
I'LL TELL YOU WHAT WE'LL DO!
THE MOST FRAGGLISH THING THERE IS TO DO!
I LOVE IT ALREADY! WHAT IS IT?
WE'RE GOING TO TAKE A SWIM!
NO! NO!
NO NO NO!
SPLASH!
A DOOZER CAN'T SWIM! IT'S IMPOSSIBLE!
WHY NOT?
SWIMMING IS THE BEST THING THERE IS IN THE WHOLE WORLD!
NO, IT ISN'T! IT'S THE AWFULLEST, TERRIBLEST, MOST DISGUSTING...
I...OH... I...RED...I'M REALLY A DOOZER!
HANG ON, DOOZER!
19

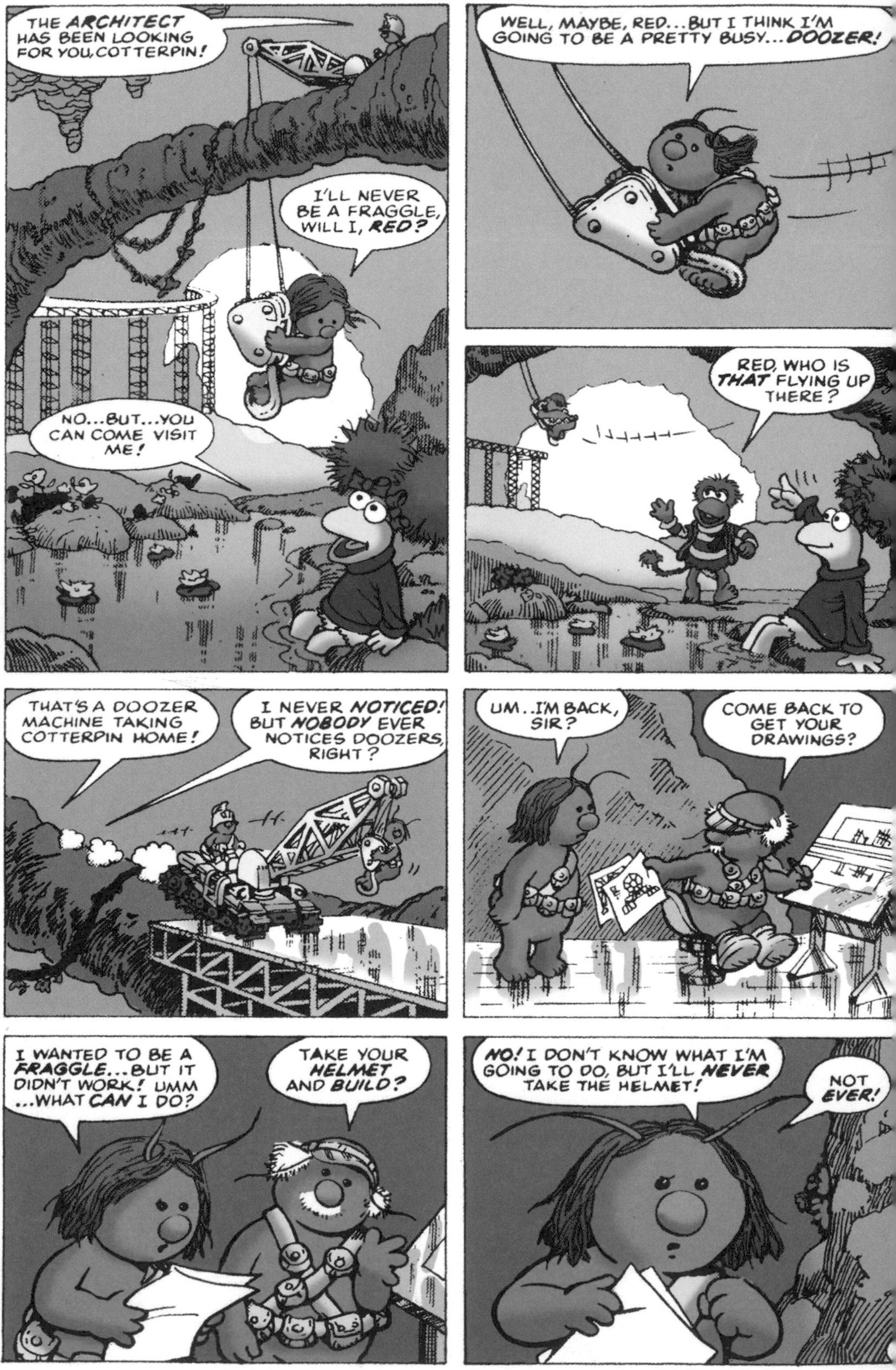
THE ARCHITECT HAS BEEN LOOKING FOR YOU, COTTERPIN!
I'LL NEVER BE A FRAGGLE, WILL I, RED?
NO...BUT...YOU CAN COME VISIT ME!
WELL, MAYBE, RED...BUT I THINK I'M GOING TO BE A PRETTY BUSY...DOOZER!
RED, WHO IS THAT FLYING UP THERE?
THAT'S A DOOZER MACHINE TAKING COTTERPIN HOME!
I NEVER NOTICED! BUT NOBODY EVER NOTICES DOOZERS, RIGHT?
UM..I'M BACK, SIR?
COME BACK TO GET YOUR DRAWINGS?
I WANTED TO BE A FRAGGLE...BUT IT DIDN'T WORK! UMM ...WHAT CAN I DO?
TAKE YOUR HELMET AND BUILD?
NO! I DON'T KNOW WHAT I'M GOING TO DO, BUT I'LL NEVER TAKE THE HELMET!
NOT EVER!

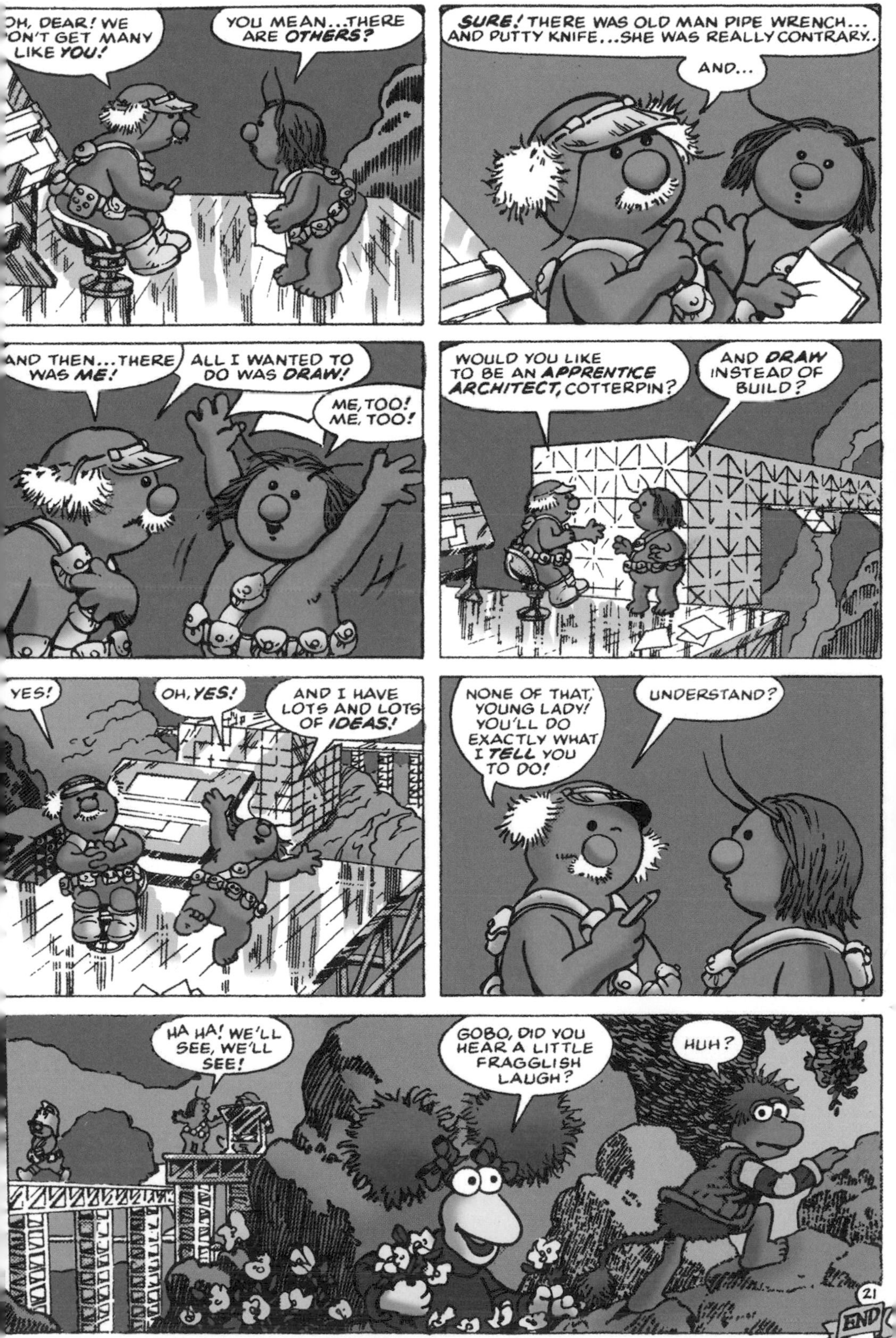
OH, DEAR! WE DON'T GET MANY LIKE YOU!
YOU MEAN...THERE ARE OTHERS?
SURE! THERE WAS OLD MAN PIPE WRENCH... AND PUTTY KNIFE...SHE WAS REALLY CONTRARY..
AND...
AND THEN...THERE WAS ME!
ALL I WANTED TO DO WAS DRAW!
ME, TOO! ME, TOO!
WOULD YOU LIKE TO BE AN APPRENTICE ARCHITECT, COTTERPIN?
AND DRAW INSTEAD OF BUILD?
YES!
OH, YES!
AND I HAVE LOTS AND LOTS OF IDEAS!
NONE OF THAT, YOUNG LADY! YOU'LL DO EXACTLY WHAT I TELL YOU TO DO!
UNDERSTAND?
HA HA! WE'LL SEE, WE'LL SEE!
GOBO, DID YOU HEAR A LITTLE FRAGGLISH LAUGH?
HUH?
21
END

The Residents of Fraggle Rock

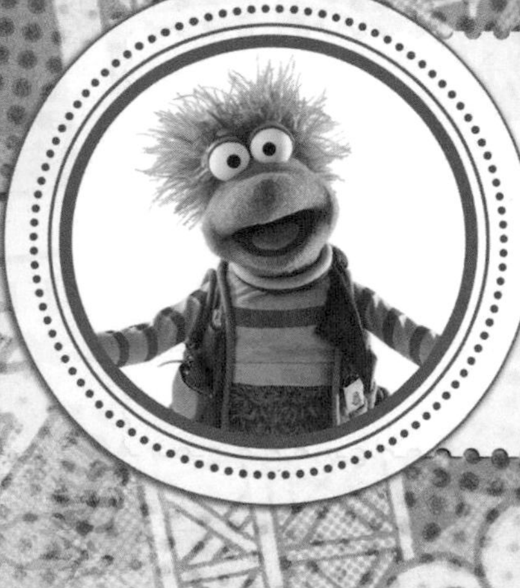

GOBO

Gobo is the natural leader of the Fraggle Five. He is an explorer, spending his days charting the unexplored *(and explored-but-forgotten)* regions of Fraggle Rock. He is highly respected by other Fraggles, although they occasionally find him a little pompous. He is also somewhat egocentric, which can make it hard for him to admit mistakes. As a leader, Gobo often provides his friends with direction, although, since he's a Fraggle, it's sometimes a fairly silly one.

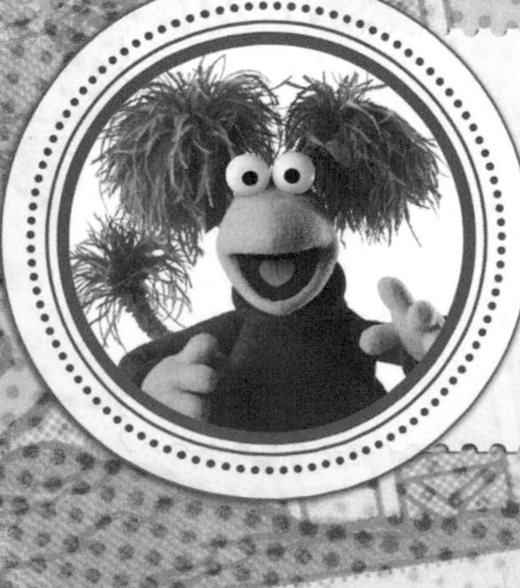

RED

Red is a nonstop whirligig of activity. To her fellow Fraggles, Red is often seen as a flash of crimson racing to her next athletic pursuit. She is Fraggle Rock champion in Tug-of-War, Diving-while-Singing-Backwards, the Blindfolded-One-Legged-Radish-Relay, and a number of other traditional Fraggle sports. She is outgoing, enthusiastic, and athletic, but take note--her impetuosity can get her into real trouble.

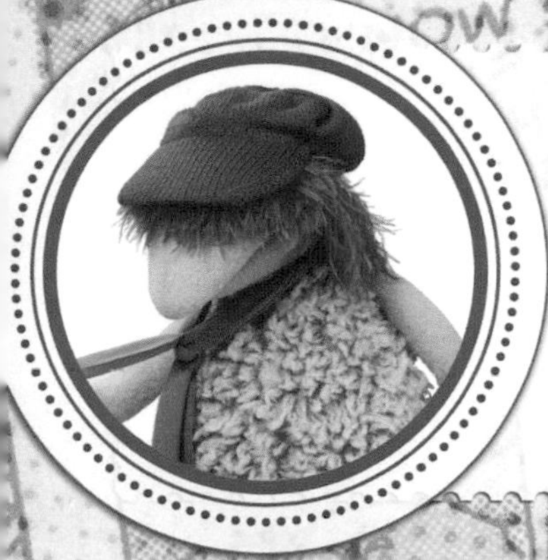

BOOBER

According to **Boober**, there are only two things certain in this world: death and laundry. Boober is terrified by the former and fascinated by the latter. He is also paranoid and superstitious. According to Boober, anything that can go wrong surely will, and when it does, it will inevitably happen to him. But Boober's negative attitude has a big plus--he can see real trouble coming a mile away, a useful attribute in a land of eternal optimists!

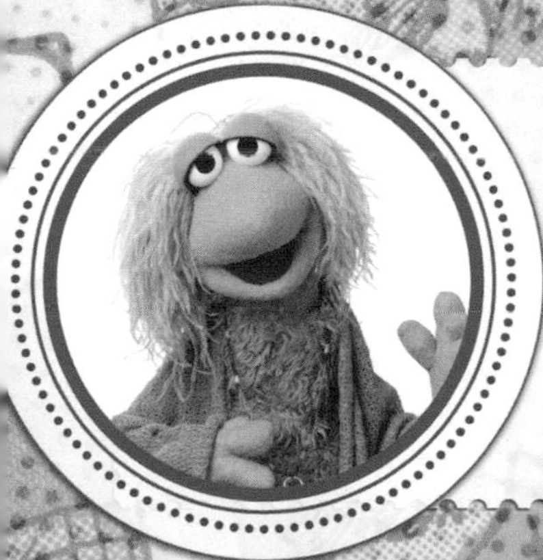

MOKEY

Mokey is an artist, poet and philosopher. She seems to be in touch with some sort of higher Fraggle consciousness. Mokey is fascinated by the beauty and intricacy of the world around her, and is always seeking new ways to share this feeling with others. Mokey may have her head in the clouds, but she's also very courageous and resourceful. Her job is to brave the Gorg garden to gather the radishes the Fraggles eat.

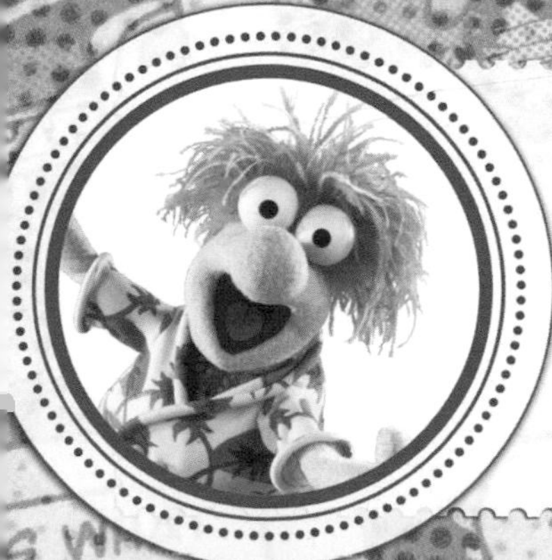

WEMBLEY

Wembley is indecision personified. He only owns two shirts, and both have a banana-tree motif. If he had any other clothes, he'd never be able to get dressed in the morning! Wembley has an uncanny ability to find merit on both sides of any issue. He is steadfast in his admiration for his best friend and roommate, Gobo. It was Gobo who encouraged Wembley to apply for his job with the Fraggle Rock Volunteer Fire Department. Wembley is the siren.

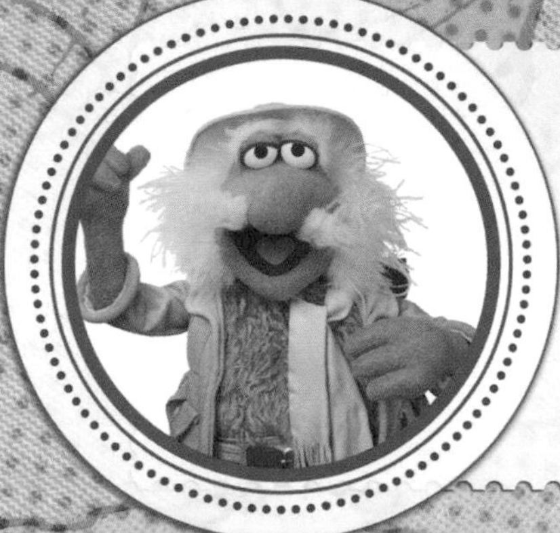

UNCLE TRAVELLING MATT

Gobo's **Uncle Travelling Matt** is the greatest living Fraggle explorer--the Fraggle equivalent of an astronaut. After completing his exploration of Fraggle Rock, he ventured forth into our world, a place the Fraggles call "Outer Space." He sends his observations back to Gobo on postcards in care of Doc.

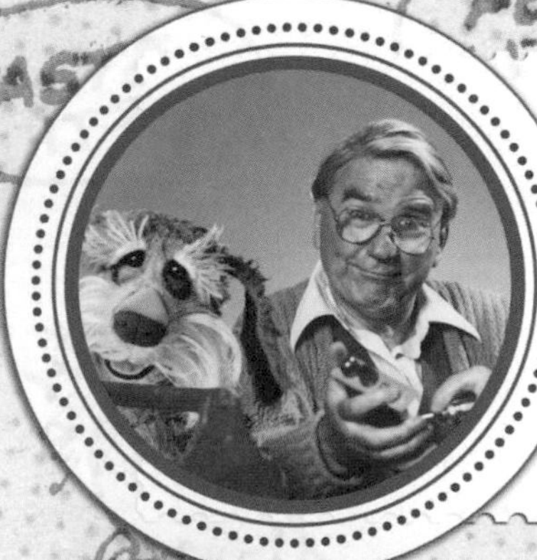

DOC & SPROCKET

Doc, the man who inhabits the workshop that contains the hole that leads to Fraggle Rock, is an inventor and a tinkerer. If it's a wee bit odd, Doc has probably already invented it. Doc doesn't know about Fraggles. **Sprocket** is Doc's extremely intelligent and expressive dog. Sprocket knows that the Fraggles exist. He's seen them lots of times... but he just doesn't have the words to tell Doc about them. This drives Sprocket crazy!

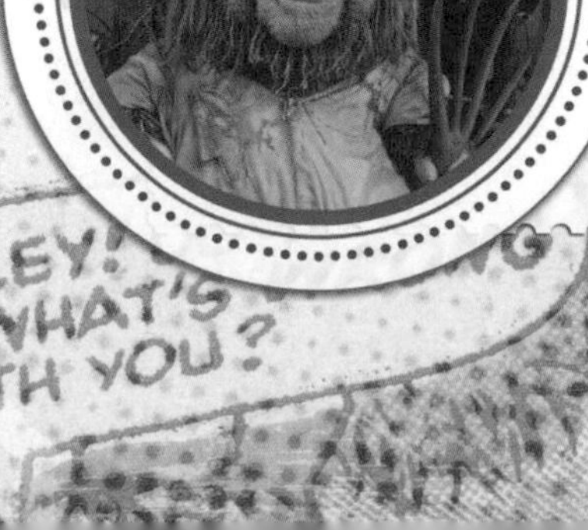

JUNIOR GORG

Sweet, loveable, galumphing **Junior Gorg** is the apple of his mother's eye and the bane of the Fraggles' existence! All he wants to do is "get those Fwaggles." Junior lives with his parents, King and Queen Gorg, in Gorg Castle. The Fraggles raid the Gorg Castle garden for radishes, and the garden is Junior's pride and joy. But the Fraggles are never really in any danger. Junior isn't very bright or coordinated, and really wouldn't hurt a fly.

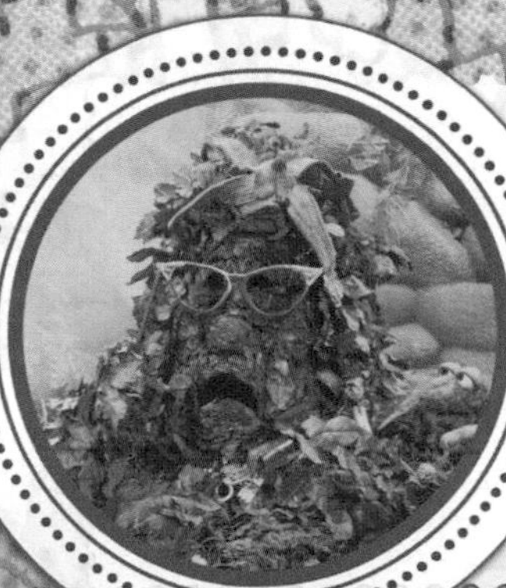

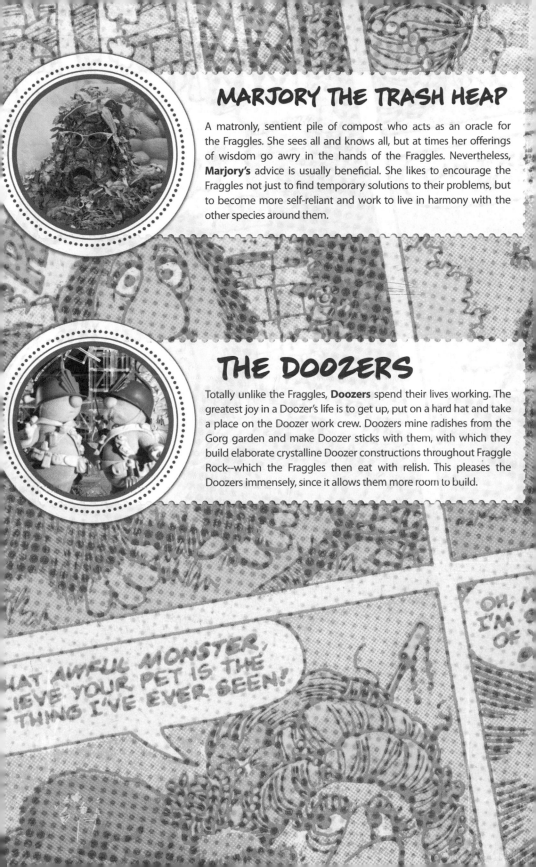

MARJORY THE TRASH HEAP

A matronly, sentient pile of compost who acts as an oracle for the Fraggles. She sees all and knows all, but at times her offerings of wisdom go awry in the hands of the Fraggles. Nevertheless, **Marjory's** advice is usually beneficial. She likes to encourage the Fraggles not just to find temporary solutions to their problems, but to become more self-reliant and work to live in harmony with the other species around them.

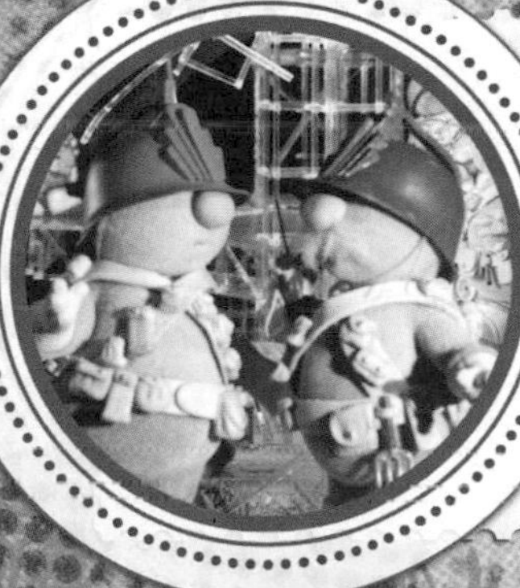

THE DOOZERS

Totally unlike the Fraggles, **Doozers** spend their lives working. The greatest joy in a Doozer's life is to get up, put on a hard hat and take a place on the Doozer work crew. Doozers mine radishes from the Gorg garden and make Doozer sticks with them, with which they build elaborate crystalline Doozer constructions throughout Fraggle Rock--which the Fraggles then eat with relish. This pleases the Doozers immensely, since it allows them more room to build.

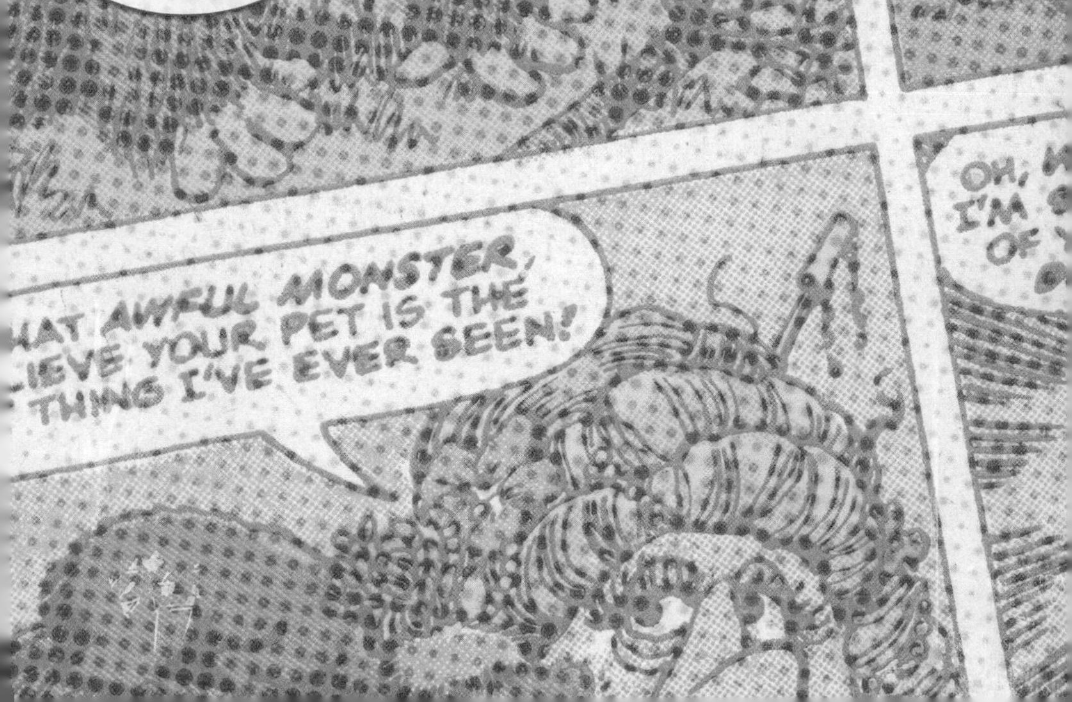
HAT AWFUL MONSTER,
IEVE YOUR PET IS THE
THING I'VE EVER SEEN!
OH,
I'M
OF